EVERYONE

Born in Bradford to Irish parents, Anne-Marie O'Connor moved to Dublin in 2000, an experience that forms the background to *Everyone's Got a Bono Story*. She now lives in Manchester, where she spends her time writing. She has written plays for local theatre and has work in development for BBC Radio 4. She is currently writing her second novel, *There's No I in Team*.

ANNE-MARIE O'CONNOR

EVERYONE'S GOT
A BONO STORY

TiVOLI

Tivoli
an imprint of Gill & Macmillan Ltd
Hume Avenue
Park West
Dublin 12
with associated companies throughout the world

www.gillmacmillan.ie

07171 3599 3

Print origination by TypeIT, Dublin
Printed and bound by Nørhaven Paperback A/S, Denmark

A catalogue record is available for this book from the
British Library.

1 3 5 4 2

This book is a work of fiction. Names, characters, places
and incidents are either the product of the author's
imagination or are used fictitiously. Any resemblance to
actual events or locales or persons, living or dead, is
entirely coincidental.

To Mum, Dad and Doug

Acknowledgments

Firstly I would like to thank my family – Mum, Dad, Sean and Sinead and Uncle Doug – for their support and for not suggesting that writing was just another hair-brained scheme;

Alison Walsh, my editor, for all of her help, advice and enthusiasm. Deirdre Nolan and Tana French for such an excellent job editing the final manuscript, and all at Tivoli/Gill & Macmillan for being so positive about this book;

Geraldine Nichol, my agent, for her unerring work, reassurance and her uniqueness;

Danny Brocklehurst for suggesting that I might be able to string a sentence together in the first place and for all his advice and encouragement;

Dot Wood and all at M6 Theatre for their continued support and to Nadia Molinari at BBC Radio 4 for the same. Chris and Judith at Northwest Playwrights for their ardent commitment to new writers;

Maurice and Moira Behan, Fiona, George and Amy Browne for putting a roof over my head when I first moved to Dublin and for keeping me in cheese (the Galtee kind, not the Barry White kind). My family in Tipperary, especially Josie and Tom O'Keeffe for all of their kindness, laughs and spotted dog over the years;

Andrew Burke for his constant friendship, counsel and hilarity;

Sarah Cannon and Martin Turton for listening to my inane witterings while writing this book and for being great housemates and friends;

And to the following; Kate Kissane for all things Kerry, Grant Louche for lots of things Rory. Steve Timmons for all the encouragement and Irishisms. Ian Scott for introducing me to Dublin. Sally Sheridan for her great enthusiasm. Heather Linnitt for having far more style and fashion sense than I have. Marcus Lanigan for his friendship while I was in Ireland. Vincent and Anna Byrne for their kindness and also for their knowledge of Dublin. Lyndsey Foulds for her legal knowledge. Sandra Dickenson for all her great stories. Julie Holt, Helen O'Donnell, Diane Tavernier, Shireen Lloyd, Kathy James, Michelle Bennett, James Holland, Becky Ascough, Nevan Bermingham, Stuart Hibbert, Brigid Callaghan, George Browne Snr, and Steve Condon, for their help, reading and feedback. Sharon Jones and Jane Chapman for their reading and help during the final mad, staring eyes, hair-combed-over-like-Arthur-Scargill stage. All who worked with me at the restaurant throughout the writing of this book, I hope this is a 'restaurant quality' novel.

And thank you and thank you again to Donal Byrne for just about everything.

Finally thanks to everyone who has told me their Bono stories. I couldn't fit them all in!

Chapter One

You've got one, haven't you? A Bono story. Go on, think about it: you might not even realise it, but somewhere, buried away in the dark recesses of your mind, it's there. You know how they go:

'Bono? Grand fella altogether. Mind you, my friend's brother was in the school choir with him – couldn't sing for shite, apparently....'

'Stood next to him in the jacks in Grogan's. He clocked me out of the corner of his eye while he was staring down at his mickey. Well, I'd finished me slash and yer man was still standing there. I said, "What's wrong, Bono, stage fright?"'

'Bono? Gobshite! Fucking loves himself. Me and the mot went out in Dalkey one night, and he was at the bar of the Queen's giving it loads. I felt like saying, "You're not at Slane Castle now, there's people trying to have a quiet pint." But herself wanted his autograph so I kept it buttoned.'

Aoife Collins didn't have a Bono story; but that was the least of her worries. After the end of the month, Aoife Collins wouldn't have a roof over her head.

'What do you mean, you're selling the house?' She stared in disbelief at her landlord.

'I'm s-s-sorry, Eefer; it's the e-economic climate, ya know the way.' The feckless, stuttering, moustachioed, bucktoothed eejit, Aoife thought. Economic climate? What he meant was that the shoebox that she and her housemates had been living in for two years was now worth close to half a million pounds. Mr Flaherty was selling it so that he could buy four or five similar shoeboxes in the back-end of Mayo, to rent to Americans as holiday homes. Aoife was fuming.

Mr Flaherty wasn't very good with confrontation. He stared at his feet and said, 'I need you out and that's all there is to it,' as if Aoife and Katie and Ian had chained themselves to the banisters.

'So what are we meant to do?' Aoife demanded. Katie and Ian shrank into the background and let her get on with it. 'I mean, we could be sleeping under O'Connell Bridge this time next week for all you care, as long as you've got your money! And don't you dare talk about the economic climate, because it's created gobshites like you!' Aoife stood shaking while Mr Flaherty's head turned an interesting shade of puce. She'd shocked herself with this outburst, but she wasn't about to let him know that.

'I have never been talked to in such a downright rude way, young lady. I was going to give you a good six or seven weeks to find somewhere else, but I want you out in two weeks' time! And you'd better leave this place as you found it, with all the bills up to date, or there'll be no deposit back for you.' With that, he marched out, slamming the front door.

'Well, you messed that up, Aoife. Thanks a million.' Katie sat at the kitchen table, looking at Aoife as if she were something sitting on the back of something the cat had dragged in.

'Messed it up? How did I mess it up? If I'd been nice and polite to him, what would he have said? "I'm sorry, lads. I won't be selling my house for half a million pounds after all; you can live in it for the rest of your lives"?' Aoife slumped down in the chair opposite Katie. 'Although it did come out a bit on the harsh side, didn't it?'

Ian looked out the kitchen window to check that the landlord had gone. 'Just a bit. Anyway, I'm with you, Aoife: he'd have fecked us out at the end of the month, no matter what, the old bollix. Fuck him. I'm not sitting around here wallowing; I'm going down to Slattery's. Who's coming?'

They headed off down to the pub, in the hope that they might find a nice three-bedroom period residence at the bottom of a pint glass. They didn't.

'What are we going to do?' Katie asked, as Aoife returned from the bar with the fourth round.

'Well,' Aoife said. 'I think that we should get the weekend over with, and then we're going to have to go on a massive house-hunt.'

'I can't bear it!' Ian wailed, hitting his head repeatedly on the table. 'For the last two years, I've been the smug bastard who lived in Rathmines for three hundred euro a month. Now I'm going to be the homeless poor bastard who has to fling himself on the *Evening Herald* as soon as it rolls off the press so I can plead with people to let me look at their houses. It's so demeaning.' Aoife and Katie agreed that it was going to be an absolute pain.

They decided on a small but perfectly formed plan of action. Tonight they would concentrate on slagging off the landlord; over the weekend they would go out and get utterly buckled and pretend that they owned a flat overlooking the Liffey; and on Monday, they would allow the panic to set in.

Katie and Ian decided to go into town to well and truly drown their sorrows, and Aoife wandered home alone.

When she was sixteen, Aoife thought, if someone had told her that in ten years' time she would have a nondescript job and would be getting turfed out of her rented accommodation, she would have laughed. Aoife had wanted to be a dress designer – she was going to be the next Lainey Keogh – but along the way she had somehow got sidetracked and had gone along with her mother's brilliant idea that she should do economics at college. 'It'll stand you in good stead,' her mammy had said.

Yeah, Aoife thought, feeling sorry for herself, *in an underpaid office job that I could have got with three passes in the Junior Cert.* She dragged her feet down the alley that led to her house. In her more self-pitying moments, Aoife thought that she really ought to do something about her career. She made most of her own clothes, and people always commented on them; she was often asked where she got them, and several times she'd been asked to make things for friends and friends of friends. But Aoife had the business acumen of a Shaolin monk, and whenever she made anything, she finished up giving it away and refusing to take any money.

As she opened the door and punched in the alarm code, she made a mental note to get off her bum and have a look in the markets around George's Street and Temple Bar, and maybe even Blackrock, to see if anyone would be interested in her designs. But by the time she slid into bed, she had already let the idea fall from the forefront of her mind and was back to worrying about how she was going to replace the roof over her head.

Aoife awoke feeling slightly the worse for wear. She pulled herself out of bed and into the bathroom. Looking in the mirror, she inspected her eyes by pulling at the skin under them; she dragged at a non-existent double chin and then arched her eyebrows to see if a look of permanent surprise might make her look slightly more presentable. She concluded that she looked terrible. This wasn't strictly true. Aoife was tall, and, with her dark shoulder-length hair and olive skin, on her better days she could pull off a fairly good impression of Andrea Roche. Today wasn't one of them.

Aoife stood in the shower for fifteen minutes, trying to wake herself up. When it didn't work, she dragged herself into her bedroom. She didn't know why she was complaining so vehemently about moving out of this room. Jaysus, it was small, she thought. In fact, it was tiny. She definitely wouldn't be having any cat-swinging competitions in it before she left. Aoife threw a pile of clothes from the floor to the bed – the same pile of clothes that she would throw on the floor again that night when she wanted to go to sleep – and rifled through them to find something clean to wear to work. She pulled on a lamb's-wool sweater, a calf-length cord skirt and comfy brown loafers – she had long ago realised that the walk into town wouldn't tolerate ridiculous work shoes – and stuffed a tiny antique diamanté butterfly hairgrip into her hair. Taking a fleeting look in the mirror, she gave herself the all-clear for a day in the office before grabbing her jacket and heading out the door.

As she neared Baggot Street, Aoife felt a familiar dread about the eight hours that lay ahead. But things had been quiet at work of late; hopefully there

6

wouldn't be too much to do, and she would be able to concentrate on hunting on the Internet for a new home.

Aoife worked for a company called Join the Dots. She had been their office manager for the past year and a half, and she still didn't know what they did – or what she did, for that matter. Well, she knew it was a search-engine company, but that didn't account for the lack of visible work that took place there. All she did know was that the fifteen employees sent one another a lot of obscene e-mails, and that most of the company's budget was spent in pubs on Baggot Street and restaurants in Temple Bar.

The office was in an old Georgian house on Merrion Square. Only today, Aoife didn't get as far as the postcard-worthy red door; she stood stock-still in the street, staring in disbelief. There were men carrying what appeared to be all of the company's computers down the steps.

She stood watching them for what seemed like a few weeks, until her brain shifted her gob straight into fifth gear.

'What the feck is going on?' she demanded of a weather-beaten man with three keyboards under his arm.

'Sorry – only doin' a job, righ'?' he said, bustling past.

'Yeah, but what *is* your job, exactly?'

'Repo, love. Your firm's up the spout,' he commented nonchalantly.

Aoife ran up the stairs. Her boss, Chris, was

standing in his office, looking like he was trying to figure out where he had put his company.

'What is the story, if you don't mind me asking?' Aoife demanded, gazing around at the half-empty office.

'No story, really. We're finished. I got a call from Montreal yesterday saying that the Dublin office wasn't making any profit. "Trying times for Internet companies," and all that shit.' He picked up some computer cables, like a dying soldier trying to salvage his own entrails.

'So what are we going to do?' Aoife stuffed her hands into the pockets of her tweed jacket with such force that her fist flew through the lining. She was getting angry.

'Well, I'm sorry to say this, but everyone has been let go. Well, everyone except me – I've been relocated to the London office.' Chris gave her a toothy half-smile.

Aoife couldn't believe he was saying it like it was the most normal thing in the world. There had been no clue that this was going to happen. Up until yesterday, she had been happily organising overpriced lunches in restaurants on St Stephen's Green, getting free weekend junkets at various castles around Ireland, and changing her job title from PA to Office Manager to Accountant depending on what mood she was in. Now she had another title – Unemployed – and she wasn't happy.

'Oh, well, as long as you're all right.'

Her soon-to-be-ex-boss gave her the smug grin that he used to cover a multitude of sins.

'Look, Aoife, don't get thick with me; I didn't know about it, honest. Anyway, there's loads of office-managery positions out there.'

Yeah, yeah, yeah, you patronising twat, Aoife thought. 'So what now, then?' she asked, looking at him as if he had just crawled out from under a laptop.

'You'll all be paid till the end of the month, and then that's it for Join the Dots – or, more like, Join the Dole Queue.' He nearly broke his ribs laughing at his own side-splitting joke, but Aoife didn't humour him; she just waited for him to finish his laugh.

'Sorry; I'll give you a good reference.' Chris shrugged his shoulders in a 'hey, don't shoot the messenger' way.

'Yeah, right. Thanks a million.' She turned to walk away.

'Aoife?' he called after her.

'Yeah?' She turned, as a burly man with a liberal attitude to personal hygiene bustled past her with a hard drive and a monitor.

'We could go out for a drink.' The shrug again.

Aoife looked at him. He was at least three inches shorter than her, weighed about nine stone with his clothes wet, had a designer beard that made him look like a pimp, and was one of the smarmiest men she had ever met.

'Yeah, we could,' she told him. 'But I'd rather eat

my own shite.' She turned around and walked down the stairs, with the walk of someone who expected rapturous applause from an appreciative audience.

She allowed herself two minutes of self-congratulation on her fantastic retort before descending into half an hour of self-flagellation about the fact that, with one throwaway comment, she had just stuffed her reference for the past year and a half.

Walking past Trinity College, Aoife headed for the river; she desperately needed some inspiration.

Chapter Two

Aoife walked down to O'Connell Bridge and stared at the Liffey. It was a cold, clear spring day; the sun was blindingly bright, and the city was abuzz with people. Aoife stood on the bridge watching as everyone rushed past her in different directions – all, it seemed, with something to do. There were people firing in and out of shops and bars; the student travel place was mobbed; even down as far as the Four Courts, people were busy doing things.

Aoife looked down at the river to see if the calming water could do anything to lift her spirits, but the Liffey had been drained, and an upturned shopping trolley and a welly weren't exactly what she'd had in mind, muse-wise. So she decided to ring Rory, her best friend; he was bound to be hanging around town somewhere, and he'd help sort her head out. She pulled her mobile from her pocket and dialled Rory's number.

'Hi, babe, how are you?'

'I'm fine, Ror – I'm….' Aoife couldn't finish her sentence; she felt her voice breaking.

'Where are you?' Rory asked with concern.

'I'm on O'Connell Bridge,' Aoife said through sniffs, trying to compose herself.

'You're not about to jump, are you?'

'No, I'm not about to bloody jump!' Aoife snapped.

'Good,' Rory replied. 'I'll be there in two minutes; I'm just round by the back of Trinity.'

A few minutes later, Aoife saw Rory jump out of a taxi by the Centra on the corner of O'Connell Bridge. He ran across the road, dodging oncoming cars and getting the finger from a few of the drivers. He had on a pair of battered Levis and a three-quarter-length leather jacket. A woolly hat was pulled over his mop of sandy hair; that hat would have made most men look like only their mammies loved them, but Rory carried it off. Aoife didn't really notice how great he looked; she was too used to seeing him, and too busy wondering what she was going to do about her predicament.

Rory gave her an enormous bear hug.

'Where's your car?' Aoife asked. Rory loved his car. It was a 1964 Jaguar E-type that spent more time in the garage, being fixed, than it did on the road.

'Never mind that! What's wrong with you?' Rory asked, pulling his head back to look at Aoife.

'I'm sorry for bawling like a big girl's blouse, Rory. It's just that I've had the shittiest twenty-four hours.'

'Has anyone hurt you?'

'No!' Aoife laughed. 'No one's beaten me up, if that's what you mean.' Rory could be more over-protective than her mother.

'Good. Why don't we go grab a drink, and you can tell Uncle Rory what the story is.'

They sat down in Pulse, Rory's favourite restaurant, and over a few beers Aoife told Rory everything that had happened. She was completely at ease with Rory. They had been friends since they'd met, eight years before, at university in Galway. Aoife had trailed Rory for a good few weeks, deciding that he was her ideal man and convincing herself that they would be together. It was only when she'd engineered a night in for herself and Rory that he'd realised she was going to make a play for him, and he had had to be honest with her and with himself. Aoife was the first person Rory had told that he was gay, and they had been each other's confidants ever since. This, however, didn't stop Rory from mercilessly ripping the mickey out of Aoife, whenever the mood struck him, about her ham-fisted attempt at pulling him all those years ago.

Aoife pulled absentmindedly at the label of her beer bottle. 'I'm up shit creek, Ror – financially, I mean; I'm bollixed. I spend money like someone who actually has some. And what have I got to show for it?' Rory was about to open his mouth, but he realised that Aoife wasn't looking for an answer. 'Nothing, that's what: nothing. Just a load of debts.'

At the word 'debts', Rory became concerned. Aoife very rarely talked about money; while she was working, she put any debts she had to the back of her mind. But now, with the grim prospect of unemployment hanging over her head, her brain had gone into debt-collector mode and she was visibly worried.

'Debts?' Rory asked uncomfortably. 'What debts?'

'Well, I've got the two credit cards – and then there's the car loan that I took out and never actually got round to buying a car with.'

'You did *what*?' Rory shrieked.

'Don't shout, Rory. That's how I paid for my ticket when yourself and myself went on holiday the other year – and then I was going to get a car, but there never seemed to be a right time, so the money just sat in my bank and got eaten up by my rent and my credit-card repayments.'

'Jesus!' Rory said. He had never thought about how Aoife got her money; he was relatively rolling in it, so money, or the lack of it, wasn't something he often thought about.

'I had a meeting with my bank manager last week.'

'The bank manager? I didn't know people still had meetings with bank managers in this day and age.'

'Well, they do. He nearly read me the riot act. I knew I shouldn't have transferred my account to Dublin. When it was in Kerry, I could get extensions to overdrafts, credit union loans ... the only question they

14

asked me was how my mammy was keeping. Not up here. He showed me a screen of what I spend, and I don't know where it all goes. I was mortified, Ror.' Aoife rubbed her forehead. 'He wants me to repay my overdraft immediately.'

'And how much is that, on top of what you owe?'

'Two grand,' Aoife whispered.

'I'll lend you some money,' Rory said.

'Don't be so stupid. I can't borrow money from you.'

'Why not?' Rory asked indignantly. 'You need to get money from somewhere.'

'That's true, but I just can't. Anyway, what I need to do is find another job and cop onto myself. I can't spend money like I'm going out with Jim Corr, not until I am going out with Jim Corr.'

Rory screwed up his face. 'Fine, babe, but there's got to be a better way for you to make money in the meantime. Anyway, Jim Corr just isn't your type; you're more of a Michael Flatley woman, I'd have thought.'

'Michael Flatley?' Aoife screwed up her face, aghast.

'Did I say Michael Flatley? I meant Colin Farrell; I'm forever getting the two mixed up. Right, I'm getting you a drink,' Rory said, before Aoife had time to protest further. 'What do you want – a Bud?'

'No, I'll have a white wine, please.'

Ten hours later, Aoife and Rory were still sitting in Pulse, having eaten lunch and dinner there and having taken several bottles of wine on board. They were well and truly past the point of sensible speech, and Aoife was putting the world to rights.

'I hate Dublin!'

'You do not! You absolutely love it, 'cause I'm here and most of your friends are here. Don't talk complete bollix.' Rory hadn't heard Aoife sounding like this in as long as he could remember. She usually took things in her stride.

Aoife snorted. 'Friends? I hardly see any of them. They're all too busy buying houses in Lucan, or being amazing at their jobs, to meet me for a drink. I haven't seen anyone but you in months.' This wasn't necessarily the fault of Aoife's friends, as Rory well knew. She much preferred spending her time with him. The two of them had a great time together, and Aoife thought that a lot of her other friends from college had turned very boring recently. But Rory wasn't about to point this out; he knew he wasn't going to get a word in edgeways for a while.

'Anyway, that's not what I was on about.' She looked at Rory, momentarily confused. 'What was I on about?' Then it dawned on her. 'Oh, yeah.... I do; I fucking hate it. Look what it's become – look at everyone.' Aoife was waving her arms around as if to indicate that the five tables of people in Pulse were representative of the Dublin populace. 'Social climbers, wannabes – everyone wants to live in Dublin fucking 4....'

'You'd give your right tit to live in Dublin fucking 4. In fact, Aoife my sweet, you'd give your right tit to live anywhere at the moment.'

Aoife was indignant. 'You know what I mean. Dublin wasn't like this fifteen years ago – it was … I don't know … undiscovered.' She was still waving her arms around.

Rory was beginning to lose his patience. 'Ah, would you listen to yourself? You are talking utter rubbish. Dublin wasn't *undiscovered*; there was just nothing to bring people here. We had no economy; our only exports were cow shit and U2. But now it's the place to be. Yes, it can be a struggle, but that's the price you pay. When you were on top of it all, you loved it, but a couple of things go wrong and you've got a face like a slapped arse. Well, cop on, girl; it's not terminal, you know. You just need to get a job.'

'I know I need to get a job! I don't need to be lectured by someone who's done precisely three days' work in his life!'

'Oh, God, are we back on this again? Stop feeling sorry for yourself.'

Aoife stared at Rory. To be precise, Aoife tried to focus, couldn't, and honed in on a lamp behind Rory's head, in the hope that it would look like she was staring at him.

'I am not feeling sorry for myself. I just think that Dublin's shite!'

Rory, who realised that she was emotional and drunk, gave up playing devil's advocate. For all his bravado, he knew how well off he was.

Rory's father was a very wealthy man who was happy to give his son money in order to keep him in the lifestyle to which he was accustomed, and out of his hair. Rory was aware that this was guilt money because of the hopeless job his father had made of actually being a father when Rory was growing up. This made it easier for Rory to take the money without too many qualms or attacks of Catholic guilt.

Rory bent forward and took Aoife's hands. 'Aoife!' he said.

'What?' She looked at him, bleary-eyed, as if she had just realised that he was there.

'Let me lend you the money,' Rory said.

Aoife shook her head from side to side, drunkenly adamant.

'Not a chance; no way.' She kept shaking her head. 'I can't take money from you. It would be just hanging over my head, and I'd be annoyed at myself for agreeing to it in the first place – and, besides, I've never taken a loan for anything before....'

'Except from the bank,' Rory interrupted.

'That's different; that's the bank, not my friend who I see nearly every day. I can just pay the bank back, and that's that.'

'Can you, though? You sounded worried earlier. *Are* you paying back your loans and stuff?'

Aoife was getting annoyed. She didn't think that Pulse was the best place to discuss the mess that her finances were in. The truth was that, even when she was employed, she had found it hard to make ends meet. When she had told Rory that she had two credit cards, she had omitted the tiny detail that they were both up to their limit. If she was honest with herself, Aoife desperately needed help. But she wasn't about to take it from Rory.

'Look, it's fine, Rory. I don't want to talk about it now; it'll keep.'

Rory knew not to press her. 'OK, fine. But I did offer. Shall we go?'

'Yeah, that's a good idea.'

After an ill-fated half-hour attempt to flag a taxi, Rory and Aoife drunkenly stumbled back to Rory's apartment in Ballsbridge. Aoife's head was swimming – they had been drinking for well over twelve hours – but this didn't stop her from accepting the glass of vodka that Rory thrust into her hand.

Aoife managed to bring the conversation back to the social climbers and wannabes in Dublin, and Rory was growing tired it. 'The thing is, Aoifey,' he said, putting on a Stevie Wonder CD, 'you would love to be one of those people that you're pretending to despise so much – farting around at the Shelbourne or the Morrison or the Bailey, rubbing shoulders with people you vaguely recognise from the Style supplement in the *Times*....'

'That is a disgusting thing to say!' Aoife hated it when Rory patronised her. 'If I was like that, I'd be at all the tin-pot parties you go to, but I'm not!' This wasn't strictly true. If anyone had given her a social ladder, she'd have been up it quicker than you could say Terry Keane.

'Oh, yes, you bleeding well are. The only ones you don't go to are the ones you're not invited to.'

'You cheeky twat! Just because you once stood downwind from Bono doesn't give you the right to criticise me!' Aoife leapt to her feet, but decided that it would be best for all concerned if she sat down, as the room was swaying.

'I didn't *stand downwind* from him, as well you know. I met him at a gala dinner in Clontarf Castle, actually.'

'Yeah, you and the rest of fucking Dublin.'

'"Yeah, you and the rest of fucking Dublin,"' Rory mimicked in a whiny, high-pitched voice. 'Listen to yourself.'

'Don't you "listen to yourself" me!' Aoife said, springing to her feet again. All of the ideas that had been rattling around in her head had solidified, making her think she'd created the greatest social theory about human society ever conceived. 'That's what's wrong with Dublin today. Everyone's got a Bono story, everyone!' Rory tried to focus on her as she paced up and down the room. 'No one takes a blind bit of notice of the people we elect into power. Bertie could cartwheel naked down Kildare Street and no one would bat an eyelid. But Bono – he only has to fart and the entire city comes to a standstill.' She was on a roll now, the ideas coming thick and fast. 'And everyone thinks they know him, or helped him on his way. Well, I haven't got a Bono story! I haven't sat next to him in a bar, or seen him at the Dandelion Market for ten pence in 1982, or had him stop in his Merc to help me with my shopping. I don't know if he's fantastic or just all right or a complete bollix – because I haven't got a Bono story!' She stood, swaying, her glass raised, like a drunk, poor man's Braveheart.

'Yeah, and you couldn't get one either,' Rory whispered, almost to himself, knowing that Aoife would hear.

'What?' She had.

Rory sat up in his chair, preparing himself for another verbal onslaught. 'You couldn't get one. For all your mouth, there's no way you'd talk to someone like Bono; you'd shit yourself.' He was winding her up, but Aoife was too drunk to realise.

'I fucking well would not! I'd talk to anyone, especially bleeding Bono.'

'I bet you wouldn't.' Rory was goading her, but, as usual, she couldn't see it.

'I bet I fucking well would.'

'How much?'

'What?'

'You heard; I said, how much?'

The next morning Aoife woke up in Rory's spare bedroom, feeling as if someone was kicking her repeatedly in the left temple. She pulled her head up off the pillow and turned it slightly towards the window to gauge what time it was. A shaft of light glanced through the curtain and Aoife felt as if her retinas had just been singed to the back of her head. She put her head back in the pillow.

Rory was up already; Aoife could hear him clanking around in the kitchen. He always did this; for someone who wouldn't know what work was if it jumped up and bit him on the bum, he didn't need much sleep. He came bustling into the bedroom with breakfast on a tray.

'Mornin', babe; here's your brekky.' He plonked the tray down on the bed next to Aoife.

'Rory, I can't eat.' Aoife turned around slowly, so as not to take her body by surprise.

'Yes you can. Oh, and here's your agreement.' Rory threw a piece of paper at Aoife. She stared at it as if she had never clapped eyes on it before; as far as she was concerned, she hadn't.

'What agreement?'

'What agreement? Christ, girl, you were buckled last night! The Bono bet!'

'Bono bet?' Aoife read down the page. The writing looked like a five-year-old's.

I, Rory O'Donnell, do bet you, Aoife Collins, the sum of 5,000 euros that you will not be the possessor of a Bono story by 31 May. The rules of the engagement are as follows:

- Your Bono story must be a conversation with the man himself, at the end of which Bono must know your full name and be in no doubt as to who Aoife Collins is – i.e. you cannot just wave at him across the Liffey as he is holding a press conference outside the Clarence.

- It must take place in Dublin, as this is where your half-arsed theory pertains.

- You cannot contact his record company to find out where he is. This is too calculating and goes against the spirit of the bet.

- No stalking. The bet is null and void if you incur a barring order against yourself.

- You are not allowed to ask Rory to get you on the guest list to Lillie's every night in the vain hope that you will meet him. This is sad and you will undoubtedly turn into a lush.

- You will not use feminine wiles to get you an introduction to Bono. This will not end in an audience with Bono but more likely in a visit to the clap clinic.

I swear on my life to abide by these rules.
Signed, Aoife Collins
Second Signature and Witness, Rory O'Donnell

Aoife shook her head. The previous night's events were beginning to clatter back into her mind.

'Jaysus, Rory, you are not serious.' She tossed the piece of paper to one side.

'I bloody well am.' Rory was only half-listening; he was checking the voice messages on his mobile.

'You'll pay me five thousand squid if I get to meet Bono?' Aoife looked from the piece of paper to Rory and back at the piece of paper again.

'Yeah, as long as you follow the rules.'

'What's in it for you?'

'Just a good laugh at your expense,' Rory said, flopping down on the bed beside Aoife.

She peered at him. 'So you want me to make a dick of myself for five grand?'

'Yeah, that's about the size of it.'

Aoife propped herself up on her side and stuck her hand out for Rory to shake.

'Right, you bollix. You're on.'

Chapter Three

Paddy's weekend in Dublin tends to be a very hit-and-miss affair. If you were to spend 17 March in New York or Sydney, or anywhere else in the world – with the possible exception of Saudi Arabia or the northernmost reaches of the Arctic Circle – then you would generally be guaranteed a great day. Dublin, however, is different.

In Dublin you can pick any night of the year to go out, and the craic will be mighty. The thing about Paddy's Day, especially if it falls at a weekend, is that it's anticipated out of all proportion, only for people to discover that there is actually a maximum level of craic that they can have. Add to this the pressure of arranging to meet people, only to miss them because their mobile phone is on vibrate in their coat, and the general logistics of getting a pint when you can't even see the bar because the place is mobbed, and it can add up to a fairly joyless night.

But if you hit on a good year, it's great – better than great; it's brilliant. Seat in the corner of your favourite bar, nine or ten pints on board, talking utter rubbish to all around you; no better way to spend the long weekend.

Aoife, Ian and Katie headed down to the Dakota Bar on Fitzwilliam Street, where they had arranged to meet Rory. The place was jammed with wall-to-wall beautiful people, all of them dressed in black; it looked like a cross between an Andy Warhol party and a puppeteers' convention. Aoife had bucked the trend and was wearing her favourite battered old jeans, which she swore she would wear until the backside actually fell out of them, and a pink top that she had made from sari material.

Rory arrived fifteen minutes later. 'Looking good, babe,' he told Aoife. 'Very mysterious and Eastern.'

'Oh, this….' Aoife said, looking down at her attire. 'It's just something I made the other week; it's not –'

'Thank you for the compliment, Rory,' Rory interrupted; 'I'm glad you noticed that I look nice, because I do.' Aoife was useless at taking a compliment, and she knew it drove Rory nuts.

'Thank you,' she said, matching his stare, embarrassed.

As the night wore on, Katie and Ian became lost in their own conversation, and Rory and Aoife were left discussing Aoife's fortunes or the lack thereof. 'Well, it all boils down to you doing one thing, doesn't it, foxy locks?'

'What?' Aoife sipped her wine.

'Don't give me "what". I've a five-grand, one-sided wager with you that you can't get to meet the lovely Bono by the end of May, remember? Or has someone removed your memory chip?'

They mulled over the different approaches that Aoife could take. Rory suggested that she should get a job in the sunglasses department of Brown Thomas, on the off-chance that Bono might sit on his fly glasses and need a new pair, but they decided that he probably had a dresser for that sort of thing. Aoife thought she might get a job on the door of Lillie's or Spy; but Rory pointed out that she wouldn't know who was really who in Dublin, and the only people she'd end up letting in would be Gay Byrne and Ronan Keating. Another idea was that Aoife should enrol with Rory's doctor, as Bono was apparently a patient there and was being treated for an ongoing throat problem, but this one bit the dust when Aoife pointed out that there were only so many times that she could sit in the doctor's waiting room faking illness before he would diagnose her as a hypochondriac. Besides, it would cost a small fortune.

In the end, they decided to go for a two-pronged attack. The first prong was for Aoife to try to get a job at one of the restaurants that Bono allegedly frequented. The second was for her to try to gain access to Bono's house under the pretence of collecting for charity. Aoife had the feeling that this one might not be such a great idea in the cold light of day, but it would have to do for the time being.

It became clear that at some stage they were going to have to move or be thrown out on their ears. Rory already had this sorted: he had guest-list passes to some new club.

The four weaved in and out of the lanes towards Wexford Street without too much trouble. True, town was teeming with people, but they were mostly in good spirits. Eventually they arrived at a steel door down an alleyway. At first, Aoife thought there was no sign on the door, but then she saw it, etched in the red-brick wall in inch-high letters; it read 'bubble'. *But of course*, thought Aoife: *the more pretentious the club, the smaller the sign*. And if there was a new up-itself bar in Dublin, Rory would have sniffed it out within three seconds of the opening.

The bouncer greeted Rory with a big, knowing smile. 'Well, Rory boy, long time no see.' He looked Rory up and down.

'I've been busy,' Rory said; he was trying to look uninterested, but Aoife could tell that he was flirting. 'So, how are you?'

'Grand,' said the bouncer, slapping his leather-clad hands together. 'And all the better for seeing you.' He winked at Rory.

'Well, I'm sure I can come and discuss this some more, once my friends are out of the freezing cold and in your club.'

The club was so dimly lit that people were bumping into things. There were low, cushioned seats scattered around, with lots of posing people trying to outdo one another in the ultra-cool stakes. To Aoife's right were three old fellas propping up the bar. One was saying, 'Jayz, Tom, there's not a fecking pint of Guinness in sight.' He was right: everyone was drinking bottles or shorts. He leant across and said to Aoife, 'Is this where you young ones come these days?'

'Well, it's the first time I've been here, but yes, I suppose it is,' she shouted over the ambient music.

'Used to be our local, and they shagged us out of it. But I made the fella on the door let us in. And look at the state of the place – they fecked it up something rotten.'

'Can I buy you fellas a drink?' Rory offered. 'Since this used to be your pub and all.'

The three old men looked at one another and agreed that it probably wouldn't do any harm.

They found themselves a group of symmetrically arranged seats. Aoife looked over at the three old fellas they had acquired; they were in a line, like the wise monkeys, and they couldn't have looked more uncomfortable if they had been hung by the ankles from the ceiling. 'You all right, lads?' Aoife shouted to them.

'Aye.'

'Grand.'

'Fine. Not a bother.'

They all sipped the Bacardi Breezers that Rory, much to his own private amusement, had bought for them. He had disappeared after giving everyone their drinks; whispering in Aoife's ear, 'Business to attend to, babe,' before heading back in the direction of the bouncer. Aoife rolled her eyes.

She took herself off to the toilet. When she came back, Katie and Ian were up dancing with the old boys and Rory was still nowhere to be seen. She sat down, deciding that watching old men dance to ambient music was probably better than joining in.

'Hi, Catherine?' Aoife swung round; the voice behind her had a broad north-side accent and was obviously, incorrectly, directed at her. 'Oh, God, I'm sorry – from the back you are the spit of a girl I went to school with.'

'Yeah, the back of my head is very common-looking,' Aoife said, and then cringed for herself.

The man smiled shyly.

'Do you mind if I join you for a moment? I'm just waiting for some friends.'

'Not at all.' Aoife shuffled up on her seat. Katie, seeing that she had some male company, waved over at her.

'They your friends?' the man asked.

'Well, two of them are my housemates, and the three old fellas we somehow acquired along the way.'

'Not joining them, then?'

'I've a fairly low embarrassment threshold, so I think I might sit this one out.'

'You're probably dead right.'

Aoife had a slight panicky feeling in her stomach; if she had thought about its cause, she would have realised it was butterflies because this man was a fine thing. But she was too busy trying to think of something to say.

'I'm Aoife, by the way,' she said, trying to play it cool and missing the mark by a mile.

'Hi, Aoife; I'm Paul.' Aoife stuck out her hand awkwardly, and Paul gave a small laugh of embarrassment as he shook it; she smiled.

Paul told Aoife that his friends were always late, and that he never usually went to trendy clubs but that he was making an exception this weekend. Aoife looked at him as he spoke. He was gorgeous. Paul had short, dark, wavy hair and bright blue eyes, and he was dressed in jeans and a black top that fit so that Aoife couldn't help noticing how broad his shoulders were. She was dying for Rory to return and confirm her suspicion that she was, in fact, talking to the finest thing in the place.

They had been chatting easily for a while when Aoife's eye fell on a man sitting opposite them. He had a champagne bucket in front of him. It appeared that he wanted it replenished but wasn't willing to leave his chair; he was clicking his fingers and waving a twenty-euro note.

'I'm so glad I don't work here,' Aoife said. 'I'd take that twenty-euro note and shove it somewhere for him.'

Paul laughed. 'He's some gobshite, all right. What do you do for a living, if it's not currency insertion?'

Aoife felt her face flush. 'Well, I'm an office manager in Merrion Square,' she said, trying to present herself as the modern working woman and not spill her guts about the shambolic state her life was in.

'Very good,' Paul said, nodding. 'How long have you been at that?'

'Oh, a while.' Aoife looked around the club, trying to be nonchalant, but her mouth got the better of her. 'Actually, I was made redundant this week,' she admitted.

She ended up telling him all about her run of bad luck. 'And so,' she concluded, 'looks like I might be on the job scrap-heap; in fact, the way this week's going, I'll probably finish up cleaning sanitary bins for a living.' Paul laughed. 'Anyway, that's enough about my woe-is-me week. What about you?'

'I work for an events-management company.'

'Really?' Aoife asked, perking up at the mention of a job that might be vaguely interesting. 'Where-abouts?'

'The office is on Ely Place, but I work all over Dublin.'

'Cool,' Aoife said, genuinely impressed.

'It pays the bills.' Paul smiled at her. 'I'd like to do something I genuinely loved, though.'

'God, tell me about it.' Aoife sighed. Paul looked at her; she had obviously thought about this one.

'So go on – what would you do if you could do anything?' he asked.

'You first; you asked the question.'

'God, I've no idea. I haven't got anything that I'm particularly good at.'

'There must be something.'

'Actually, yeah, I'm secretly brilliant at football; I would be a striker for Manchester United, but I don't like working evenings and weekends.' Aoife laughed. 'Or I'd be a rock star; I think I could really handle the lifestyle. And I can play the tin whistle, so I suppose that's a start.' Paul smiled at Aoife. 'What about you? If you could do anything, what would you do?'

She didn't even have to think about it. 'I'd design clothes.'

'Is that something you're into?' He seemed genuinely interested.

'Yeah, I make most of my own clothes.' Aoife said excitedly, and then realised that she might be offering slightly too much information, simply because she wanted to convey to Paul that she was interesting and that he shouldn't run off just yet.

'Well, if what you're wearing is anything to go by, then I think you could make a fair living at it.'

Aoife blushed and was thankful that the club was dark.

'So,' she said, deciding to steer the conversation away from herself, 'have you ever met Bono?'

'Have I what?' Paul looked at her in confusion and amusement.

'You heard. As a budding rock star, have you ever met Bono?'

'Well, he hasn't asked me to accompany him anywhere on a Learjet, if that's what you mean.' Paul took a slurp of his drink. 'No, I haven't met Bono. Although I did see him in a restaurant in Temple Bar where a friend of mine worked. They didn't sell Guinness, and he asked her if she'd go and get him a pint from over the road.'

'Did she go?' Aoife asked, smiling.

'Course she did. It was Bono. Anyway, why do you ask?'

Aoife was about to tell him about her bet when she saw Rory weaving towards them through the crowd. 'Just wondering,' she said. Rory eyed Paul and raised a complimentary eyebrow towards Aoife.

'Ror, this is Paul; Paul this is Rory.'

'Pleased to meet you,' Rory said, smiling his charming smile and sliding into a seat. Aoife, who had initially been glad to see him, realised that he was going to hold court and immediately wanted him to go away again.

He didn't. Instead he started waxing lyrical about St Patrick's Day and how all the plastic Paddies were out in droves. Then Paul spotted one of his friends walking in.

'Listen, it was really good talking to you.'

Aoife's heart sank; there was still no sign of Rory budging. 'Yeah, and you.'

Paul seemed to realise that Rory wasn't going to give them a minute's peace, and obviously decided to bite the bullet.

'Do you fancy meeting up for a drink – sometime this week, maybe? I'll be around on Thursday – there's a band playing at Whelan's that I wanted to see. Would you like to join me?'

'Yeah, that'd be great!' The words were out of Aoife's mouth before her brain could tell her to act cool and calm. Rory's head was whipping from side to side like he was enjoying an afternoon at Wimbledon.

'What's your number?' Paul took his mobile phone from his pocket and keyed Aoife's number into it. 'That's great. I'll give you a buzz during the week, then. How's that?'

'Great, yeah.' Aoife smiled, trying not to catch Rory's eye.

'Well, good luck,' Paul said, smiling and heading over to his friend.

Once Paul was safely out of earshot, Aoife turned on Rory.

'Gobshite!'

'Who?' He looked at her innocently.

'You!'

'Why, what have I done?'

'It's what you *didn't* do that's bugging me.'

'What's that, exactly?'

'You didn't get up out of it when I was talking to that guy.'

'Get up out of it? How Kerry.' Rory sipped his drink casually and gazed around the club.

'Rory!'

'What? You gave him your number, didn't you? I don't see what the problem is. He'll ring you, you'll go out, it'll be fine. That is how heterosexual relationships work, isn't it?'

'Arghhh!' Sometimes Aoife couldn't understand how she let Rory wind her up.

'Cool it, babe.' He tickled her under the chin, and she slapped his hand away. 'Fit as fuck, mind you.'

'I know, Rory, and it's been ages since I've had so much as a sniff of anyone I like.'

'That's true. So it's better for you to play it a little bit cool – and if that meant me sitting there till he went, and you not running after him, then surely to Christ that's a good thing, isn't it?'

'Oh, God, I suppose so,' Aoife admitted, throwing her eyes skyward. She had seen this before. Whenever she received any male attention, Rory became all knowing about men and what was best for her.

'Anyway, he's going now,' Rory said. Aoife looked around and saw Paul waving over at her as he left the club. 'His friend obviously couldn't afford the extortionate prices.'

'Either that or he fancied a Guinness.' Aoife looked after Paul. 'Look at him, Ror – he is fine, though, isn't he?'

'I wouldn't kick him out of bed for farting, if that's what you mean.' Rory shrugged dismissively.

'Jealous, are you?'

'Not at all,' Rory said haughtily. 'In fact, I've just been attending to business of my own.' He waved a scribbled beer mat at Aoife.

'Oh, yeah? Who's that?' Aoife asked

'The bouncer; me and him have unfinished business,' Rory said enigmatically.

'Really?' Aoife said in an all-knowing tone, trying to mimic Rory's. Her mind was still on Paul.

'He had a Bono story as well – which reminds me,' she said, draining her drink, 'have you thought of any more plans re: Bono?'

'That's not for me to do, now is it, babe? Where's the fun in that? What about you – what have you come up with?'

'I have got a plan, actually,' Aoife said, trying to look smug and secretive.

'Oh, yeah?'

'You know I said I was going to get a job in a restaurant? Well, do you know Blues, the restaurant on the Green? I remembered, while you were doing whatever you were doing outside, that Bono was spotted there last year. Bernie Curran, a girl I used to work with, saw him.'

'Just because Bernie Curran saw him there once, it doesn't mean he goes all the time.'

'I know, but it's fairly swanky – and, anyway, I could do with the money.' Rory rolled his eyes, pretending to find all of this talk of money vulgar in the extreme. Aoife ignored him. 'Besides that, I'll just keep my ear to the ground.'

'What ground would that be, then? Do you hear a lot about celebs and their whereabouts lying prostrate on the Rathmines Road?'

'No, you sarcastic twat, but whatever ground you keep your ear to seems to come up trumps, now and again.'

Rory shook his head. 'No, no, no, that won't do, I'm afraid. The bet's with me; I can't help you.'

'Why not?' Aoife was indignant.

'Oh, sorry, am I getting all of this wrong? I'll tell you what – I'll just pop to the bank, get five grand out and give it to you, how does that sound?'

'Ah, Rory!'

'Ah, Rory, nothing. It's no fun if I do all of the groundwork for you. I don't mind helping you if you need a lift somewhere, or if you need a bit of moral support; but other than that, you're on your own, babe. Anyway, doesn't it say in the agreement that I won't help you?'

'It says you won't help me get into Lillie's, that's all!' Aoife slumped back in her chair, pretending to sulk. Rory tickled her under the chin.

'Ah, come on, babe; that's fair enough.' He took a swig of his Canadian Club and grimaced. Then something dawned on him.

'When have you ever worked as a waitress before?'

'Em….' Aoife floundered.

'Have you seen the staff in there? They're very good.'

'So? I bet I could do it as well as them.'

'Ah, Aoife, no more stupid bets for you; you're up shit creek as it is. Waitress, indeed…. Anyway, cheers – happy St Paddy's Day!' Rory raised his glass and looked over at Ian, Katie and the three old fellas, who were causing mayhem on the dance floor, doing the conga to Massive Attack.

Chapter Four

Aoife's one claim to waitressing fame was that she had worked in a café in Kilbane for a day at the age of sixteen. She had been unceremoniously dismissed for pouring a pot of tea into some old boy's lap, rather than his cup. But, Aoife reasoned, how hard could it be to carry a couple of plates?

As she walked into Blues on the Green, Aoife was greeted by a tall, wiry man who was rushing around like a mad thing. This was Martin, the manager, whom she had met briefly at her non-interview the previous afternoon, when she had popped in to see if they needed any staff. He had asked her about three questions and then told her she could have a trial shift.

'Oh, hi, Aoife – haven't got much time to spend with you tonight – sorry, probably a bad night to start you – we're two waiters down, so although you'll be shadowing Carmel for the evening when she gets here, you'll find yourself doing quite a bit – but that shouldn't be a problem if I show you the general gist, should it? Now then, if you follow me through....' He almost ran into the main body of the restaurant, gesticulating wildly in no particular direction. 'This is the main room – tables run one to forty-five, clockwise.' Martin swooped his arm around the top of his head like a lasso, presumably to indicate 'clockwise'. Aoife ducked to avoid his returning swing.

'Your section will be tables ten to fifteen – fourteen and fifteen are a table of eight, so they're to be laid together – OK, kitchen.' He flew through the double swing doors into the kitchen; Aoife followed, not having understood a word of what he had just said.

'Boys, this is Aoife – Aoife, Pete is the head chef. During service, what he says goes – John, Connor, Luka, Finty....' None of the names sank in; they just floated past Aoife as she tried to keep up. 'Right, check goes on here – call check on – starters come out here, mains come out here – always call away – that goes without saying, I know I don't really have to tell you – dirty plates here, dirty cutlery here – left door is in from restaurant, right door is out – here's a copy of the menu – any specials, lads?'

'Give us a fucking minute, will you, you fucking gobshite,' said the head chef. Aoife was slightly taken aback. Anywhere she had worked before, people had at least had the decency to pretend that they liked each other. This didn't seem to faze Martin; he looked at the chef as if it were polite banter and walked out of the kitchen, still in full flow.

'Right, so, we'll get the specials in a bit – I'll show you the till – any questions so far?' He stopped dead mid-stride, and Aoife nearly walked straight into his back. She was very aware that she had put herself in a position that she couldn't really get out of and of which she had no comprehension whatsoever. Rory had been right. She was up shit creek, and she didn't even have her boat with her, never mind her paddle.

'Em, no, not so far.' She tried to smile confidently, but finished up looking like she was trying to disguise trapped wind.

She turned her attention to the till as Martin ran through its basic functions. From what Aoife could gather, even its basic functions were so advanced that it could probably have landed a space shuttle on a postage stamp in the Nevada Desert. She was baffled and out of her depth.

Martin told her to cut the fruit for the drinks. Within five seconds of picking up the fruit knife, she cut herself and proceeded to drip blood over the lemons and limes.

At six o'clock a woman came bustling in and announced to Aoife, in what seemed like the friendliest voice she'd ever heard, that she was Carmel and that she was sorry that she was late. Aoife could have kissed her. She felt an instant, clinging-to-driftwood bond with Carmel. Before she had time to stop herself, she had admitted that she had never waitressed before and that she thought she was going to make a complete mess of it. Carmel told her not to worry and that she would help her out.

Aoife also admitted that she was hoping to find Bono there. To which Carmel replied, as she rushed around getting everything ready for service, 'I've never seen him here, although I know he's been in, but I saw him swinging out of the top of the castle gate near the Queen's in Dalkey. Oh, and I stood next to him in the chipper once. He got five lots of cod and chips and a batter burger.'

By the start of service at seven o'clock, Aoife knew what most of Martin's tirade had meant, she knew the house wines and she had been shown how to carry three plates. This in itself was something she had never thought she would achieve.

As customers began to arrive, Aoife decided to just smile, look like she knew what she was doing, keep disasters to a bare minimum and, if they did occur, share them only with Carmel. She hoped the rest would follow. Most of the lads in the kitchen were being as helpful as possible, but the head chef, it seemed, could spot a non-waitress at fifty yards.

'Go on, two medium beef, one duck and a lamb,' he was shouting to all around him. 'Right, new wan, take this lamb and beef to table twelve – that's the lamb and that's the beef, just in case you didn't know.' Aoife decided not to throw any sarcastic comments back; he didn't look like he should be messed with. 'Well, off you go; it's getting fucking cold.' *Twat*, thought Aoife.

By nine o'clock she was getting into the swing of things. Her only serious mistake of the night had been dripping raspberry coulis into a customer's handbag when she was clearing her plate, but the woman hadn't noticed and Aoife had thought it prudent not to say anything. Things seemed to be getting a little easier.

Then the door opened and in walked Chris, her ex-boss, of 'I'd rather eat my own shite' fame. It looked like she was going to have to.

'Hi, Chris. What brings you here?' Aoife asked through gritted teeth.

'Well, pleasure rather than work,' he said with a smug grin, looking Aoife up and down as she stood there with the menu and wine list in her hand. 'So what brings you here? Lack of funds, I presume.' His dinner companion – fat, spiky-haired, wearing dangly parrot earrings – nearly wet herself laughing. Aoife noticed that she laughed like a field of baaing sheep. It was nice, she thought bitchily, that Chris had managed to find himself someone who had smacked off as many branches as he had on the way down the ugly tree.

Aoife checked the booking list; they were booked on table fourteen, one of her tables. *Oh, goodie,* she thought with utter dread.

'So, really, Aoife, what *has* brought you here?' Aoife was clearing the starter plate away from Chris and Sheep Woman.

'I'm looking for Bono,' she said, scraping some lollo rosso off of the plate and onto Chris's leg. 'Shit, sorry.' He wiped his trouser leg and gave her that 'Now, Aoife, who's being a silly little girl?' look that he used to use at work. She could have belted him.

'Why are you looking for Bono?' Chris asked, with an incredulous sneer towards Parrot Earrings, who laughed herself silly again.

'I've got a bet with a friend,' Aoife said, taking his empty beer bottle away.

'There are easier ways of getting to meet Bono than getting a job here, I'm sure. You want to go down to Coast in Howth. I've seen him there loads of times. Stood next to him in the loo of the pub up by the church. Nodded hello to him, like you do – you don't like to bother a man mid-piss, do you?' The sheep were baaing again. 'He's sound, apparently; went to school with my brother's friend.'

'Well, thanks for the advice, but I'm quite enjoying this waitressing thing, to be honest. Anyway, as you told me, there are lots of office-managery positions out there. So I'll go get one when I decide to get round to it.'

She was just about to walk away when Chris beckoned her in conspiratorially. She leaned forward and he whispered, 'It's nice to see you again, but if you don't mind, we'd like some privacy for the rest of the meal.'

Aoife breathed deeply and said, 'I'll see to it that

you are not disturbed, Sir and Moddom.' She took a
long look at Parrot Earrings, who was smiling the
smile of the smug at her fantastic partner, and shook
her head as she walked off, wishing she could strangle
him with his own napkin.

Chapter Five

Aoife rang the intercom and slumped in the doorway, waiting for Rory to answer. Rory ran down to greet her.

'Oh my God, it's the dying swan! What is wrong with you? You look like you've had a death in the family.'

'I've been trying to ring you. Both your phones kept going to the answering machine.'

'I'm screening my calls this morning, avoiding my father. He had me round at his house last night, trying to impress some fellas that he'd dragged up from the country. I was there as chief custodian of wit and repartee, from what I could gather. My dad had me following the usual script.'

Aoife sighed. Rory's father's wealth and status had an enormous hold over Rory. When Rory and Aoife had left college, both with degrees in economics, Rory had framed his certificate and done little else with it since. He had spent the best part of his time at college building up his record collection and DJ-ing at parties; upon moving back to Dublin, he had carved out a much-vaunted, if short-lived, career as a DJ around the city, but his own nerves when playing in front of large crowds, coupled with an innate desire to please his father, had made him retire from the decks at the ripe old age of twenty-four.

Rory's father was a self-made man. He had opened his first pound shop in 1962, and by the end of the 1980s he had had a chain of thirty 'Eoin's Pound Emporiums' dotted around the country. And as people can't resist a bargain, or a gimmick, he had made a mint and coasted into the twenty-first century on a sea of money.

Eoin O'Donnell, however, was too much of a control freak to let his son anywhere near the reins of the family business. Although this rankled with Rory, he had to acknowledge that he wasn't really a pound-shop person; he didn't know a bag of Flumps from a can of Silvikrin hairspray. So he lived in one of the five apartments his father owned in Ballsbridge, and every month his father flung a set amount of cash his way from the rental of the other apartments. The problem was that Rory felt that his father had him tightly by the balls; he was accustomed to the calls telling him to be at Eoin O'Donnell's office on Ormond Quay at the drop of his Burberry hat, only to have some in-decipherable order barked at him.

Aoife plonked herself down on the settee. 'What, you pretended that you worked with your dad again?'

'Yeah, I had to,' Rory said, sitting down in an armchair.

'You didn't *have* to do anything. I thought that was your main bone of contention with Daddy dearest – the fact that he wheels you out to do the son-and-heir bit every time he needs to look good?'

'It is!'

'Well, say something to him!' Aoife said in exasperation. She had heard all this a million times.

'I would, but what would it achieve?'

'Well, he might actually let you *be* son and heir.' Rory slumped down in the chair. 'But you don't really want that either, do you?'

'I don't know – well, I do, but I'd rather not think about it at the moment; he wrecked my head yesterday. So come on, what's wrong with you? You look a bit worse for wear.'

'I'm wrecked!'

'Oh my God!' Rory shrieked. 'Sorry, Aoife, I completely forgot! How is being a waitress?'

'Murder. But good murder.' Aoife told Rory about the previous night, and he ummed and ahhed and 'he didn't, did he?'d in all the right places. Aoife had only just got over the mortification of her ex-boss showing up.

'Well, you came out of it alive, by the sounds of it. When are you there again?'

'I've said I'll do this Saturday night. And then I find out what I'm working next week. I've said I'll do as many shifts as they have going. It's not like I've got anything else to do.'

Aoife went quiet again and lay across Rory's settee.

'Come on,' Rory said, knowing self-pity when he saw it. 'What else?'

'That guy from the club never called.'

'Never mind, babe,' Rory said, trying to be flippant for Aoife's sake. 'Fuck him; he was probably shit in bed anyway.'

'But he seemed so genuine, Ror,' she said pathetically, craning her neck to look at him.

'Does the door need oiling?' Rory asked.

'What?'

'Just wondering where that squeaking, whining noise came from.' Aoife threw a cushion at him. 'Why don't you go down to Whelan's? He said that was where he was going.'

'Not a chance. If he can't bother his arse to ring me, then fuck him!' she said, but without any real conviction.

Rory decided to change the subject. 'So are you any nearer to procuring a nun's habit to help us gain access to Bono's premises?'

'Funny you should mention it. I've decided that I'm going to bite the bullet on Sunday morning and go visit my mum's cousin, the nun, up in Whitehall – old bag that she is. And I've got a few little ideas up my sleeve that I'm going to put into practice in the unfortunate event that we do not get to meet him when I am dressed as a nun.'

'And they are?' Rory asked.

'Never you mind.' Aoife said, hoping to sound enigmatic. The truth was that all her ideas had been so far-fetched that in the end she had just decided to see how she got on with the nun plan, but she wasn't about to tell Rory that.

Rory raised an eyebrow and decided to take the wind out of her sails. 'How's the flat-hunting going?'

Aoife groaned. 'A nightmare.' She had seen enough hovels in the back of beyond, all claiming to be in central Dublin, to last her a lifetime.

'I can't believe there are that many people out there looking for places in Dublin.'

'Well, why would you? You live in the lap of luxury here.'

'Well, why don't you join me?' Rory asked.

'What, live with you?'

'No, there's a car-park space downstairs you could pitch a tent in. Of course, live with me, you idiot.'

Aoife hesitated before answering. 'Ror, I couldn't. I mean – well, I'd just feel like I owed you too much. Anyway, we've been through this before; it would just give me a false sense of the world. And then at some stage I'd have to come back down to earth.'

'Back down to earth? I live in Ballsbridge, not Bel Air. Come on – just till you get yourself sorted.'

'No, Rory, don't; it's too much of a temptation. Honestly, I'd rather get somewhere myself. But if things get really desperate I'll kip here for a couple of nights, if that's all right.'

'You know it's all right to kip at mine; I just wish you'd stop being so stubborn.'

'I am not being stubborn.'

'No, you're not, of course you're not,' Rory said. 'Why sit in a nice comfy chair when you can sit on a spike, that's my motto too.'

He was right, of course, Aoife thought. What was she doing? She was being offered a room in Ballsbridge, and she was turning it down because of some half-arsed principle that she didn't really understand herself.

'Look, why don't I have one last go at finding somewhere with the other two, and if it doesn't work, I can move in with you.'

'Whatever, but I hardly think the others are going to be crying into their pillows if you say you're not moving with them. They are big enough to look after themselves.'

'No, you're probably right…. All right – let's do it! I'll tell them tomorrow and see what they say.' The fact that she had just reached accommodation Nirvana was slowly dawning on Aoife. 'Only if you're sure, though….'

'Aoife!' Rory shouted. 'Cop the feck on, would you?' He had been here a few times, trying to get Aoife to move in with him. She had always said that it was too easy, as if living in a boxroom made her a better person than she would be if she went the way of the devil and moved in with a friend who had a nice place.

The penny finally and suddenly dropped from a great height. 'Oh my God, Rory! Ballsbridge, in a nice flat with my best mate! How good is that?' She jumped up and smothered him with kisses.

'If I'd known I was going to get that reaction, I wouldn't have bothered offering,' Rory said, pushing her off. 'You couldn't run down to the docks and hire a navvy to do that for you, could you?'

'Thank you, thank you, thank you!' Aoife shouted.

Rory rolled his eyes. 'Just one thing.'

'What's that?'

'Can I have a week or so before you move in?'

'No problem. Why?'

'I just want to appreciate my last days of freedom, that's all,' Rory said, giving Aoife a mischievous wink.

Chapter Six

The elephant was hitting his trunk repeatedly against the top of a Mini, making an atrocious row. The noise got louder and louder until Aoife realised that the elephant was tap-dancing around some vacant corridor of her sleeping mind, and that the thumping noise was someone banging on the front door. She pulled herself out of bed and threw on her dressing-gown. The thumping continued.

'All right, all right, I can hear you, for fuck's sake!' Aoife shouted as she marched down the stairs. Halfway down she realised that she recognised the silhouette through the glass of the front door: it was her mother. What was she doing in Dublin? She hated Dublin! In fact, that was one of the reasons Aoife stayed there.

She opened the door to see her mother, plump and red-faced, with Roddy skulking behind her. *Shite!* Aoife thought. What was *he* doing there?

'Jaysus, Mary and Joseph, girl, I thought you'd died. What's all this I've been hearing from Michael? You're near destitute, says he, and you've no job! If I've told you once, I've told you a thousand times: this place is like Sodom and Gomorrah. I don't know why you don't stop being so stubborn and come back down to Kerry.' Bridie had bustled her way past Aoife during this speech and was now standing in the kitchen, hands on hips, looking around as if she expected to find a man hiding under the kitchen table. Roddy followed, looking uncomfortable.

'How are you, Aoife?' he asked Aoife's cleavage. He couldn't help himself; any time Roddy spoke to a woman, his eyes fell to her breasts. Aoife could see him willing it not to happen, but this just made it worse.

'Fine, Roddy, and yourself?' she said, pulling her dressing-gown tightly around herself and folding her arms.

'Good, good, and all the better for seeing you,' Roddy replied, his gaze not budging. Aoife wished she had ventriloquist skills, so she could make her chest answer Roddy; that'd put some manners on him. She rolled her eyes and turned her attention back to her mother.

'So, what is all this about? You never come here. What has that gobshite Michael been saying? He's in bloody Australia, Mammy, and I hadn't heard from him for a good month until he rang the other day.'

'Your brother is no gobshite, Aoife – he is concerned about you.'

'Concerned about me? He's just a big shit-stirrer! Wouldn't you'd think he'd have a beach to lie on, or something else better to do with his time than ringing you and telling tales on me?'

'He is not telling tales, girl.'

'Yes, he is. He just loves winding you up, and you always go for it – but not usually to the extent that you land in Dublin. So what exactly has he told you?'

'He says that you've no job.'

'I have got a job; I'm a waitress.'

Bridie blessed herself with the speed and precision of a martial-arts expert.

'Waitress? What sort of job is that?'

'A job, Mammy, just a job.'

'Just a job? I don't know what's gotten into that head of yours. I hope no one in Kilbane finds out that you're a waitress.' Bridie was up and hunting around the kitchen like a velociraptor.

'What are you looking for, Mother?'

'A toilet.'

'Well, you're not going to find one in here. Top of the stairs, on the left.'

As the bathroom door shut, Roddy moved towards Aoife. 'Your mother is only looking after your interests, young lady.'

He stood next to Aoife, a bit too close for comfort. He always did this. On her more charitable days, she put it down to the fact that he wasn't aware of other people's personal space, but on most days she just thought he was a borderline pervert.

Roddy had been Aoife's father's childhood friend. Aoife's da had died when she was ten; Roddy, who had never married, had begun to do odd jobs around the farm for Bridie, and had somehow managed to assume the role of ineffectual stepfather into the bargain – all this without ever really getting his feet under the table, or his hands anywhere near Bridie. The fact that Aoife had missed her father terribly had done nothing to endear Roddy to her. He was never going to replace her father – not that that had ever been his intention; he just wanted his meals cooked and his clothes washed.

As soon as the toilet flushed, Roddy dived into a kitchen chair. Bridie's voice came from the top of the stairs: 'Roddy, would you have a look at the cistern for the lads? I don't think it's safe.'

'Mammy, I'm moving out next week; it doesn't matter!'

'Well, if you're up to your eyeballs in shite and ballcocks, don't come crying to me.' Bridie bustled down the stairs and back into the kitchen. 'You're moving, you say? I thought you were destitute. Michael said it was near impossible to get houses up here.'

'Well, it can be, but I'm moving in with a friend.'

'What *friend*?' Bridie came down on her like a sack of spuds.

'Rory.'

'That nancy-boy that you went to university with?' Bridie asked in complete shock.

Roddy decided to stick his two cents in. 'That fairy that you brought home once?'

Aoife was incensed. 'I don't know what you two are on about. You thought he was a – and I quote – "lovely young man" until Michael told you he was gay. You didn't have a clue, did you? You thought he was my boyfriend, for God's sake. And why wouldn't you? It's not like he minces around like Graham Norton.'

'Who?' Roddy asked.

'She's on about that fella off the telly that you like,' Bridie explained.

Roddy thought for a moment. 'He's not gay, that fella. He's just on the telly!'

Aoife couldn't believe that she was discussing Graham Norton's sexuality with her mother and Roddy on a bright Saturday morning. 'Look, I'm moving in with Rory because he happens to be a very good friend and he lives in a very nice flat. And, anyway, it's not permanent.'

'No,' sighed Bridie. 'Nothing ever is with you.'

Aoife bit her tongue. 'Why don't we have a cup of tea?'

'Have you got a teapot?'

'No,' Aoife said, firing teabags into three cups.

'Good Lord above. In the cup'll have to do, I suppose. Roddy, are you all right having your tea like that?'

'Well, I suppose I'll have to be.'

Aoife rolled her eyes. She couldn't believe that they hadn't phoned to say they were coming up, and she was still unsure how long she was going to be subjected to this for.

Not that long, it transpired. It had taken them five hours to drive up to Dublin. They had set off at six o'clock in the morning, and Roddy didn't like driving in the dark, so they would have to start back again by two o'clock, just to be on the safe side.

Bridie insisted on taking Aoife to Dunne's and buying her some food. Roddy wandered around moaning about everything from the price of the food to the size of female customers' backsides. Bridie employed selective hearing.

Once they had bought enough soda bread to open a village coffee shop, they headed down to the local church. Bridie wanted to light a few candles; her theory was that the more twenty-cent pieces you slung at the Lord, the more chance you had of having your prayers answered. Aoife scanned the church for devotion lights. In a corner was an electronic candle-stand. Bridie was disgusted. 'You see, Roddy, that's what Vatican II did for us. Pushing electronic buttons instead of lighting candles – it's unnatural.' Even so, she was not to be outdone by Dublin, Vatican II, or technology; and she lashed about three euros' worth of twenty-cent pieces into the collection box. She then pushed every button on the stand.

'Got a lot of people to pray for, Mammy?' Aoife inquired as she knelt beside her mother in front of the candle-stand, which now looked like a night-time view of the runway at Knock Airport.

'Not really; they're all for you.' *Jesus,* thought Aoife; by her mother's standards, she was obviously in deep trouble. To her knowledge, even dead relatives only ever had five candles lit for them at one time. Aoife made the sign of the cross and looked up at the picture of Mary, who looked more like Julian Clary than the mother of Christ. Roddy shuffled uncomfortably close to her and coughed incessantly. They knelt there for a good ten minutes. Suddenly Bridie blessed herself violently, and they had their cue to leave.

Outside, Aoife asked her mother and Roddy what they wanted to do with the hour and a half they had left in the capital city. Bridie wanted to go to Bewley's on Grafton Street for tea and a cake.

Saturday afternoon on Grafton Street was like a cattle stampede at the best of times. Aoife persuaded them to leave the car at her house and get the bus into town.

'Look at this place – the traffic's at a standstill!' Bridie declared to her daughter, Roddy and the rest of the passengers on the bus.

'Mammy, it's fine; it'll move in a minute.' Aoife peered ahead at the front windscreen as if she were actually trying to see what the hold-up might be.

'You wouldn't have this in Kerry,' her mother huffed.

'Sure you wouldn't; there'd be uproar if the roads came to a standstill like this,' Roddy said. Aoife looked at them, wondering how many times she'd been stuck behind a tractor with the pair of them, back in Kerry, while they grumbled about the inconvenience.

'I'm not moving back home, if that's what you're at.' Aoife folded her arms across her chest in defiance and looked out the window, hoping in vain that this would end the conversation.

'Stubborn as a mule, you are, girl. Well, it's there if you want it.'

'I know, Mam, I know.'

'Look! Look!' Roddy said, bouncing up and down in his seat and pointing through the window. 'Those people are walking faster than the bus!'

Bridie looked disapprovingly and then turned her attention back to her daughter. 'So what happens when this friend of yours decides that he's had enough of you? Where are you going to live then?'

'He's not about to do that, Mammy.' Aoife knew that Rory would have her at the flat indefinitely, but her mother had a point: she had to stand on her own two feet at some stage. Not that she was about to admit that to her mother.

The bus finally reached the top of Grafton Street, and Bridie forgot that she was badgering her daughter to move back to Kilbane and decided that she wanted to see St Stephen's Green, for old times' sake – what old times, Aoife wasn't sure. As far as she was aware, her mother had been to Dublin only twice before and had hated it both times.

Aoife watched with horror as her mother and Roddy tried to negotiate their way across the road. After sticking their feet between the oncoming cars a few times, as if they were testing bath water, they finally threw caution to the wind: Roddy held up both hands to the now-stationary traffic, while Bridie casually strolled across the road like a visiting dignitary. Aoife ran across with her head bowed, not wanting to be associated with them, and dived through the gates of the Green.

The spring flowers were just appearing and it was a cool, clear day. Aoife thought the park looked beautiful. Her mother obviously had a different opinion. 'Gone to wrack and ruin,' was all she said before turning on her heel and marching back out of the park to kamikaze the traffic again.

Aoife finally packed Roddy and her mother off at about half past two. She managed to avoid Roddy's clinch by standing back from the car with her arms crossed firmly. Bridie, not the most tactile person in the world, gave her a cursory hug. 'Well, I expect I'll see you soon. I don't like thinking of you up here on your own like this.'

'I'm not on my own, Mammy. I've got my friends.'

'Friends are all well and good, but in a time of crisis it's family that you need.'

'I'm fine, honestly.'

'Aoife, I don't think you know your own mind at the moment. It's family she needs, isn't it, Roddy?' Roddy shrugged. 'I worry about you, girleen. I'll see what I can do. Good luck.' With this, Bridie got into the car and slammed the door. Through the window Aoife could see her telling Roddy to put his seat-belt on. They pulled out, beeped the horn twice and drove off down the road.

Aoife realised that she was holding her breath and let out a huge sigh – but it wasn't one of relief. What had her mother meant by, 'I'll see what I can do'? Surely to God she wasn't going to have some long-lost relative spying on her every move, was she?

At least, she reasoned, she could rest easy that that was the last time her mother and Roddy would turn up unannounced. Bridie's hatred of the big city had been reconfirmed over the past few hours.

Chapter Seven

'What do you make of all that, then?' Bridie asked Roddy as she rummaged around in the glove compartment for some Milky Moos.

'How do we get out of this place? It's like a fecking labyrinth, so it is.' Roddy had stopped the car at a T-junction and was scanning the empty road as if he were about to squeeze his Toyota Corolla in between the lead cars at the Grand Prix.

'I think she wants help, but won't ask for it. Stubborn, just like her father was.' Bridie unwrapped a sweet and handed it absentmindedly to Roddy. He grabbed it from her without taking his eyes off of the road. After a good three minutes of waiting to see if anyone might venture down this particular thoroughfare today, he saw a car coming and pulled out, swinging the Corolla around, veins bulging in his head; he looked as if he was trying to parallel-park a tank.

The driver behind had to slow down rapidly and beeped his horn. Roddy shook his fist at him.

'Eejits, the lot of them. He won't get where he's going any quicker if he's in traction for the next six weeks, now, will he?' Suddenly Roddy panicked. 'Where are we going now? Where is it we're going?'

'We head into town and out by that park, same way we came in, and then follow the signs for the motorway. We'll be grand; we've plenty of time.'

At four o'clock, Bridie and Roddy were sitting just outside Inchicore, behind a Bus Éireann bus, moving approximately one inch per hour. Roddy was concentrating on bursting a blood vessel. 'I don't know why you couldn't have just rung her like you usually do. Dragging us all the way up here so that we can sit in traffic....'

Bridie, who usually let Roddy's drivel pass, suddenly became agitated.

'Now, you listen to me. I came up here because I was worried about Aoife. She's a good girl, and I don't like thinking of her up here on her own. And if it meant me coming back again and again to make sure she's not wasting her God-given talents serving food to people, and to see she's not sleeping on the streets, God forbid – because that's far from an impossibility in this city – then that's what I'd do.'

Roddy knew when he had been put back in his box. Finally he muttered, 'Well, don't expect me to come back up here again.'

'Sure, no one's asking you to do anything.' They drove in silence for half an hour, until they reached the Red Cow and saw the reason they had been held up for so long. Two of the three lanes of traffic, just before the roundabout that was the gateway from Dublin to the rest of Ireland, were blocked by workmen. Roddy and Bridie began talking again, as they now had something in common to moan about.

'Would you look at that?' Roddy spluttered. 'They're only working on about twenty square feet of road!'

'Not the sense they were born with,' Bridie agreed. 'Wouldn't you think that they'd see to one lane at a time, wouldn't you? It's ludicrous.'

'Stupid, bloody stupid,' Roddy said.

'Well, I'll tell you something for nothing,' Bridie said, rifling around for another chew.

'What's that?' Roddy asked, getting the car comfortable in the slow lane.

'I'll be getting the train next time.'

Roddy ignored the comment. Bridie knew he was hoping that she was speaking purely hypothetically. He wouldn't fancy the idea of fending for himself in her absence. He had a hard enough time getting himself dressed in the morning.

Chapter Eight

Aoife had had a very tiring shift at the restaurant the previous evening, and wasn't in the best form to be dragging herself out of bed and across Dublin to try and acquire a habit.

It had been five years since she had darkened the doors of the Sisters of the Lamb and Cross convent in Whitehall. As she rang the doorbell, she wondered how on earth she'd got herself into this situation. Bridie's cousin, Mary, was a nun – well, Mary was what she had been baptised, but no one had called her that for years; she was Sister Immaculata. Sister Immaculata scared Aoife silly. She was an imposing woman who took great delight in preaching about the sins of the world and the evils of money. This was the same woman who had single-handedly negotiated the sale of ten acres of Lamb and Cross land, just outside Ballsbridge, for around fifteen million pounds. It was for this reason that the Sisters were driving brand-new

Peugeot 206s and using PowerPoint displays on their Dell laptops to spread the word of God throughout Dublin.

The door opened slowly and a frail little woman peered at Aoife.

'Yeesss?'

'Oh, h-hello – I'm looking for Sister Immaculata; I'm her niece – well, sort of…. Em, if you could tell her that Aoife Collins is here to see her….'

'I will, but she is in contemplation at the moment. Won't you come in, and I'll get a cup of tea made for you.'

The last time Aoife had paid the Sisters a visit, it had been under duress from her mother and it had been an unmitigated disaster. She had visited a week after a young Dublin girl had died after taking an Ecstasy tablet, and Sister Immaculata had subjected her to a tirade about 'youngsters' taking 'yokes' and 'killing themselves for fun'. Aoife had come away feeling like a crack addict who had just received an audience with the Pope.

The little old nun guided Aoife down the corridor to the huge kitchen at the back of the convent. The housekeeper, Mrs Reagan, greeted her with a wide smile; on Aoife's few previous visits, they had always got on well. 'How are you, Aoife? It's great to see you. I'll make you a cup of tea while you wait for Sister Immaculata.' She filled the huge kettle and put it on top of the even huger Aga. It looked as if they were preparing to tea the five thousand.

Mrs Reagan quizzed Aoife on what she had been up to of late, and Aoife told her the bare bones of the last five years before diving into the real reason she was there.

'Mrs Reagan, I wonder if you could help me.'

'I'll certainly try, dear. What's wrong?'

'Well, I've started running evening classes in art at the Tech in Rathmines.' Aoife wasn't quite sure where this little fable was coming from, but she knew where it was leading, so she soldiered on. 'And, well, as one of the modules we have to do life drawings with themes that are relevant to life in Ireland today.' The story was clarifying in her head now. 'So I was thinking that, as we've become a wealthier nation, there's been a distinct move away from the Church.' She was losing her audience, Aoife realised, as Mrs Reagan looked at her with a blank expression. 'Oh, I don't mean people like you and me, but you know – people in general.' The audience was back with her. 'Anyway, I wanted to do something that spoke of religion, so I've decided to do a piece with a nun in it – you know, someone dressed as a nun – so that it's like a commentary on the fact that the community still needs its ecclesiastical orders and....'

'So you want to borrow a habit?' Mrs Reagan stopped Aoife in her tracks. She'd been quite enjoying her role as art teacher.

'Em, yes, but –'

'You don't want Sister Immaculata to find out?'

'Well, no, I don't.' Aoife hung her head.

Mrs Reagan smiled and said in a hushed voice, 'Right, so; I'll have it in a carrier bag for you when you leave, but you'll have to leave by the back door. I'll leave it by the bin so that you can collect it without being seen. Sister Immaculata would go mad if she knew.'

This was turning out to be a lot easier than Aoife had envisaged.

'But promise me one thing.' Aoife looked up at Mrs Reagan's serious face. 'It's not for a fancy-dress party, is it?'

'No, no, no, no, no!' Aoife shook her head violently. 'Of course not!'

'I'm sorry, Aoife; it's just that we do get weirdos coming round, making up all sorts of excuses so they can borrow the habits, and they're usually just after them for a hen night or a fancy dress. I'm sorry, love. I know you're very respectful of the Sisters.'

Aoife wanted the ground to open up and swallow her. If Mrs Reagan had only known the real reason she wanted the habit, she would have probably lost her faith in humanity entirely.

At that moment, Aoife heard the familiar clacking of rosary beads as Sister Immaculata made her imposing way down the corridor to the kitchen.

She looked at Aoife without warmth. 'Well, it's nice of you to finally make an appearance.'

Aoife stared at her and thought, *You could've got*

off your fat arse and come to visit me while you were
playing property tycoon on the south side, you old
bitch, but she took the more diplomatic route.

'I'm sorry; I've been very busy – you know how it is.
But I thought I couldn't leave it any longer. So how are
you?'

The old woman swept across the kitchen, beads
clacking, and sat down with a flourish in a chair by the
sink. 'I am as well as can be expected in these trying
times.' Aoife braced herself for the onslaught. 'We are
having a real battle with the divil here in Dublin at the
moment, as you will know. There is so much greed.
Fancy cars, fancy houses – it's all material with people
of your generation. No thought for God or what he
has done for us.'

Something started playing 'The Lord is My
Shepherd' on what sounded like panpipes. Sister
Immaculata rummaged around in her habit and
produced a tiny, sleek mobile phone. 'Hello! Hello?
You're cutting out. Call me on the land line; the
reception's terrible here.' She deposited the phone back
in the folds of her habit. 'Now, where was I? Yes – I
can't see any redemption for the lost souls of Dublin at
the moment.' Aoife was lost for words – not that it
mattered; Sister Immaculata had enough for both of
them. 'So you are experiencing a time of crisis, I
believe?'

'Where did you hear that?'

'Your mother rang the other day.' *No way,* Aoife

thought. She was going to strangle her mother. So this was who she'd had in mind when she said that Aoife needed family to keep an eye on her.

'Well, it's not entirely true. I've lost my job and I'm moving house, but it's hardly a time of crisis.'

'I'm sure that your mother has cause for concern. She's not a dramatic woman by nature.' Not dramatic? Aoife could have screamed. Her mother could have taken the lead in any amateur dramatics production, and her speciality was melodrama.

'Well, my mother came to visit the other day and I'm sure I'll be fine. I'm sorry, Sister, but I can't stay for long; I have to be at 4.15 Mass. I'm doing a reading.' *That stopped the old cow in her tracks,* Aoife thought triumphantly.

'Mass? You?' The look on Sister Immaculata's face was one of pure incredulity.

'Yes, me. But if I don't go now, I'll miss it. I was just in the area and I thought I should drop in – Mammy was asking after you yesterday, and I told her I'd come and see you. You seem in great form, so I'd better get going.'

'Well, there was no need, really; sure I'll be seeing your mother soon enough, won't I?'

'Are you going back down to Kerry?'

'No, she's coming here. Next Saturday.'

Aoife's jaw fell open so quickly that her chin nearly smacked off the floor. Sister Immaculata seemed to enjoy the reaction. 'Oh, you didn't know? She's staying here for a couple of weeks. She wants to keep an eye on you, which is only fair; you are her only daughter, and she knows what an evil place Dublin can be – I've told her.'

Aoife's mind was reeling. How was she going to talk her mother out of this one? Sister Immaculata had pushed herself up from her chair and was waiting for Aoife to move – she didn't want her being late for Mass – but Aoife's body had gone into temporary shock. Sister Immaculata coughed, snapping Aoife out of her trance.

'Well, that was short and sweet,' the nun said.

'Em, yes – yes, it was.' Aoife was wondering how she was going to go out by the back door, to get the habit – which, after all, was the only reason she had endured this painful encounter. Sister Immaculata headed out of the kitchen and towards the front door, and Aoife panicked; she knew she had to do something quickly.

'I ... I need to go out of the back door, please.' Aoife was floundering.

'What on earth for, girl? We've a perfectly good front door.'

'Well, I'm ... I'm just a bit, em, superstitious about it. When Mammy visits the priest, she always leaves by the back door – you can ask her when she gets here – and, well, it's just stuck with me, whenever I visit religious houses. I drive poor Father McNooley mad, up in the Sacred Heart in Rathmines – out of the back door every time – he thinks I'm nuts…. Anyway, must go….' Aoife was babbling. She stepped forward to kiss Sister Immaculata goodbye, but the nun stood stoically staring at her, so she backed off and headed for the back door.

Beside the big bin was a carrier bag. Aoife bent down and quickly stuffed it in her rucksack. As she straightened up, she saw a puzzled-looking Sister Immaculata at the window, obviously trying to work out what on earth she was doing. *Shit*, thought Aoife; *if she tells my mother, she'll think I'm scavenging for food, on top of everything else.*

Chapter Nine

Aoife rang Rory's doorbell. He ran to the door, expecting the return of the triumphant hunter-gatherer; when he saw Aoife's face, he thought that her mission must have been a failure.

'No luck with the habit, babe?'

'Yeah, I got one, it's in here,' she said distractedly, pointing at the bag. Rory was beside himself. He had been convinced that they'd end up in a fancy-dress shop, paying through the nose for an unconvincing nun's outfit, and here they were with the genuine article.

'So, why the long face?' he asked, rummaging in the bag.

'I've just been informed that my mother is coming to stay – for two whole weeks, by the sound of things!'

'Your mother? But she hates Dublin. And she was here only yesterday.' Rory dragged the habit out and laid it on the floor to have a good look.

'I know. Wouldn't you think she'd leave me in peace? She's coming up to stay with Sister bloody Immaculata, of all people, so that she can have her head filled with shite about the evils of Dublin and how I've got myself into bad ways.'

'I'll tell your mother if you want me to. I'll say, "I've been trying to get in her knickers for years, Mrs Collins, and she's having none of it. Pure as the driven snow. Hymenus Intacticus." '

'Cheers, Ror, but I don't think the possibility that I've had sex has ever crossed my mother's mind. She's more worried that Kilbane might find out that her daughter is a waitress and living with a gay man. Imagine! She could die a social death if that sort of information got out.'

'God, is it made out of horsehair for extra puritanical pleasure?' Rory was fingering the habit.

'I don't know, but it's a bit on the smelly side.' Aoife screwed her face up at the garment. 'What d'you reckon?'

'Smells of frustration, if you ask me. Come on, then; let's see you in it. I'm sure you'll make someone a lovely Bride of Christ one day.'

Aoife decided that, unless she was willing to endure a severe amount of chafing, she had better wear the habit over her clothes. She struggled to get it over her head.

'Rory, stop laughing!' Her shouts were muffled by the tangle of hessian-like material.

'I'm not laughing,' Rory said, nearly swallowing his own tongue and pulling at the gown. 'Now, did you get any of those horrible big rosary beads? The ones that could kill an ox with one swipe?'

'Shit, no; I forgot. But I think I've got some small ones at home.'

'Well, it's true what they say: you can take the girl out of Catholicism, but you can't take the Catholicism out of the girl.' It *was* true. Aoife had her rosary beads stashed in a box under her bed. If the box had had a label, it would have read, 'Things that I can't throw away because I'm scared that God will strike me down if I do.' Alongside the rosary beads lay a half-full bottle of stagnant holy water shaped like Our Lady of Lourdes, a triptych of the Holy Family that was on its last legs, and – the pièce de résistance – a picture of the Sacred Heart of Jesus that, when fitted with an AA battery, lit up and gave the illusion of pulsation. Aoife made a mental note to do something with the contents of this box when she moved out.

'Actually, you know, I think I have a set of rosary beads that a friend brought me from Hamburg the other year.' Rory disappeared into his room and re-emerged with the beads. 'They glow in the dark. Put them round your wrist.' Aoife did as she was told. 'Oh, Sister, you do look the part now! And if darkness descends on Killiney Hill, they won't lose you with those, will they?'

Aoife gave herself a once-over in Rory's full-length

mirror. She looked like a complete lunatic; but she did look like a nun.

'So what's the story now, Sister Blister? I think this needs further planning.'

'No way! I'm going now if I'm doing it at all. I've had a traumatic enough day already, without you sitting around telling me how I'm going to break and enter Bono's house.'

Rory refused to drive to Killiney. He told Aoife that the car was on the blink again, but Aoife had her own opinion on the matter. 'You just want me to get the DART dressed like this, don't you?'

'How dare you?' Rory asked in mock disgust.

At the Lansdowne Road DART station, the young nun and the attractive young man garnered a lot of glances from the commuters of Dublin. The train, when it finally arrived, was jammed. Rory stood back.

'After you, Sister.'

'Would you ever fuck off?' she whispered, without moving her lips.

Every man and his dog had decided that it might be a good idea to go to the seaside, and they were all crammed into the same carriage as Aoife and Rory. Aoife didn't get the Dublin obsession with the coastline. Dubliners all leg it to Sandymount as soon as the sun peeps out from behind the clouds, only to discover that the sea is so far out you can walk to Wales and that fifty per cent of the view is obscured by the Poolbeg towers – which, even on a good day, look like something out of Chernobyl.

Aoife was winding herself up into a ridiculously bad mood. Rory was busy whispering words of non-encouragement to her, and she wanted to knock his lights out. Suddenly there was a tug on her habit.

'Excuse me?'

Aoife looked down to see a little girl with curly blonde pigtails. 'My gran wants to know if you'd like to sit down.' Aoife smiled. Then, as Rory shook with suppressed laughter, she realised why the girl's grandmother was taking such an interest in her.

The woman was wearing a tea cosy on her head, a camel-hair winter coat that was buttoned up to the top even though it was an unseasonably warm day outside, and a pioneer badge pinned to her collar to denote that she had taken a pledge to be teetotal in the name of the Lord – not that *He* seemed to mind about alcohol; half the priests Aoife had encountered had been roaring drunks. The woman was beaming at Aoife with the delirious smile that is only ever seen in the truly devout, or the truly mad.

By the time the DART pulled into Killiney station, Aoife had had a full discussion about the merits of the sisterhood and the evil ways of the world. The woman was convinced that Aoife was the reincarnation of St Thérèse, the patron saint of small deeds. She even pulled out a dog-eared old holy card from her pocket, to prove that Aoife looked like the saint. The young girl with the pigtails was in complete awe of Aoife; she was obviously at that age where constant prayer and superstition are the only things between yourself and the bogeyman.

As Aoife got off the train, the woman shouted, 'God bless you, Sister – there's not enough left of ye in this evil world!' Rory was struggling so hard to hold in his laughter that he thought he was going to buckle under his own weight. As the train pulled away, the bemused passengers observed a Sister of the Lamb and Cross looking disparagingly down at a young man clinging, doubled over in hysterics, to the hem of her habit.

'Will you fecking well cop yourself on, or I am not going through with this!' Aoife was getting really annoyed at the amount of enjoyment Rory was getting from this.

'I'm sorry, babe; you just make such a good nun!'

Aoife was thawing; she couldn't stay angry with Rory for any length of time.

'Come on. We've a mission to accomplish.' She held out her hand to help Rory up from his crumpled position.

Aoife was getting irritated with the habit. It was making her neck itch, and she was baking because she had on two layers of clothes, one of which appeared to be made of Brillo pads. Rory was showing no sign of getting bored with her outfit; in fact, he was all for her keeping it so that he could wear it to London Gay Pride.

They were trudging down the Vico Road. The houses were set back in their grounds and were obscured by high walls, like mini-castles. All that could be seen was whitewashed walls and huge manicured trees, and through the gaps in the trees the Irish Sea stretched out, calm and blue in the spring light. If Aoife hadn't been so preoccupied by her situation, she would have been taken aback by the grandness of the road.

'Where's Bono's house?' she asked Rory.

'You're like a kid saying, "Are we there yet?" It's just up here, about another five minutes away. How's the temperature in the nun suit?'

'Fantastic; it's only about a hundred and twenty degrees at the moment.'

'Grand, so.' Rory got a piece of paper out of his pocket and studied it. 'That's the one – over there, with the wooden gates. Come on!' He tugged at Aoife's habit sleeve.

As they reached the gates, Aoife got a huge sense of the stupidity of what they were about to do. 'What the fuck am I doing here, Rory?'

'Pretending to be a nun. Now get in character and focus.' Rory took Aoife by the shoulders and looked her in the eyes, as if he were briefing a boxer who was about to get in the ring. 'You are Sister Immaculata of the Lamb and Cross. You got a calling at the age of eight, when you promised God that you would become either an Olympic long jumper or a nun. When you realised that you were never going to make it past four metres, you turned your attention to the Lord. You became a nun at the age of eighteen, and it saddens you that, in this secular time of ours, there are so few young girls who want to go into the sisterhood. You do find the life austere and sometimes hard, but then you remember your calling and your devotion to Jesus, and that fills you with the courage to carry on. The reason you are here today is that you are collecting for the Good Shepherd Fund. The fund was set up in 1967 by Father Eamonn Brennan, in the parish of St John and the Blessed Martyrs, Whitehall, and it is for the Cancer Hospice.'

'I cannot pretend that this is all for a cancer charity! I'll get struck down! Jaysus, Rory. And what happens if they give me some money? I'll fecking burn in hell. Can you imagine if it got out that I've done this? I'd be in the *Sunday World* as "Evil Nun-Impersonator Aoife Collins" and they'd get my age wrong by about ten years on purpose. I'd be hounded out of the country. Nicking money off Bono for a pretend cancer charity, for fuck's sake! My mother'd have a fucking heart attack!'

Rory was shaking his head at Aoife. He had the feeling she was going to bottle out. 'Don't be so stupid. It's not a made-up charity; it exists. My da used to know Eamonn Brennan. So if they do give you some money, you can just give it to the charity, and you haven't done anything bad.'

'Except impersonate a nun.'

'Well, how the fuck else are you going to meet Bono? Now cop yourself on and get in there.'

They both turned around to look at the gates. The house was hidden from view and there was a CCTV camera on the wall.

'It doesn't look how I expected it to look.'

'Why, what did you expect? A big sign saying "Bono's House" and the fecking Joshua Tree growing in the front garden? Stop arsing around and buzz the intercom. What's the worst that can happen? They tell you to feck off. No big deal.'

Aoife decided to bite the bullet. She pressed the intercom. There was a crackling noise, and a male voice boomed out of it.

'Hello?'

Aoife nearly collapsed. 'I – hello, I am here on behalf of ... well, I am ... sorry, I....' Rory kicked her, in the hope of jump-starting her. 'Sorry, let me start again. My name is Sister Immaculata, and I am a Sister of the Lamb and Cross. I am here on behalf of the Good Shepherd Fund. It's a fund for the Cancer Hospice in Whitehall.' Aoife looked nervously at Rory and winced.

'Ah, God bless you, Sister; my auntie was in that hospice. You do great work,' came the voice on the intercom. 'Let me buzz you in.'

Aoife wanted the ground to open up and swallow her. As they walked up to the house, she whispered to Rory, 'And who the fuck are you meant to be?'

'I'm the *lay* minister,' Rory said, grinning cheekily.

'Lay minister, me arse.'

'Don't be getting all nasty, now, just 'cause you're feeling guilty about the cancer thing. My little petal, we have just gained access to the house of one of the most famous men in the world. This could be the easiest five grand you ever make.'

A tall man in his mid-fifties was at the door, beaming from ear to ear as if he couldn't have enough visits from nuns and lay ministers. One thing was definite, though: he wasn't Bono.

'Hello, Sister; welcome. Come on in and I'll get you a cup of tea.' He showed them through the ornately decorated hallway.

'That'd be grand, thank you very much.' Aoife suddenly realised that she was talking like an eighty-year-old, for some reason. She looked at Rory; they were both thinking the same thing. Had they got the wrong house?

'My name's Tom; I'm looking after the place at the moment.' Aoife's heart sank. *Where the feck is Bono?* she was thinking. But she couldn't very well admit that she was only there to see the owner of the house. Tom showed them into the kitchen, where there was a woman who was definitely not Bono's wife; she was probably old enough to be his grandmother. Tom introduced her as Annie, the housekeeper. Aoife's eyes were darting around the kitchen to see if there were any photographs of the man himself. Nothing.

Annie put the kettle on. 'It's lovely to have you here, Sister. What is it you're collecting for?'

'For the Good Shepherd Fund; the money will go towards the hospice in Whitehall.' Aoife felt sick to her stomach.

'Yes, Sister Immaculata works very closely with the hospice and has collected thousands of euro over the past few years.' Aoife stared at Rory, who was busy avoiding her gaze. 'The other year she received a commendation from the Pope for her work.'

Aoife butted in just as Rory was explaining how Nelson Mandela had heard about her work and invited her to South Africa.

'How long have you lived here? It's a lovely house.' Aoife was playing dumb, on the off-chance that the couple would say, 'Actually, we only lodge here, but if you look upstairs in the front bedroom, U2 are just running through their set list.'

What Annie actually said was, 'Oh, we're just looking after it while the owner's away.'

'Oh.' Aoife found it hard to keep the disappointment out of her voice. 'What does the owner do?'

Annie poured the boiling water into the teapot and set it to one side. 'She owns racehorses. She's over in the US at the moment.' Aoife gave Rory a dirty look. She had asked him a million times if he was sure he knew which house was Bono's, and he'd promised her faithfully that he did.

'A horse owner?' She was going to get something

out of this if it killed her. 'There are a lot of wealthy people around this area, aren't there?'

'Oh, yes,' agreed Annie, as she poured the tea. 'Enya lives a couple of houses down.'

'And Damon Hill's got a house around here,' said Tom.

'Doesn't that singer from U2 live around here somewhere?' Rory asked, hoping he could get a result that would prevent Aoife from beating him up as soon as they left the house.

'Yes, he lives next door,' Annie said, sipping her tea and missing the fact that the nun's eyes nearly popped out of her head. 'Lovely man. An absolute gent, isn't he, Tom? He's always got the time of day for everyone. My brother went to school with his father at Brunswick Street Secondary. They didn't have two ha'pennies to rub together, but they were happy.' Aoife was half-listening to the woman's Bono story while mulling over the best way of killing Rory. '... But I haven't seen him for a while. They're over in the US doing their touring, aren't they, Tom?'

Aoife thought she was hearing things. *The fecking States! Rory must have known, the gobshite.* She looked over at him; he was knocking back his cup of tea like he was afraid it was his last.

'Well, thank you both for your hospitality, but we really have to be off – don't we, Mr O'Donnell? We have to get around all the houses in the area before the end of the day.'

'Oh, that's fine – we completely understand. Sure, no rest for the wicked, eh, Sister?' Tom was evidently not averse to the odd side-splitting joke.

As they stood up, Annie reached for her handbag and took out a ten-euro note. Before Aoife could register what she was doing, Annie was prising her hand open and forcing the money into her palm, like an aunt giving you money that she doesn't want your mother to find out about.

'No, no, no, Annie, please – I don't want to take any money from you. I only thought that the richer among us would be able to spare a few euro. If you just pray for us, that will be fine.' Aoife was hurriedly thinking of a way out of this. Rory was standing back, watching the spectacle unfold.

'No, Sister, it's only a little bit of something – ten euro for all the good work you do. Here, take it.'

Aoife felt like an absolute fool. Annie was not going to take the money back, and Tom was rooting around in his pockets. So Rory and Aoife left the house of the racehorse owner with twenty quid and no Bono story.

Aoife smiled good-bye to Annie and Tom through gritted teeth. As soon as the automatic gate closed, she let rip. 'You fucking dickhead!'

'Sister, there is no call for that sort of language from one so devout.'

'Stop pricking about! I am really pissed off with you! Not only do we get the wrong house and get money from people who think we are collecting for a cancer charity, but we find out – or *I* find out – that fucking U2 are on tour on the other side of the Atlantic.' Aoife was so annoyed that she was having trouble spitting out the words. 'You fecking *bollix*!'

She turned to see an open-mouthed Tom holding her luminous rosary beads.

'Sister, there's obviously tensions here that I don't really want to get involved in, but I thought you might want your rosary back.' Tom held out the beads.

Aoife wanted to rewind her entire day; in fact, rewinding her entire life seemed like a good idea. Right back to the beginning, so that she could structure a life where she was a cool, calm, collected young professional. One who'd bought herself a little pad off the South Circular Road around 1994, and watched it quadruple in value. One who had her own successful web-design company because she was a computer whiz and had a knack for knowing exactly what was right for the time. One who drove an MGF or one of those nice new Beetles. And, above all, one who didn't get roped into dressing like a nun and making an absolute fool of herself.

Tom walked away, looking like a man who'd just lost his religion. Aoife turned her back on Rory and headed up the Vico Road.

Chapter Ten

'Aoife, I didn't know that was going to happen, honestly!'

'Would you ever feck right off, Rory!' Aoife was holding up the habit so that she could walk faster.

'Babe, you have to believe me. I really thought I'd got the house right. Come on – I was only one out.'

'They're on fucking tour, Rory. You must have known that when we agreed to all this.'

'Why would I? You didn't know. The only thing I know is that, when tickets went on sale for their Dublin concert, there was nearly war outside HMV. That is my sum total of U2 gig knowledge for this year. I might be a cruel bastard, Aoife, but I'm not about to march you up and down Killiney Hill, dressed as a nun, just to amuse myself.'

'Yes, you would!' Aoife shouted at him.

'Well, maybe I would, but I didn't. I honestly thought that we might be in with a chance of meeting him.'

'Well, we're not, are we? Because I'm not even in the same country as him.'

'He'll be back. You don't think he's going to stay over in the States for the duration of the tour? They have planes these days, you know.'

'That's not the point, Rory. The point is that you, Mr fucking Man-about-Dublin, didn't know that U2 were touring. You know if one of Westlife catches a fecking cold, because one of your showbiz hanger-on friends tells you, but you didn't know that U2 were on the first leg of a world tour!' Aoife stormed off, veil blowing in the wind. As she marched past a side gate, it opened and Aoife slammed straight into the person who was walking out of it.

'Watch where you're go…' The man stopped in his tracks as he recognised the young nun who had just barged into him. Aoife stood staring in shock. She was face to face with the guy from Bubble who had promised to call her and hadn't.

'Aoife?'

'Yeah – sorry … Paul, isn't it?' *What was that about?* she thought. Of course it was Paul. She didn't forget an ego-bruising that easily.

'Yeah. Jaysus, I'm so glad I ran into you! I'm really sorry I didn't call – I had my phone stolen the day after we met, and I knew you must think I was a complete shite – you know, for not calling – and I…. Why are you dressed as a nun?'

Aoife looked down at the habit and then at Rory. 'Do you want to tell him or shall I?'

'If you've quite finished bawling me out in the middle of the street, then I'll tell him. If not, I'll leave the honour to you.'

'Sorry, Rory, I know you didn't do it on purpose,' Aoife said, rolling her eyes in exasperation.

'Do what?' Paul asked; he was even more confused now.

'Well, I've got a bet with Rory, and it involved dressing up like this and trying to meet … Oh, God, it doesn't matter. Look, nice to see you again, but we'd better get going so that I can get changed.' Aoife was mortified and wasn't too sure that she believed the mobile story; she wanted to get out of the situation as quickly as possible.

'I'm going into town; maybe I could give you a lift,' Paul suggested.

'Em….' Aoife looked at Rory, who shrugged. 'Yeah, that'd be great.'

'That's my car there.' Paul pointed at a Passat.

'Nice car,' Aoife said. She heard Rory the car snob sniff, and threw him a look that suggested he was better off keeping quiet.

'It's a work car, but it does the job,' Paul told her. 'In you get, then.'

Rory sat in the back. Aoife took her habit off before getting in.

'So, what are you doing in Killiney?' she asked Paul.

'I live in Killiney,' Paul said, starting the car.

'What, *here*?' Aoife asked in wonderment.

'God, no! We're organising a function in town for the fella who lives in that house there. He's a businessman with about as much party spirit as the Pope, and it's happening on Tuesday. He's flapping and needed to go over the details.'

'On a Sunday?' Aoife asked.

'Yeah. I was raging at having to work on a Sunday, but I'm glad now because I bumped into you.' Aoife felt Rory's knee dig into her back.

'So, where do you live, then?' Rory asked from the back seat.

'Oh, where I live is a lot less grand – bottom of the hill,' Paul said. Then he asked, 'You weren't looking for Bono, were you, by any chance?'

'Actually, we were!' Aoife looked round at Rory, wide-eyed, as if Paul was a genius to have guessed. He rolled his eyes. 'How did you guess?'

'Well, that's why most people go up the Vico Road – not usually dressed as nuns, though. And last week you asked me if I'd ever met him, remember?'

While Aoife explained the bet to Paul, Rory sat passively in the back like a child who had been told he could have some sweets if he was quiet. Occasionally he would force his knee into Aoife's back, just to let her know that he was still there and that the mating ritual unfolding before his eyes was making him ill.

Halfway into town, Rory piped up, 'You've missed the turn-off for town.'

'Oh, shit,' Paul said, suddenly becoming alert. 'What am I thinking? I drive this way every day. It's all the talking.' He peered out of the window and found the right turn-off. Rory fell back into silence, and Aoife and Paul went back to getting on like a house on fire.

Paul dropped Rory and Aoife by the American Embassy in Ballsbridge. 'Thanks for the lift, Paul,' Rory said. Then he turned to Aoife and said, with a knowing look, 'I'll be in the flat when you're ready.'

'I won't be a minute,' she promised.

Paul leant across the passenger seat so he could see her properly. 'Was your friend all right? He seemed a bit quiet.'

'Oh, we'd just had a bit of an argument, that's all – about getting the wrong house. I think he's still in a bit of a fouler about that. He's not usually that quiet – in fact, you usually can't get a word in edgeways; he's normally twittering on about anything that comes into his head....' Aoife realised she was describing what she was doing at that moment, in order to put off saying goodbye to Paul.

'Aoife, do you fancy going out – not to Whelan's; somewhere nice where your feet won't stick to the floor?' Paul said. 'I honestly had my phone nicked – look, new phone.' He held out his phone for her to inspect. 'The only numbers I've got programmed in are work and my ma; how sad am I?'

Aoife laughed. 'I might be persuaded.' She hated hearing things like that come out of her mouth. She felt like she had walked onto the set of a Meg Ryan film.

'Well, how about Wednesday night at Halo in the Morrison Hotel?'

Aoife thought about her shifts for the week; she was free that night. 'Yeah, that's fine,' she said, impressed with herself for playing it so cool.

'Great. I'll meet you there at eight – is that OK? Here's my mobile number. Can I have yours again?' Aoife gave it to him and he keyed it into his phone. 'If there's any problem, give me a call. I'll book the table.'

'Great,' Aoife said, beaming from ear to ear.

'See you Wednesday,' Paul said. 'Nun attire is optional.' He waved as Aoife shut the car door.

She watched him drive off round the corner and thought with glee: *I am going to the Morrison, the fecking Morrison, on Wednesday!* She skipped into the house. *Wait until I tell Rory!*

'I smell a rat,' Rory said, as he let Aoife into the flat.

'What do you mean?' Aoife was indignant.

'Well, did you clock that accent? There's nothing Killiney about it, babe. That accent is as near to the Liffey as you can get without falling in.'

'You are such a snob! Listen to yourself! Your father's from just outside Ballymun, and that's where you'd still be if he hadn't had the idea of flogging everything for a quid when he did.' Aoife flopped down on the sofa next to Rory.

'I am not a snob! I just think it's weird that he lives in Killiney but doesn't know the way into town from there, that's all.'

'What do you mean?'

'Didn't you notice? Well, no, I suppose you didn't; you were too busy batting your eyes like a geisha.'

'Notice what?'

'The roundabout before Blackrock! He didn't know which way to go into town.'

'Rory, would you stop being so bloody suspicious of everything? You're like fecking Columbo. Just because I've got a date for a change.' Aoife waited for the onslaught.

'Oh, a date? You've got a date with the lovely Paul? Is this going to be like the last date you had with him?'

'Rory, he lost his fecking phone! Are you jealous or something?' It had been a long time since Aoife had been out with anyone. It had been over six years since she had split up with Aidan, her long-term boyfriend, whom she had gone out with in college and lived with when she first came to Dublin. Since then she had had a couple of two-monthers, a few dates here and there, and a one-night stand that was best forgotten. But whenever another man paid any attention to her, Rory became possessive.

'Jealous! I'm just thinking about you, that's all. I don't want you getting hurt.'

'I'm going for dinner at the fecking Morrison, Rory; I haven't agreed to be the mother of his children.'

Rory slumped back on the sofa. 'Okay. But are you going to play it cool?'

'Yes, I am.'

'And you'll do what Uncle Rory tells you and not start punching him on the arm like you're having a fight with your brother, will you?' Aoife cocked her head to one side and gave Rory a look of incredulous scorn. 'What's that look for? You know what you're like.'

He was right, of course: Aoife was terrible at flirting.

It had all started when she was fifteen and there was a disco in the next town. Aoife went to an all-girls school, so her access to the opposite sex was, at best, limited. The only men she had any real contact with were Michael, her brother; Roddy, who didn't count; and Joe, the next-door neighbours' seventeen-year-old son, who wasn't allowed out after the episode where he'd bitten a chunk out of his own dog's backside ('Well, he bit me first').

The village disco had been a bit of a breakthrough in Aoife's quest for awareness of the opposite sex. It was there that she had her first kiss. The kisser's name was Phelim Kissane, and he edged over to Aoife about halfway through the night. He was about six foot four and so skinny that his Adam's apple looked like an extra head, and he'd apparently been shovelling cow shit in the same boots he was wearing to the disco, but she wasn't overly concerned; he looked like Jason

Orange out of Take That, and that covered a multitude of sins.

Aoife noticed that other girls from her class, who had the same limited access to boys as she had herself, seemed to take to this a lot better than she did. Aoife's tactic was to stand in the corner of the room, laughing like a drain and hitting Phelim on the arm every time he said anything remotely amusing. Sinéad Carroll and Mary Finch, however, were in the opposite corner, dancing to the slow set, with their tongues down some young lads' throats, while the lads felt the girls' rear ends like they were kneading dough. Aoife was talking non-stop, for fear that, if she paused, Phelim might do something. He might kiss her – and she might not know what to do, or put her tongue somewhere she shouldn't, or have a heart attack from the sheer momentousness of it all.

In the end, he said, 'Would you like to dance, so?'

'Em, yeah, that'd be grand,' Aoife said, thus beginning a long career of saying inappropriate things at potentially romantic moments. Not that that moment turned out to be romantic.

Phelim clung to her hips as Chris de Burgh sang 'Lady in Red'; then he lunged forward, with his tongue stuck straight out. If she hadn't opened her mouth in surprise, he could probably have broken her two front teeth. After thirty seconds of waggling his tongue and grappling with her backside, eyes screwed tightly shut, Phelim removed his face from Aoife's and grinned triumphantly – not at Aoife, but at three young fellas who were in the corner sneaking poteen into their Cidona.

Rory, who knew what Aoife was like with the opposite sex, decided to back down. She would be bad enough as it was, when the date came around, without him giving it loads. He changed tack. 'I'll come round and help you get ready if you want.'

'Well, OK, but I'll do my make-up myself.'

'I wasn't suggesting I'd do your bloody make-up for you – do you think I've gone soft in the head? I might be gay, but I wasn't born with a propensity to apply make-up and arrange flowers; anyway, you'd only finish up looking like Bosco. I meant we'll have a beer, *you* can glam up and I'll give you a pep talk.'

'OK. I'll need some Dutch courage; I'll be shitting a brick by then.'

'I don't know why, babe. I've told you a thousand times: you're gorgeous. You could have any man in Dublin, if you stopped acting like you wanted to be their sister.'

'Cheers, amigo,' Aoife said, planting a kiss on Rory's head. 'I think.'

Chapter Eleven

Getting changed for the third time in five minutes, Aoife looked at Rory and Carmel, who also had the night off from the restaurant. Ian and Katie were out house-hunting. Aoife had been reticent about telling them that she was moving in with Rory; she felt that she was somehow letting them down. But she needn't have worried. They were delighted for her: they had called her a jammy cow and threatened good-naturedly to sleep on her floor for the next six months, until they found somewhere to live that was within their budget and this side of Roscommon.

'What do you think?' Aoife asked. She was wearing a vintage slip-dress with fishnet tights and high-heeled black satin shoes.

'You look amazing.'

'She's right, babe,' Rory agreed. 'So how are you going to play it this evening? Are we going to see a new Aoife Collins? Are you going to sweep in there and act mysterious and aloof? Or are you going to do what you usually do?'

'Which is what, exactly?' Aoife asked, flinging off the slip and dragging on a black vest and a skirt that she had made out of kimono material.

'Which is act like you're there to interview a potential new best friend. You know: spill your guts about everything that's ever happened to you; tell him how much you wanted to be on the football team at college, and how, when you weren't allowed, you picketed the matches – much to my embarrassment.' Rory said the latter aside to Carmel, before continuing, 'Slap him on the back when he says something funny … the usual.'

Aoife gave Rory a look of despair. He got to his feet and took her by the shoulders. 'Think mysterious and aloof, mysterious and aloof.'

Aoife let one knee go and cocked her head to the side like a sulking child. Rory turned to Carmel again. 'There's no helping some people, is there?'

Aoife, who was nervous enough as it was, had had enough. 'Right, you two – tell me what to wear, or leave me in peace.'

'I think you should stick with the first outfit, the black shift dress,' Carmel said, looking at Rory; he was nodding. 'I can't believe you make all this stuff yourself, Aoife. It's amazing.'

'Oh, it's all right – and I don't make all of it,' Aoife said dismissively.

'Would you never think of selling these in town – you know, in one of those boutique places?'

'Oh, now and again the thought enters my head, but I never have the time.'

Rory stifled a laugh. 'What with juggling a career and a family, not to mention all her charity work, she just doesn't have time.'

Aoife shot Rory a look. They had talked on numerous occasions about her trying to sell her clothes, but Aoife always lost her bottle when she tried to do anything about it. She had approached shops with a portfolio, but never followed up. She had made a good twenty pieces for a stall in the George's Street Arcade, but had refused to hand over the goods, claiming they weren't up to scratch. The truth was, Aoife was afraid of her work being rejected, so she avoided this by not putting herself in a position where that might be a possibility.

Aoife turned to look at herself in the mirror for at least the fortieth time that evening. She thought she looked quite good – no, better than quite good; she looked great.

Rory had offered to drive her into town; his car had miraculously recovered now that she wasn't wearing a nun's outfit. 'Can I come in and meet him again – make sure his intentions are honourable?' he asked.

'Rory, feck off; you'll frighten him.'

'Can I come in?' asked Carmel. 'I'll just say a quick hello.'

'What is with you two? Jaysus, leave me alone! I'm only going out for a meal with the poor bloke. Anyone would think he'd proposed!'

'Ooo!' exclaimed Rory. 'Touchy, babe, touchy.'

Rory and Aoife pulled up outside Eliza Blues just before eight.

'Thanks for the lift.'

'No problem. And remember: mysterious and aloof.'

'OK,' Aoife shouted, waving goodbye as Rory revved off. She looked across the Millennium Bridge, at the Morrison Hotel, as if she were about to walk the plank.

Rory headed up the back of Dublin Castle, towards Camden Street. His phone had rung three times, and when it rang a fourth time, he pulled up at the lights near the Bleeding Horse and answered it.

'What now? ... I'm just busy at the moment.... Yeah, it is something that I can do another time, but ...Well, can you give me twenty minutes? ... I'll see you there.' He threw the phone into the back seat and headed back round to Stephen's Green. The call had been from his father.

The sprawling Georgian houses that now housed businesses, instead of families, blurred in Rory's side view as he sped along Merrion Square. The heavens opened and he turned on the windscreen wipers as he drove back along the Liffey. He wondered what on earth could be so urgent. Then again, the last time his father had done this, two weeks before, Rory had hared across the city only to be presented with the new office curtains and asked if he thought they were too dark for a working environment.

As he approached the glass front offices, Rory hoped that, for once, his father had something *really* urgent to share with him. He feared he might lose the will to live altogether if he appeared at the office at this hour only to be asked his humble opinion on the best position for an umbrella plant.

Just as he pulled the car into one of the parking spaces behind the office building, Rory noticed a couple huddled in the doorway of a coffee shop, sheltering from the rain. The man was holding the woman, stroking her long red hair. He kissed the top of her head gently, then looked her in the eyes and talked intently to her. Rory squinted; he was sure he knew the man.

He turned the engine off; the wipers stopped and the windscreen became blurred with the lashing rain. He saw the woman wave goodbye to the man as she braved the weather and ran off in towards Smithfield. The man pulled his hood up and made a run for it in the direction of the river. Rory sat back in his seat and took a deep breath.

He wasn't one hundred per cent sure. He wasn't even eighty per cent – he couldn't be; it was raining too hard, and he hadn't got a proper look at the man's face. But Rory felt sure he recognised the man who had just been part of that intimate goodbye. It was Aoife's dinner date for the evening. It was Paul.

Chapter Twelve

The Morrison was packed. Aoife headed towards the bar to buy herself a drink. She couldn't see Paul anywhere, but she wasn't too worried; he had texted her to say he was running fifteen minutes late. She got herself a beer and found a seat.

Looking out the window, Aoife watched the rain bouncing off the road and was thankful that Rory had given her a lift; the last thing she wanted to do was look like a drowned rat on their first date. When Paul came in, his hood was pulled up tight, but he was still soaked through.

'Thought I'd been stood up,' Aoife said, smiling.

'Sorry about that. I've had a mad busy day at work and I didn't get in until about seven. I'll just grab myself a drink – you OK for one?' Paul asked.

'I'm fine,' Aoife told him, watching as he took off his coat and went to the bar. He was dressed in dark jeans and a zip-up top. His dark hair was dishevelled. All in all, Aoife decided, he looked great.

Paul came back from the bar and sat down opposite Aoife, and they smiled nervously at each other. Aoife took a swig of her beer.

'You look great,' Paul told her.

'Thanks. You don't look half bad yourself.'

'So, have you been in here before?' Paul asked. '... Jaysus, did you hear that? That was nearly "Do you come here often?", wasn't it?' He grinned at himself and Aoife laughed.

'Not at all. And yes, I've been here. I came to the opening with Rory.'

'Very swanky.'

'Well, yeah, I suppose it is; but it's Rory that gets all the invites, not me.'

'Why's that?'

'He used to be a DJ a few years ago. When he did his final gig, he got some friend of his father's who's in PR to hype it around the city. The place was mobbed, and since then he's had this kind of legendary status around town. He'd get a fortune if he decided to do another gig – he's always being asked – but he tells people that he wanted to go out in a blaze of glory and that's what he did. Anyway, that's the reason he ends up getting invited to stuff – just because people vaguely knew of him; you know what Dublin's like. And, because he hasn't got a job, he can generally be relied upon to turn up at whatever the glitterati have decided is the thing to do that week.'

'He's not DJ Monkey Business, is he?'

'The very same. How on God's earth did you guess that?'

'I was one of the people who fell for the hype; I was at that gig. Jaysus, that's mad! That was a brilliant night.'

'Yep, I know. I got free drinks all night.'

'Why did he stop DJ-ing?'

'Well, one explanation – and this is the one he tells everyone – is that he gave it up because he could. He's not short of cash. But the real reason is that he got unbearable stage fright. Used to chuck his guts up before and after every gig.'

'Bloody hell, that is such a shame. He was brilliant. Next time I see him, I'll probably get star-struck.'

'So you're a bit of a raver, are you?' Aoife decided to change the subject slightly; she didn't want Rory stealing the limelight even when he wasn't there. 'Or was that before you became a responsible man?'

'I used to go clubbing quite a bit, but – at the risk of sounding like an old fart – it's not the same any more.'

'You do sound like an old fart.' Aoife grinned at him.

The maître d' showed them through to their table, and they stayed there all evening. Aoife couldn't believe how well they were getting on. Paul told her all about growing up in Dublin, and how he'd worked in every job known to mankind before landing himself a temporary job in the company where he was now an account manager. 'It was back in 2000, and they'd have made a monkey in a suit permanent if it proved it could answer a phone,' he told her. Aoife knew he was right; back then, there had been more jobs than people.

In return, Aoife, true to form, told him everything about herself, ensuring that mystery and aloofness went straight out the window. She kept picking up things that proved to her just how alike they were – but, in all fairness, if the waitress had pointed out that they both had heads or that they were both sitting on chairs, Aoife would have taken it as a sign that they were perfect for each other.

After the second course and the second bottle of wine, Paul leant forward and, resting his chin on his hands, looked intently at Aoife.

'What?' she asked. She was nicely buckled from the wine.

'I'm just looking.'

Aoife pulled her head back and eyed him suspiciously. 'At what?'

'At what? The picture on the wall behind you is slightly crooked. What do you think I'm looking at? I'm looking at you.'

'Ah, right. Work away, then,' she said, trying to sound flippant.

'I'm going to say something now, and I might have to shoot myself once the words are out of my mouth, but....'

'Just say it. I might walk out, but look on the bright side: you've had a nice meal.'

'OK. I think you're great.'

Aoife burst out laughing – her natural reaction was to dismiss the possibility that he might be serious – but then she looked at Paul, and he seemed crushed. She could have kicked herself. She always had this knee-jerk flippancy when anyone showed any interest in her. What she really wanted to do was agree with him and tell him how much she liked him. She didn't want the night to end. There had been no gaping silences, no embarrassing gaffes, no indications that Paul was affiliated to any weird sects. And he was funny. He didn't just think he was funny, like a lot of men did in Aoife's experience; he genuinely was. And she fancied him like mad. He'd be telling her something, and her mind would just wander off and imagine him naked.

She leant forward and smiled at him. 'Sorry. I've got some form of mental block when it comes to people saying nice things to me. I actually know exactly what you mean. In fact,' she said, taking a sip of her wine and mulling over the wisdom of what she was about to say, 'I can honestly say that I haven't got on with someone this well in as long as I can remember.'

Paul relaxed back into his smile again. 'Great,' he said. 'Shall I get the bill, and maybe we could head somewhere else?'

'Yeah, we could.'

Just then, Paul's phone rang. ''Scuse me a minute –

sorry about this,' he said to Aoife. He got up and moved away from the table to take the call. Aoife heard him say, 'I don't know what time ... with a friend....' and then he was out of earshot.

When he came back, Paul had a look of consternation on his face.

'Everything all right?' Aoife asked.

'Yeah, fine,' Paul said. 'Fine. Just my housemate – forgot her keys and wanted to know when I'd be back. But she's just going to stay at a friend's.'

'Housemate?' Aoife asked, and then immediately regretted it, hoping it didn't sound like she was fishing.

'Yeah, she's lived there for a few years.' Paul looked at Aoife and smiled, as if he had just remembered why they were there. 'Won't be a minute,' he said. 'I'll just grab the bill.'

Chapter Thirteen

Rory took the lift to his father's office. The doorman had given him a knowing nod, and Rory wondered briefly if his father made this man nervous too. He saw no reason why not; Eoin O'Donnell wasn't about to make an exception for a doorman, not when the rest of the Western world trembled every time he spoke.

The offices were deserted. Even Eoin's long-suffering PA, Niamh, was nowhere to be seen. But then again, it was half past eight; she'd probably got off nice and early – about eight or so. He knocked on his father's office door.

'Come!' boomed the voice from within. *Come?* thought Rory, as he did every time he visited his father's office; *what was that all about?* 'Come in,' fair enough, but 'Come' was just pompous.

Rory pushed the door open. 'Hello, Dad.' His father swivelled round in his chair to face him; it was all very James Bond.

'Good man yourself,' Eoin said, leaping from his chair. 'I need figures for the flats in Ballsbridge, and I need them now. I've a meeting with the board tomorrow and Niamh is in at seven in the morning to put together the presentation, so I need to know how much rent I've had from each apartment in the last quarter.'

Rory sighed. 'Well, you have all that information already. I make sure that Niamh has a running tally of the rent from the flats, and it hasn't changed in the last few months. No one's moving anywhere, Dad – people are over the moon to be living in an apartment in Ballsbridge – so the figures have been constant.' Rory couldn't believe his father had dragged him there for this. The man owned five apartments in a block in Ballsbridge; Rory lived in one of them, and the other four were rented out for 1,200 euros a month each. It didn't take Stephen Hawking to work it out.

'That might be so, but I needed to hear it from the horse's mouth.' Eoin was throwing a stress-relief ball with the O'Donnell Properties logo on it from one hand to the other. He was concentrating on the ball and not looking at Rory, which was making Rory want to throttle him.

'Well, there you go. Four apartments at one thousand two hundred euros per month, over three months, makes...' Rory checked his mental arithmetic. 'Fourteen thousand, four hundred euros.'

'I see the old cogs are still intact. We might have to

put you to some use around here soon, when I can think of something I need you to do.' Rory took a deep breath. His father had an amazing knack of offering a combination of flattery and despair. 'It's a long time since you graduated, and I don't see you developing much in the way of a career off your own bat.'

The thing that annoyed Rory most was that his father was right. He didn't really do anything. Granted, he had been one of Dublin's most sought-after DJs for a very brief spell, but that was about as useful as a batwing jumper from 1984 – great at the time, but not much good to anyone now.

He sat looking at the great man around Dublin, Eoin O'Donnell. He was well known, well feared and well respected. Rory thought of the tyrannical way he had run the house when Rory was a child. They had never been particularly close, but they had spent a lot of time together when Rory was younger; his father had been priming him to be the heir to the throne.

The gap between them began to inch wider when, at the age of fifteen, Rory had the full, terrifying realisation that he was gay. As far as he was concerned at the time, people didn't have sex unless they were married and going to have babies. The feelings he was experiencing were so different from anything he could talk about that he just ignored them and hoped to God they would go away.

At the age of seventeen, he went on a school trip to London, got himself lost accidentally on purpose and, quite literally, found himself in Soho. After that, Rory had slowly inched his way out of the closet. He had lost people on the way – people who couldn't cope with the fact that he was gay – but he had gained more friends than he had lost.

But his father ... his father was different. Rory always had the feeling that he was somehow letting his father down. Eoin didn't mind wheeling him out when a friendly face and idle chitchat were required, but that was about it.

As a result, Rory was in a constant state of frustration with his father. He didn't want to feel like he had disappointed him, but he didn't want to do things just to impress him. He didn't want to work for him, but he wanted the opportunity to be there. He didn't want to take his money, but it was too easy, so he did. He wanted to stand up to his father and tell him that he thought he was a bully, but anything like that would be meaningless because, by being financially dependent on his father, he had given up his right to an opinion. Most of all, he wanted to tell his father that he was gay; but there was a promise he had made, eight years before, that meant he couldn't.

'Well, is there anything else, or can I go?' Rory asked.

'No, that's it. Just write the figures down on a Post-it and stick it on Niamh's computer, and that'll be grand.' Rory took a pen from his father's desk and did as he was told. 'I'll call you next week.'

I'm sure you will, thought Rory. 'OK, good luck, then.' His father went back to throwing the stress reliever around as Rory made his own way out.

Rory headed along the Liffey wall, towards Parliament Street; he was meeting his friends, Dave and Gavin, in the Front Lounge. He was thinking that he really needed to sort out the situation with his dad. It made him feel weak and dependent – and, if he was honest with himself, that was because he was. He needed to do something about it once and for all.

But, as always, as his annoyance with himself and his father faded, so did his will to do anything about it.

Chapter Fourteen

Bridie stood at Killarney station, tutting and sighing. The train was late, and she was in no mood for delays; she'd had a trying enough day as it was, getting ready for her stay in Dublin. Roddy had kicked up a fuss to the point where Bridie had thought he was going to hold his breath until she promised to stay.

'I don't know what's gotten into you, woman! Haring off up to Dublin at the drop of a hat,' he had said, sitting at the kitchen table and watching Bridie label two weeks' worth of meat, potatoes and veg for him.

'I am not haring off,' she had told him. 'I'm going to stay with Mary at the convent – it's all arranged: she's picking me up at the station at three o'clock, and then we're driving over to Whitehall. I'm going to go and see Aoife in the morning.' Bridie piled pre-cooked bacon and cabbage into another Tupperware container. 'Now, listen – you put these in the microwave for five minutes on defrost, yes?'

'Yes,' Roddy said, kicking the table and staring at the floor.

'And then you put them on full power for another two minutes, yes?'

'Yes,' he said sulkily.

'Now, there's enough there for the two weeks, but if I'm away longer, there's some frozen meals in the freezer; you just need to follow the instructions on the packets.'

'More than two weeks? You never said anything about that! Sure, two weeks in Dublin is a lifetime, woman. Why on God's earth would you be staying up there longer than that?'

'I don't want to stay there at all, but I might have no choice,' Bridie told him, absentmindedly clutching at the crucifix around her neck.

'She's lost her job, for God's sake; she's not been sold into white slavery.' Roddy was getting to the end of his very short tether.

'You saw how she was, Roddy, as well as I did. She doesn't know whether she's coming or going.' Roddy frowned; Bridie decided to ignore the look. 'If I just sit here and let her lose all interest in herself, then what sort of mother am I? Sure, didn't the Lord say we have to act in times of crisis in order to enter the Kingdom of Heaven?'

'Did he?' Roddy furrowed his brow.

'Well, I don't know, but that's what I'm doing and that's that,' she told him, hoping that would end the discussion. It did, in a way. Roddy pushed himself away from the table and stood up so quickly that he nearly sent his cup of milk flying.

'Well, good luck yourself! But don't come crying to me when you want to come back here.'

Bridie looked at him as if he had gone mad. 'What would I do that for? I'll catch the train back, same as I'm catching the train there.'

'Good!' Roddy shouted. 'Off you go, but don't expect a lift from me.'

'I don't. I've called a taxi,' she had replied. Roddy had nearly taken the hinges off the kitchen door making his dramatic exit.

The train finally arrived at the station twenty minutes late. As Bridie chose a seat, her mood lifted. For the first time in as long as she could remember, she had no one to look after, and it felt good. She put her glasses on, spread her magazines out in front of her and settled back in her seat.

Bridie thought about Roddy for a moment and worried; but then she reasoned that she had left him with food and ironed some shirts for him, so he should be fine. Anyway, she was more concerned with getting her daughter back on track. Aoife was twenty-six years old now, Bridie mused, and there wasn't so much as a sign of a boyfriend in her life, let alone any hope of her settling down. And as for the job situation ... well, Bridie had already done something about that herself.

Bridie sat back in her seat as the train pulled out of

the station. Pulling out her flask of tea, she made herself comfortable in her seat. She thought to herself that her visit to Dublin would be fairly cut and dried. She would sort her daughter out, get her back on the straight and narrow, maybe even persuade her to move back to Kerry. She would spend some time with her cousin Mary, and then she would return home.

Chapter Fifteen

'I'm in lust!' Aoife had announced to Rory.

His response had been pretty much what she expected. 'You got your end away, babe! You hadn't sealed up after all!'

'I didn't shag him, for God's sake, Rory. You have a one-track mind. Besides, my bed is too small; we just cuddled.'

'*Cuddled*?' Rory had pulled a face of disgust. 'And in your bed? Your horrible embarrassment of a single bed? Not his Killiney shag-pad?'

'There were no taxis,' Aoife had explained. 'Anyway, I'm meeting him again tonight, so you never know – I could be Killiney-bound.'

'Where's he taking you? He'll have to do something to top the Morrison.'

'We're just meeting in O'Neill's on Suffolk Street.'

'Dear me,' Rory had said with disdain, 'I'd nip that

in the bud as soon as possible. O'Neill's is full of students and tourists; deeply uncool.'

As soon as she got through the door of the pub, Aoife started to see Rory's point. O'Neill's was huge and it was mobbed. She was late. She had been trying to get hold of her mother, who wasn't answering her home phone or her mobile phone, in order to dissuade her from coming to Dublin. Aoife made a mental note to try again the following morning. She still had a couple of days.

She pushed through the crowd on the ground floor and was just about to check upstairs when she felt a tap on her shoulder. She spun round to see Paul grinning at her.

'How'ya?' he said, leaning forward and kissing her. Aoife's stomach did flip-flops so quickly that she found herself clenching her buttocks.

'I'm good, how are you?' she grinned.

'Fine, but I thought I might never find you in this place.' Paul was looking at Aoife as if he were five and had just unwrapped Action Man on Christmas morning.

'I know; it's mobbed.' Aoife realised that they were mooning over each other and that an onlooker would probably find them sickening, but she decided not to care.

'You want a drink?'

'A pint of Miller, thanks.'

When Paul returned from the bar, he and Aoife

managed to find a seat and began admiring each other again. Aoife hoped to God that no one she knew saw her in this lovestruck state; they'd be forgiven for thinking she had joined a cult, going by the beatific look on her face.

After about an hour of being enthralled with each other, Aoife and Paul found themselves suddenly and unceremoniously interrupted. Two women were trying to squeeze into the seat next to them.

'Room for a little 'un?' one woman asked. The other one let out a piercing squeal of a laugh. Fair enough, Aoife thought – it was ironic all right, as the woman's friend had an arse the size of Kilkenny, but it wasn't *that* funny.

'Em, yeah,' Paul half-heartedly agreed, moving over so much that he was almost in Aoife's lap.

'Here y'are, Kath, get yersen sat down here.' The woman waggled her backside as if to demonstrate how comfortable the pub bench was. 'Phew! That's better, i'n't it, Kath? Christ on a bike, we've been standing up all day; me poor feet are killing.' Aoife and Paul smiled as politely as they could, but their eyes just weren't in it. 'Sorry to barge in, loves; you two carry on with your conversation.' Aoife felt that her usual verbal diarr-hoea was amateurish by comparison and suddenly couldn't think of anything to say – not that it mattered; the woman had decided not to leave them to it after all.

'Are you two from Dublin?' she asked.

'Yeah.' Aoife found her voice again. 'Well, I've been here long enough – you know the way.'

'We were just saying, weren't we, Kath, we love the Dublin accent, don't we?' Kath nodded. 'It's so poetic. Not like ours – we sound like bit parts on *Emmerdale*, don't we, Kath?' Kath could have sounded like a bit part from *Knotts Landing* for all Aoife knew; she hadn't got a word in edgeways. 'We're from Yorkshire. A place called Shelf, like what you put books on.' Kath shuffled uneasily in her seat and put her mouth to her bottle on the table.

'Oooh!' the other woman exclaimed. 'Aren't I rude, not even introducing myself! I'm Jeanine and this is Kath.'

'Hi; Aoife.'

'Howya; Paul.'

Aoife decided to add something to the conversation.

'So what brings you to Dublin's fair city?' Sometimes Aoife despaired of herself; she sounded like a Bord Fáilte advert.

'Well, we come to Dublin about four times a year, don't we, Kath?' Kath nodded again and ripped at the label on her bottle. 'We're members of the U2 fan club.' Kath smiled wistfully and stared at the table. Paul nudged Aoife. Jeanine carried on, 'We've seen them all over – the States, Australia, Japan…. We were members of the Yorkshire U2 fan club, but I had a to-do with the fella in charge of subs and we decided to part company, so it's just me and Kath at the minute.'

Aoife had perked up. 'So have you met them?'

'U2? Yes, lots of times.' Kath suddenly came to life. 'They're always really polite, you know. Bono is an absolute gentleman – isn't he, Jeanine?' Jeanine nodded; she was about to say something, but Kath didn't give her a chance. 'He gave me his jacket on the Zooropa tour, didn't he, Jeanine?' Jeanine nodded again. 'He said to me, "Ah, Jayz" – sorry, I can't do the accent very well....' Kath went bright red, and Aoife and Paul cringed. '"Ah, Jayz, Kath, yer freezing, let me give you this jacket."'

'He did not!' Jeanine interrupted indignantly. 'He said, "Ah, Jayz, *love*, yer freezing, let me give you this jacket."' Paul nudged Aoife; the accents weren't getting any better.

'He bloody well did, and you know it!' Kath had jumped to her feet and was shouting into Jeanine's face. 'He said my name; he knows my name! We've met him enough times – why wouldn't he? He said "Kath", he definitely said *"Kath"*.' Kath was close to tears; she turned away from the table and pushed through the crowd in the direction of the toilet.

Jeanine seemed unperturbed by the whole incident. She leant forward and whispered, 'She hasn't done this for a while. I'm sorry. It's a bit of a sore subject. You see, we were in Manchester, and we were outside the Palace Hotel where they were staying, and ... well, don't get me wrong, Bono did give her a jacket, but he never said her name. But you try telling her that. I don't like mentioning it, but every now and again it surfaces and I have to put her straight. I mean, making up that Bono said your name? It's a slippery slope from that to a barring order for stalking; I've seen it all before.' Jeanine gave them a knowing look, sipped her drink and resumed a pose that was meant to indicate she hadn't been talking about her friend in her absence.

Kath returned from the toilets, dabbing her eyes and trying to look composed. She leant forward and whispered in Jeanine's ear.

'Yeah, that's fine.' Jeanine looked up at Paul and Aoife. 'Well, it's been nice meeting you, but we'd best be off; doesn't do to let the grass grow under your feet.' She nodded her head quickly sideways towards Kath. 'Goodbye.'

They were just about to head off when Aoife stopped them.

'You don't know if Bono's in town this week, do you?' she asked.

'He was meant to be here the other day, but you've just missed him; he's back in America now. We're going up to Raheny, aren't we, Kath?' Kath nodded. 'Going to see where Larry Mullen did his paper round.'

'Bye.' Aoife smiled.

'Good luck.' Paul winked after the two women.

There was a pause as they waited for the two women to leave the pub, and then both Aoife and Paul fell about laughing. 'Larry Mullen's fecking paper round?' Paul asked. 'Have you ever heard anything like it?'

'Yep,' said Aoife. 'Loads of times. But for every person who's met Larry Mullen, or seen Larry Mullen, or stood next to Larry Mullen at their brother's girlfriend's nephew's christening, there are another ten who've seen Bono. There's no one else in Ireland like it. Van Morrison? Handful of people will say they met him somewhere, or saw him play; he was quiet, kept himself to himself, and that was it. Sinéad O'Connor? Same again: everyone can comment on her – I mean, even my mother knows who she is.' Aoife mimicked her mother: '"Ah, isn't it a pity about that young wan Sinéad O'Connor? A real beauty, but mad; her mother must be fierce disappointed." But nobody claims they've met her. There are a lot of famous people to come out of Ireland, but for some reason Bono is the one everyone thinks they know.'

'I'm going to get a drink,' Paul said, 'and when I come back, we're going to have a chat with quite a few people in this bar.'

'What for?' Aoife asked.

'I want to test just how watertight your theory is.'

'You are so fecking right!' Paul said in disbelief. It had become more and more apparent that Aoife's theory was correct.

'Go on.' Aoife was smiling the smile of the smug. 'Which one's your favourite?'

'I don't know; there's a fair few to choose from. I liked the fella with the big red head, over on the stool, who said that he kicked the living shite out of Bono for being a gobby little bollix when he was thirteen.'

'I know! Can you believe that he actually thinks that Bono can sing as high as he does in "With or Without You" because that lunatic kicked him in the nuts when he was prepubescent?'

'Actually, no, that's not my favourite. I like the fella who said he went to audition as a bass player for them after seeing a notice pinned up at school, but when Bono turned up and started throwing his weight about, he told them they were shite and he wouldn't be in the band if you paid him – and now he's in a U2 cover band! That is some story, if it's true.'

'Yeah, if it's true – but that's not the point; the point is that everyone's got one,' Aoife said, settling into the comfort of her theory.

'I think you're becoming obsessed with this,' Paul told her.

'I am not!' Aoife exclaimed. 'Oh, OK, maybe I am.'

'Shall we go?' Paul asked.

'Yeah, fine.' Aoife was thinking that she might like to stay in Killiney tonight, or at least in a double bed. As they left O'Neill's, she wondered how to turn the conversation round so that she could say, 'Can we stay at yours?' She gave up wondering and said, 'Pa-aul.'

'Ye-es,' he said, mimicking her.

'Sorry, that was pathetic of me; I'll start again. Paul?'

'Yes?' he said, mimicking her sincerity this time.

'Can we stay at your house tonight?'

Paul coughed and took a deep breath. 'I'm sorry, and I was going to tell you, but we can't.'

'Oh, OK.' Aoife backtracked.

'It's just that I've got builders in and the place is a tip,' Paul said by way of explanation. There was a short silence as they wandered along the street, and then Paul spoke again. 'I have, however, taken the liberty of doing something that you might think is really bad, so you can say no if you want.'

'What?'

'I've booked us in at the Shelbourne.'

'What?' Aoife shrieked.

'Well, if you want to go, that is.'

'I'd love to! It's just that it's really expensive.'

'We get a discounted rate from work. So it's only half a fortune.' Paul smiled, and Aoife felt the butterflies in her stomach get on their bikes and start pedalling round in circles. 'I just thought it would be a treat, and it means not sleeping with my face pinned to the wall in your bunk again.'

Aoife laughed and mulled it over for a nanosecond. 'Fair enough.'

Paul was in the middle of giving her a big hug when his phone began to ring. He pulled it out of his pocket.

''Scuse me a minute,' he said to Aoife. He moved

ahead, obviously wanting to take the call in private. Aoife heard him say, 'Hello.... I'm in town.... A friend.... Why do I have to explain everything to you? .... Ah, come on, don't start that again.... Don't put the phone d.... Bollocks!'

'Family shit. Sorry about that,' Paul said, staring at his phone and shaking his head.

'What's the matter?' Aoife asked.

'I'd rather not talk about it, if that's OK.' Paul took Aoife's hand and started in the direction of the Shelbourne.

'No, that's fine – if you don't want to talk about it, that's fine,' Aoife said, but she didn't really mean it. She felt slightly uncomfortable: she had told Paul all about herself, and he didn't even want to explain a phone conversation. But as they walked up Grafton Street, Aoife reasoned that she was being ridiculous. Paul was treating her to an evening in the Shelbourne, and he obviously didn't want to spoil it by going on about whatever family problems he was having. She put the phone conversation to the back of her mind and thought about the evening she had ahead of her.

Aoife awoke slowly the next morning and spent a good few seconds daring herself to open her eyes. When she finally did, her joy was confirmed: yes, she was in a suite in the Shelbourne, and sleeping next to her was the most amazing man she had ever met.

The previous evening had been fantastic. Aoife had

been nervous about sleeping with Paul – it had been a long time since she had slept with anyone – but she was so absolutely mad about him that all her fears had disappeared, and she had just wanted to rip the clothes off him as soon as they were in the room.

Paul stirred, rolled over and pulled Aoife into him. 'Morning, missus,' he said, kissing her on the nose.

Aoife bounced up in the bed. 'I can't believe I'm in the Shelbourne! This is mad!' She jumped up and ran to the window. 'Would you look at that?'

'Yeah, I bet you never thought you'd be looking at Stephen's Green stark bollock naked, did you?'

Aoife ran back to the bed and jumped on top of Paul. 'Thank you, thank you, thank you! This is brilliant!'

'No problem; you deserve it.'

'Nobody *deserves* this; this is pure luxury,' Aoife said, curling up in his arms.

After a minute, Paul rolled over, propping himself up on his elbow, and looked down at Aoife. 'Do you know, I can't remember a time when I felt this at ease with a girl? It's all happened so quickly … it's amazing.' There was a pause; Paul seemed to be gathering his thoughts. 'Aoife, I really need to tell you something.'

Aoife felt a strange jerk of fear in her chest. *Oh, my God*, she thought, *he's going to tell me that he loves me*. She really liked Paul, but she wasn't ready for undying love to be thrust upon her.

So she put her hand over his mouth. She couldn't

believe she was doing it; she felt like Alexis Colby silencing some half-bit love interest in *Dynasty*. All she needed to do was say, 'Don't say anything. Let our bodies do the talking,' and she'd have been there – Denver, Colorado, circa 1984.

What she actually did was take her hand from his mouth and kiss him. They both started laughing, simply because of the sheer confusion of the situation. Paul took the hint and didn't continue with what he had been about to say; he returned the kiss, and they both dived under the quilt.

Chapter Sixteen

Paul and Aoife strolled up Leinster Road towards Aoife's house. Paul pulled out his mobile to call the office and let them know that he'd be in at about eleven o'clock.

'Oh, shit, that reminds me,' Aoife said, fumbling for her own mobile in her jacket pocket; it had fallen through the lining and she had to chase it. 'I've had it diverted all night.'

Aoife's voice mail informed her that she had four new messages.

'Message one: "Hi, Aoife, it's Katie. Listen, can you give us a call as soon as you get this message? Talk to you soon." Message two: "Aoife, it's Ian. Presume you're out with lover boy. Come on, switch your bloody phone on; I have to speak to you before I go to work." Message three: "Aoife, long story short, your mother's here and she's insisting on waiting here for you. Because you're not home, she thinks you're dead in a ditch. I was going to tell her you were probably riding the arse off some fine thing from Killiney, but I thought that might push her over the edge. What are we meant to do with her?" Message four: "Aoife; Ian. I gave your mother the keys and told her to wait there for you. I can't guarantee that she hasn't called the guards looking for you. I suggest you get your arse home ASAP." '

By this time, they were nearly outside Aoife's house, and her jaw was nearly on the floor. Paul put his phone away and looked at Aoife, who was muttering, 'Oh my God, oh my God....'

'You all right? You look like you've seen a ghost.'

'It's my mother. She's here; she's in my house. Oh my God, Paul, you have to go, honestly; I cannot inflict my mother on you.' Aoife wasn't being entirely truthful. What she meant was that she didn't want to pierce her mother's bubble just yet; and, armed with the fact that her daughter had been out all night and was walking home hand-in-hand with a man, Bridie might finally put two and two together. Aoife had a vision of her mother blowing a chip in her brain and steam coming out of her ears.

But it was too late. Bridie had obviously had her face glued to the window since Ian and Katie had left for work. The door to Aoife's house flew open and there she stood.

133

'Aoife Collins, I have been worried sick! Where have you been?'

'Ma, what are you doing here?'

'You might well ask what I'm doing here. I've come to keep an eye on you.'

'But when I saw Sister Immaculata the other day, she told me you were coming up on Saturday. I was trying to get hold of you last night to tell you not to come.'

'I had my phone off because of the trains,' Bridie said, giving no explanation. She turned her attention to Paul, who was smiling politely at her. 'Well, hello,' she said accusingly.

'Em, this is Paul, Ma. He's my –'

'Friend, very good,' Bridie finished.

'Hello, Mrs Collins. Pleased to meet you.'

Bridie nodded her head. 'Likewise, I'm sure.'

Paul, realising he was being dismissed, turned to Aoife. 'Listen, I'd better head. Thanks for making sure I got home OK last night; I feel much better now.' He looked at Bridie. 'Food poisoning,' he said. 'Your daughter's a lifesaver – brought me home and made sure I was all right.'

'No problem,' Aoife said, picking up on the story. 'No problem at all. Thanks for the loan of the bed.'

Paul went to kiss Aoife and then remembered that he was just a food-poisoned friend.

'Well, good luck. Nice to meet you, Mrs Collins. I'll give you a buzz later on, Aoife, OK? Tell you how the tummy is bearing up.'

Aoife looked forlornly after him. Bridie glared after him like a hawk.

Aoife gave her mother a kiss on the cheek; Bridie screwed up her face as if waiting for someone to stick a needle in her. 'Have you been standing at the window waiting for me?'

'Actually, I was waiting for the guards.'

'*What*?'

'Well, I called them and they weren't very helpful, I can tell you. They said that they would take it seriously, but that people reported within a couple of hours of disappearing usually turned up safe and sound, and that I wasn't to worry too much. I told them … I said, "What sort of rubbish is that? She could be raped and murdered for all you people care." I put the phone down on them. But then I thought to myself, I'll tell them the house has been ransacked; that'll get them out. So they're sending someone round.'

'Ma, you can't do that! You'll be prosecuted for wasting police time!'

'And I might very well prosecute them for wasting my time. An hour I've been at this window, and I could've been giving this filthy house of yours a good scrub if they'd turned up and done their job.'

'Ma, I wasn't missing. I was out with friends. Jesus!'

'Don't blaspheme, Aoife.'

'Oh, for God's sake!' Aoife grabbed her phone and rang the guards.

'Hello, I'd just like to tell you that my mother rang

to say there had been a burglary, and...' That was when Aoife noticed the garda car pulling up outside. 'Sorry to bother you. The guards have just arrived. Thanks; bye.' Aoife threw her mother a look of despair. Bridie was standing with her arms folded and a self-satisfied smile on her lips, ready to greet the guard who had just got out of the car.

'Hello. We have a call about a burglary; which one of you two ladies reported it?'

'Well, there's been a bit of a mix up....' Aoife began, but her mother cut in.

'I called you. Come in. You'll have a cup of tea?'

The guard looked a bit taken aback, and refused politely. He got his notepad out and tried to look officious as Bridie explained her actions.

'I thought she was dead!' she said, talking about Aoife as if she were nowhere to be seen.

'Now, Mrs Collins, I appreciate that,' the policeman told her, 'but you should really have checked with her friends; she seems to think that they had an idea where she was.'

'"Friends" you call them? They just told me not to worry, she'd be home and everything would be fine. But they couldn't tell me where she was, could they?'

The guard pieced together what Bridie was telling him, and arched an eyebrow. 'You should count yourself lucky that you aren't being charged with wasting police time. I've been called here on a charge of burglary, and there hasn't been a burglary – has there, Mrs Collins?'

Bridie wasn't used to being in trouble. 'No, there hasn't,' she said, in a little mouse-voice that Aoife had never heard come out of her before.

'Well, I'll leave you to think about it. But in future, when you turn up unexpectedly at your daughter's house at the crack of dawn and she's not there, will you give it a few hours before you call out the search parties?'

'Yes, Guard. I was only worried about her, and–'

'Yes, Mrs Collins.'

'I'll show you to the door,' Aoife offered. Her mother sat on a chair, swinging her legs like a chastised child.

At the door, the guard said to Aoife, 'Off the record and all, you've got your work cut out there, haven't you?'

'She wasn't even meant to be coming up until the weekend!' Aoife whispered.

'She here for long?'

Aoife shrugged; she didn't want to jinx herself by setting a time limit on her mother's stay.

'Well, good luck.'

'Thanks a million, and sorry again for the hassle.'

Aoife went back to the kitchen to find that her mother had stopped her quiet leg-swinging and was back in indignation mode.

'He was barely out of short trousers! Talking to me like that – I don't know who he thought he was!'

'A guard, Ma; he thought he was a guard. And I thought he was very fair with you; he could have read you the riot act.'

'Fair? I was only concerned about you; I thought you were dead in a ditch!'

Aoife wondered why her mother's first assumption was always that she was dead in a ditch. Ten minutes late for tea when she was five years old and playing hide-and-seek in her friend's barn: dead in a ditch. Stopped to watch the young lads playing hurling on the way back from the shop: dead in a ditch. Didn't call from university for two weeks once, due to lack of funds: dead in a ditch again. She couldn't help thinking that she'd be hard pushed in Dublin to find a ditch to finish up dead in, but she decided not to share this particular observation with her mother.

'Well, I wasn't,' Aoife sighed. 'Ma, can we get a few things straight?'

'Such as?'

'Well, first of all, you seem to be convinced that my life has somehow gone to the dogs.'

'Well, I wouldn't go that far, but it's getting there, isn't it?'

'No, it's not! Things are fine. I am perfectly happy.'
Happy she was, but if someone had told her a month earlier that she could look forward to the pleasure of being a waitress, she would have laughed in his face. 'And another thing is that I don't really see what good

you being here in Dublin is going to do. You don't even like the place.'

'I know, I detest the place, but if it means getting you back on track, then I'm prepared to be here. This is not about me; it's about you, my girl.'

Aoife smelled burning martyr. She decided to take a different tack.

'Ma, what would you like me to do?'

Bridie looked at her as if it was obvious. 'Sort yourself out, with a roof over your head, and get a proper job. I didn't put you through college so that you could go off and serve food to people.'

'I will, but it takes time. I got the job at the restaurant so that I'd be working again straight away.' This wasn't entirely true, but she didn't want to tell her mother that she was also hoping to run into Bono. If Bridie knew about the bet, she might think that her daughter had lost it altogether and decide to camp down in Dublin for the foreseeable future.

'Have you thought about the plot of land back home?'

'Not really. To be honest, I just can't see myself moving back home.'

'What?' Bridie was utterly dumbfounded.

'I don't know; I just feel at home here.'

'How can you be at home somewhere where you haven't even got a house? What sort of rubbish is that? I think you need to have a good long think about what you're doing with yourself.'

'What does Roddy think about you being up here?' Aoife was desperate to steer the conversation away from herself.

'He's grand,' Bridie said dismissively. 'I've cooked him his dinner for two weeks and frozen it, so I think that should do him.'

Aoife rolled her eyes, for two reasons. Firstly, she couldn't believe that her mother had cooked food for Roddy so that he wouldn't go unfed in her absence. Secondly, she now knew for sure that her mother intended to stay for two weeks. *Brilliant,* she thought.

'So what have you got planned for today?' she asked her mother, who had managed to produce a clean dishcloth from somewhere and was busy wiping the cooker.

'Nothing, really. I thought I might carry on trying to get you a job. I made a couple of phone calls, and I've got you an appointment at one of those places that gets young girls jobs.' Bridie made it sound as if she were talking about an escort agency.

'What, a recruitment agency?' Aoife asked in astonishment.

'Yes, that's what they're called, isn't it? Spoke to a lovely woman. I have it written down somewhere. It's at one o'clock on Monday, I think. Somewhere on Grafton Street – you know where that is, don't you? Near the Bewley's we were in.'

'Mother, you cannot just go making appointments for me without telling me first.'

'You'll be fine,' Bridie said reassuringly. 'They'll just ask you a few questions and do some tests, so she told me, and then they'll get you a job. I told them that I was ringing for you because you were just recovering from tonsillitis and were resting your voice. Didn't want them thinking that a twenty-six-year-old has her mother getting jobs for her.'

Aoife let out a huge sigh of exasperation. 'Right, I'll go. But I can organise these things myself, you know.'

'Well, I'm just giving you a little jump-start. Now then, I need to head off into town; I'm meeting Mary at twelve. We're going to somewhere where there's lots of homeless people. She's having a Novena for them. I'll let you know how I get on; I bet there's a few people there who were in the same boat as you, swanning along and thinking they were going to be fine, and now they've no roof over their heads. I'll ask them.'

Aoife had given up. 'I'm not homeless, Ma.'

Bridie gave her a look that said, 'Not yet, you're not!' while simultaneously taking the enamel off the cooker with a scouring pad.

Chapter Seventeen

Having successfully parcelled her mother off, Aoife received a phone call from her about two hours later, to say that she had just got in the door of the convent and that the traffic in Dublin was 'fecking diabolical'. Bridie also asked Aoife why they hadn't thought to widen the roads. She told Aoife that she should ring Dublin City Council and suggest that they improve their transport system. Bridie was a great woman for ideas.

Aoife decided that she was going to sit down and do something normal – well, relatively normal, anyway. She was going to make a list of her own – a list of ways to meet Bono.

She made herself a cup of tea and sat at the kitchen table. *Right,* she thought, *come on, Aoife: get the old office-manager head on.* She had always been super-organised in her professional capacity as PA/Office Manager/Coffee-and-Sandwich Monkey; she had to be

– that was the point of the job. But in her own life she was organisationally disastrous. So she pretended the list was a task for work, to focus her mind.

At 12.15 her mobile rang; it was Rory's number. Aoife picked the phone up and was greeted by the sound of Elvis singing 'Viva Las Vegas'. She put the phone down and looked at her list; she had nearly finished. She didn't have time for Rory arsing about playing CDs down the phone.

The phone rang again straightaway. Aoife picked it up again. 'Speak!' she instructed.

'Well, I don't know who you think you are – Lady Muck? The King rings you and you haven't got so much as a "good morning" for him,' Rory complained.

'I'm busy. I'm writing a list of ways to hunt down Bono.'

'Very good. And what have you come up with so far?'

'I'm not going to tell you yet; you're breaking my train of thought.'

'Fair enough, but we need to arrange the big move. How's tomorrow?'

'Fine, but I could put most of what I own in a Dunne's carrier bag and there'd still be some room left over.'

'Don't talk rubbish. You've got loads of beautiful things; they've just been packed away because the capsule you call a bedroom isn't big enough to accommodate anything other than you,' Rory said.

'Tomorrow morning. Ten o'clock. You'd better have your carrier bag ready or there'll be trouble. Byeee!'

Aoife put down the phone and looked at her list; it was starting to take shape.

Number 1 went as follows: 'Call U2's management company and get a list of tour dates. Check with Rory that this doesn't contravene the rules of the bet as it's not the record company. Pretend to be calling from a UK-based magazine, trying to set up an interview with Bono. If they ask which magazine, tell them it's called *The Table*' (this stroke of inspiration had come from the fact that she was writing on a table) 'and it's based in Manchester. It's highly unlikely that you'll get an interview with Bono, the man being fairly busy and all that, but you should find out where he's going to be.'

Aoife had decided to hedge her bets and try to make her approaches fairly diverse. So Number 2 read: 'Go to the Clarence. Get dressed up, take Paul or Rory or whoever is available, and ponce around in the bar. Ask the bar staff how often Bono goes in there, and pretend to be a reporter for *The Table*, doing an article on what it's like when your boss is world-famous.'

The page was full of ways to meet Bono, but most of them were based on the management company being helpful enough to tell her where and when he was going to be in Dublin over the next month. Aoife wasn't completely convinced that this would work, but at least she had something to be going on with.

There was a knock at the door. Aoife went to

answer it; there, smiling from ear to ear, was Paul. He picked her up in a big bear hug. 'Sorry, couldn't keep away.' Aoife threw her arms around him and gave him a deep kiss.

'What brings you here, then? I thought you were working,' she said.

'I am, but I need to collect some stuff from one of our clients in Sandyford, so I was driving this way. And I've brought you something.' Paul rifled around in his pockets and pulled out a newspaper clipping; the headline read, 'Micky Callaghan: Psychic to the Stars.' Aoife scanned down the article, trying to work out which bit could possibly be relevant to her. 'It says he's the psychic for loads of famous celebs, and there's a bit that says he's done some work with U2 – granted, it's a bit sketchy about his connections with them, but I thought he might be worth a visit. And anyway, you could always get your fortune told while you're there.'

Aoife smiled gratefully; anything was worth trying at this stage.

Paul couldn't stay for long – he had to get back to work – but he and Aoife curled up on the couch together for a few minutes. Aoife thought how nice this was, and how much she wished Paul didn't have to go to work.

Paul broke the silence. 'Aoife?'

'Yeah?' She turned her face to look at him.

'Do you ever get fed up of Rory betting you to do things for money?'

'What do you mean?' Aoife was trying to keep a defensive note out of her voice.

'I don't know – I just mean … well, you said that he makes bets with you all the time, that's all.'

'I did, yeah.' Her tone was telling Paul to tread carefully.

'I was just thinking that, if I had a friend who bet me all the time, when he had more money than me and could afford to do that, then it would wind me up a bit. But … Oh, God, ignore me. You've known me for like three seconds, and you've known Rory for donkey's years. Sorry – ignore me. It was just a small thing I was wondering.'

'Well, you don't have to wonder anything,' Aoife said, shifting closer to him on the sofa. 'Rory's my best mate – he'd do anything for me – and that's that. The betting thing is something we've always done; it's just messing, really.'

'I'm sorry; I've no right to say something about you and a friend of yours. I'm a complete gobshite sometimes. It's obvious that Rory thinks the world of you.' Paul kissed Aoife. 'I'd better get me arse in gear.' He kissed her again. 'Listen, I can't see you tonight; I'm away.'

'Where are you going?'

'Just Belfast; I'm working there all day tomorrow, and I can't face the drive in the morning. But I'd love to see you tomorrow night, if that's OK.'

'I can't tomorrow night – I'm working. What about Saturday?'

Paul grimaced. 'I've got to work.'

Aoife looked crushed. 'On a Saturday?'

'Yeah, but how about Sunday? Night or day. I'll take you somewhere nice.'

'No, *I'll* take *you* somewhere nice.' Aoife was determined not to have Paul pay for everything. 'As long as your idea of "nice" is McDonald's, I don't think I can go too far wrong.'

'Great,' Paul said. 'I'll see you then. I'll call you later.' He kissed her again before leaving, and walked out backwards so he could wave goodbye.

Aoife stayed on the sofa and thought about what Paul had said about Rory. The more she thought about it, the more she thought that maybe Paul had a point. Rory could afford to get her to do stupid things if he wanted to, just because he was rich.

It had always been like that. At college, he had bet her five pints that she wouldn't dress up as Toto to his Dorothy; she had done it because she didn't have any money to go out that night. He had once got her to tell some American tourists that the carved wooden salmon at the end of the Salmon Weir Bridge in Galway was, in fact, a wooden penis and was there in honour of the old Celtic god of fertility. The Americans had swallowed this, hook, line and sinker, and Aoife had won twenty quid.

It occurred to Aoife that there was a definite pattern

running throughout their relationship, and that she was going to have to have a word with Rory about it next time she saw him. But at the moment she had more pressing things to consider – like the fact that, even though she hadn't let Paul finish what he wanted to say in the hotel, she had a feeling in her stomach that she hadn't felt in a very long time. She wanted to think it was just nerves, butterflies or even trapped wind, but she couldn't deny it to herself. The feeling she had was Aoife falling in love.

Chapter Eighteen

Rory sat in the foyer of his father's office, tapping his fingers on the chair arm. To the casual onlooker he might have looked like a nervous interviewee, rather than a son summoned by his dad. Eoin's secretary, Niamh, was fussing around as she always did. She wrecked Rory's head, probably because she reacted to his father in much the same way as he did himself.

'Are you sure you won't have a cup of tea there, Rory?' she asked for the twelfth time in five minutes.

'No, Niamh, I'm fine,' Rory said through gritted teeth. *And I won't want one in three nanoseconds when you ask me again,* he thought.

'You look well,' she said with a girlish giggle.

'I try my best,' he said dismissively. When Niamh had first started working for his father, Rory had been amused by the fact that she blatantly fancied him. Like most Irish women Rory had come across, she never even considered the possibility that he might be homosexual, Irish gayness best being left to celebrities and clergy. Rory used to flirt outrageously with her, to the point where, every time she saw him, her face was purple with embarrassment before he even opened his mouth. He had soon tired of this and now just kept his contact with her to a minimum.

The intercom crackled into life.

'Niamh!' She involuntarily threw her handful of papers into the air, and ran to press the reply button.

'Yes, Eoin?' Her voice was very nearly trembling. She dragged her foot around like a minesweeper, desperately trying to retrieve the papers.

'Is my son here?'

'Yes, he's here; would you like me to send him through?'

'In a minute. Ask him if he wants a cup of tea or something.'

'I did. He said he's fine and –'

'Do you know where the figures are for the third quarter of 2002? I told you to file them in the file behind my desk.'

'I did; they're in the file that says "Third Quarter Figures 2002,"' Niamh said, with the patience of the Union of Saints.

'I've got that here in front of me, and there's no figures…' Eoin's voice trailed off for a split second. 'Oh, here they are; you mustn't have filed them in the right order. Right, so. Tell Rory I'll be five minutes and then he can come through. That'll teach him to be late.' The intercom went off.

Niamh gave Rory a sympathetic smile. He didn't want her sympathy; it drove him mad to see how she let his father treat her, and that reminded him that he put up with the same treatment. And the last thing Rory needed was to be lumping himself into the same category as downtrodden Niamh. But then, Eoin O'Donnell had this great levelling effect on people. Rory was sure that the man could reduce George Bush to tears, given half an hour and some missing sales figures.

He tried to formulate how he was going to have this word with his father. He visualised what he was going to say. In his head, he swaggered into the office like Bobby going to see JR Ewing, and thrust his hand out for his father to shake, but this thought didn't last long; it was shunted aside by the image of Eoin looking at his hand and snapping, 'Sit down, Rory, what are you playing at?'

He was just wondering if he should go and knock on his father's door when Eoin came through the door of his office. Niamh nearly collapsed.

'Hi, Eoin, I was just....' She was just picking up the last of the papers.

Eoin ignored her. 'Well, you'd better come on through, I haven't got all day.'

'Hello,' Rory ventured.

'What?' his father barked. Of all the words that ever

came out of his father's mouth, it was the word 'what' that unnerved Rory the most. It wasn't the actual meaning of the word; it was the way Eoin delivered it, which always left Rory feeling as though he had been shot in the ear.

'I was just saying hello, Dad.'

'Well, hello yourself,' Eoin said, waving Rory through to his office. He shut the door and walked around behind his desk, leaving Rory on the other side as if this were an interview after all.

Eoin O'Donnell was an imposing man in more ways than one. He was very tall, and this allowed him to do deliberately what a lot of tall people do without realising it: he threw his height about. When he was standing, very few men could make eye contact with him, and he enjoyed watching them try. He was very broad, with hands like turf shovels; a handsome man for his age, he wore his distinguished looks like he wore his tailor-made clothes – very well. His booming voice wielded authority, and on this occasion it was trying to wield it over Rory.

'I want to have a word with you,' Eoin said, gesticulating at the chair on the other side of the desk. Rory looked at it and wandered over to the sofa in a corner. This had the desired effect: his father came out from behind his desk. Once out of his comfort zone, he looked around to see where he could anchor himself, and finally perched on the front of his desk. Rory felt a sense of self-satisfied one-upmanship.

'What about?'

'I would have thought that was obvious. I want to talk about what exactly you're doing with yourself, and where you see yourself going.' Eoin O'Donnell held his son's gaze. Rory pulled his head back a little, wondering where this line of thinking was heading. 'I think you need more direction in your life, from what little I see of it.' Rory opened his mouth to speak, but his father steamrollered on. 'For example, I hear you talk about women you know, but I never see any.'

Rory's mouth dried up. 'Well, I'm hardly likely to bring them down to the office and parade them in front of you, am I?'

'No, true, true. Anyway, I'm having one of my dinner parties next week; I was thinking you could come along and bring someone.'

Rory took a deep breath. He felt sick. He could just imagine turning up with his latest fling on his arm: 'Hi, Dad, this is … sorry, what was your name again? Joe? Sorry, Dad, we only met two hours ago – but he's got great cheekbones, hasn't he?' Rory wasn't big on long-term relationships at the moment. He had spent three years of emotional turmoil with his previous partner, Alan. Alan was a guard from Maynooth and wasn't in any hurry to tell anyone he knew that he was gay. Sometimes Rory had caught Alan making homophobic comments, such was the extent of his denial.

In the end, Alan had got engaged to a nurse and broken Rory's heart into the bargain. He came sniffing around now and again, but one thing that Rory had inherited from his father was an iron will, and he always told Alan to get lost. It had taken a while for the message to sink in, but Alan had eventually got it. Rory had bumped into him once in the past twelve months; he had been in Tomato, wearing a gold band on his wedding finger. Rory hadn't bothered to ask; the thought of Alan going through the pretence of a wedding with that poor unsuspecting nurse had made him feel sick.

'Yeah, that'd be great,' Rory finally said.

'Anyone in mind?' Eoin's eyes bored through him. Rory winced; he hated being put on the spot. Also, it really annoyed him that his father presumed he was straight – but, then again, Rory had to admit that he had never given him any reason to think otherwise.

Rory had promised his mother, shortly before she died, that he wouldn't tell his father of his sexuality. She had said that the shock would kill Eoin. Aoife had always said that this was utter bollocks and that his mother had been completely unfair in asking anything like that, but Rory would not discuss it. He had made a promise, and that was all there was to it.

'Em – yeah, there might be someone.'

'What are they like?'

'Oh, she's really nice; you'll love her.'

'She? Has *she* got a name?'

'Aoife.' She was going to kill him.

'Isn't that the young one you went to college with?'

'Yeah, but ... well, we're moving in together.'

'Really? And when did all this happen?' Rory put his father's incredulity down to the fact that he had been so flippant about such a commitment.

'Well, we've been talking about it for a while, but we've only just decided. It makes sense, really.'

Eoin raised an eyebrow. 'So, you'll be bringing this Aoife to the dinner party? Fine.' He went back behind his desk. 'It's eight for eight-thirty, Thursday.' He pressed the intercom. 'Niamh, any sign of John Farley?'

'He's just on his way up; he rang me from the car park.'

'Offer him a cup of tea, will you? I'll be out in a minute.' Eoin switched the intercom off and looked at Rory. 'Well, that's it. I want to talk to you about a role I think you can play in the business, but that's for another time. I think it's about time I saw a return on my investment in you.' He boomed laughing at the alleged joke. Rory flinched.

'I wanted to talk to you about that as well.' Rory felt a creeping humiliation, tinged with anger, pawing in his stomach. 'I wanted to talk to you about the money situation. I'm not happy taking money from you all the time, and –'

The intercom sounded. 'John Farley's here to see you, Eoin,' Niamh announced.

'Grand; I'll be out in a minute.' He turned his attention back to Rory; if he picked up on the fact that his son was annoyed, he didn't acknowledge it. 'Well, that's great; we both seem to be singing from the same hymn sheet for once.' Eoin stuck his head out the door. 'Well, John, are you having a cup of tea?'

'No, I'm gr–'

'Niamh, have you offered the man a cup of tea? Come through, come through.' He did not introduce Rory. 'Back in a minute, John; take a seat.'

Rory said goodbye to Niamh, who was putting the kettle on, and went to the lift. His father followed him. 'Good to see you seem to be having a think about what's important.'

The lift opened, and Eoin O'Donnell took his son's hand and shook it. It was a textbook handshake – firm, brisk and businesslike, eye contact maintained – but Eoin held it a fraction too long for comfort, and he twisted it so that his hand was on top and his son's underneath. It didn't take Sigmund Freud to work out that he was letting Rory know who was boss. As the doors of the lift closed, Rory rolled his shoulders back and pulled himself up to his full height.

He stepped out into the bright Dublin sunlight and thought, *Bollocks*. He had managed to achieve precisely nothing – well, other than a dinner date for himself and Aoife. Rory decided not to break the news to her until she was well and truly ensconced in the apartment, the following day. Given the fact that he would be putting a roof over her head, Rory reasoned, she couldn't really say no to pretending to be his partner for just one evening.

Chapter Nineteen

Rory's spare room had been transformed. The first thing Aoife saw was the flowers. Her favourite flowers were lilies, and there were about five vases of them dotted around the room. Rory had placed candles on the dressing table and had hung sari material for curtains, and there was a huge helium balloon that said, 'Welcome Home, Aoife!'

She couldn't believe it. She jumped on Rory and gave him a huge bear hug.

'I love you!'

'I know you do, why wouldn't you?' Rory took a bottle of champagne from an ice bucket on the floor, popped the cork and poured them a glass each.

'Here's to us, babe, and all who sail in us!'

Aoife took her glass and giddily looked around.

'Cheers, Rory – this is fantastic!' was all she could manage to say; but the look that she gave him said 'thank you' a million times.

They sat on the couch, drinking the champagne. Aoife was feeling a nice warm glow. But she had been thinking about the conversation she and Paul had had, about Rory betting her, and it was making her feel slightly wound up.

'Rory,' she said finally. 'I've been thinking – well, it was more something someone said to me yesterday.... I mean, I said it to them, but –'

'Spit it out, babe; you're going to choke on it. It wasn't *Paul* who you had this conversation with by any chance, was it?'

'As it happens, yes, it was Paul.' Rory rolled his eyes. 'Don't be like that, Ror. Just let me finish.'

'Go on, then.'

'OK. Well, I just think that … well....' She was on the verge of an outburst. 'I always end up making a right dick out of myself for your amusement, and it's always because of a bet – and I end up making money out of it, so it's almost like prostitution!'

Rory had a bemused look on his face. 'Dramatic, Aoife! Simmer down on the theatrics, will you? Name a time, before the Bono bet, when I've bet you and given you money.'

'The salmon penis.'

'OK, that's just one.'

'The time you bet me that I couldn't climb to the top of the Burke statue outside Trinity and sit on his head.'

'You fell off.'

'But I still did it. And the time you had me try to

158

blag my way into Lillie's as an Italian fashion designer, and the bouncer told me to fuck off because I couldn't speak a word of Italian and he was fluent....'

'What were the chances of that happening? A multilingual bouncer – who'd have thought it?'

'That's not the point, Rory. The point is that you get me to do things so that you can have a good laugh, and I look like a fecking eejit. The Lillie's thing was a case in point: you can get us in there free any day of the week.'

'So, why do you go along with it?' he asked innocently.

'I don't know. I just think that maybe I shouldn't any more.'

'Look, Aoife....' Rory was serious, which made her sit up and take notice; this wasn't a regular occurrence. 'I don't want you thinking that I only do stuff like that to make a dick of you. I love you to bits; you know that. The thing is that you are generally up for a laugh, and you enjoy it as much as I do – or at least I thought you did.' Rory grabbed her hand. 'Is it Paul who's made you think like this?'

'No!' Aoife said defensively.

'OK, OK, I was just asking. Look, if you don't want to go ahead with the Bono thing, that's fine. I don't want to put any pressure on you.'

'I know I'm being melodramatic. I'm sorry. It's just that – I don't know.... No one else seems to get themselves into the stupid situations that I do. And the stupid situations seem to have a common defining factor.'

'What?'

'You!'

'OK, OK! So, are we going to scrap the whole thing, then?'

Aoife sipped her wine and thought about it.

'No. I've done enough daft things because of you over the years; I might as well stick with this one.'

'Right, so.' Rory swiftly changed the subject. 'Are you working on Thursday night?'

'I don't know the shifts until tomorrow, but I can always swap with someone,' Aoife said hopefully, thinking that Rory was going to tell her that Bono was in Dublin on Thursday.

'Good, because I've told my dad that you're my new girlfriend and that we're living together and that you'll come to a dinner party with me at his place on Thursday evening,' Rory said, all in one breath.

'Fuck that!' Aoife shook her head adamantly.

'Ah, come on Aoife, it's just one night.'

'That's not the point, Rory. You're pandering to your father again and I don't want to be part of it. You should just tell him to shove it.'

'Do you think I enjoy the way he treats me?' Rory asked, his face clouding over with anger. 'The fact that he thinks I'm so fucking good-for-nothing that he has to pay me to keep out of his way?' He had raised his voice, and Aoife wasn't used to it.

'You don't have to take his money,' she said, matching his tone. 'You could fend for yourself. Christ knows, Rory, if you went back to DJ-ing you could make good money.'

'I couldn't do it.' Rory shook his head. 'I used to be in bits, Aoife, remember? I used to puke my ring up five times a night. That's not working – that's fecking torture.'

'Loads of people hate their jobs, Rory. And they have better reason than you. It's not like you were shovelling shit off of the street.'

'What do you know about jobs? You're a bloody waitress – that's how great your career is!'

Common sense told Aoife that the best thing to do would be to bite her tongue, but her need to have the last word overruled it.

'You were playing music in front of a thousand people who thought you were great. So don't make out like you're the most hard-done-by person on the planet, Rory, because it won't wash.'

'Fuck you, Aoife! I accept money from my father because I put up with enough shite from that man to last me a lifetime, as well you know. The man used to beat the living crap out of me if I didn't do exactly what he said. Discipline, in his book, is character-building. Well, I'll tell you something: I must have the fecking character of ten men.' Rory stopped for a moment. Aoife was stunned; she had never seen him like this before, and it seemed to have come out of nowhere. He went on, 'So, in some fucked-up way, I think he owes me. And if you can't see that, Aoife, then you must be fucking blind.'

Aoife had her hand over her mouth. She thought it was probably the best place for it.

'I'm sorry, Aoife,' Rory said finally. 'Well, I'm sorry for the way I said it. I just … well, I know I shouldn't let my dad have so much control over me. But he does. He's got me by the knackers and he knows it.' Rory sighed and shook his head.

Aoife wanted to say something, but she mulled it over for a moment first; she didn't want to get it wrong.

Then she said, 'Why don't you tell him on Thursday that you don't want his money any more? You must have some money saved. And why don't you try to DJ again?'

Eventually Rory nodded his head slowly. 'You're right, you know. Maybe now I'm a bit older I'd be better equipped for it – you know, not as nervous. Or am I just having myself on? What do you think?'

'You'd be headlining in no time. You could stage a comeback.'

'Christ, listen to us! Who says that the kids today want to hear some old fucker spinning tunes? I'm so out of touch these days, I'll be mixing bleeding Christy Moore into Van Morrison just as they're all coming up on their pills.'

Aoife laughed. 'Well, you can but try. And if they

laugh you out of the place, we'll go up to Johnny Fox's and see if they need a resident DJ there.'

Rory went over to Aoife and hugged her. 'Aoife, I am so sorry for shouting like that. I'm just so stressed about my old man....'

'I know, Ror. It's fine.'

'Are you going to come on Thursday?' he asked, a look of hope spreading across his face.

Aoife squeezed his hand. 'Oh, all right,' she said. 'I might as well.'

Chapter Twenty

By the following evening, Aoife felt fully settled into her new home. She sat on her bed and pulled out the newspaper clipping that Paul had given her – 'Micky Callaghan, Psychic to the Stars'. At the bottom of the piece was a number to contact Micky, in case any stars might be in need of psychic assistance.

Aoife lay on her bed staring at the article, wondering if she could contact someone who had superimposed his head onto a picture of the body of Krishna; surely that constituted blasphemy. Finally she decided she had nothing to lose; she picked up her mobile and dialled the number.

An abrupt voice barked down the phone, 'Yeah!'

'Oh, sorry – I think I've got the wrong number…. I was looking for Micky Callaghan.'

'Sorry, love. I'll just get him for you. One minute.' There was a lot of shuffling, and the phone was dropped on something solid; then Aoife heard shouting.

'Mr Callaghan, there's a young wan on the phone for you; could you approach the phone?' There was some coughing, and then a deep voice that obviously belonged to the same person said, 'I shall.'

Mr Callaghan 'approached' the phone. 'Hellooo,' he drawled, in a bad impression of a Dublin 4 accent.

'Hi, I was looking for Micky Callaghan, psychic to the stars,' Aoife said.

'Yes, that is I.'

'Right. Well, I want my fortune told, if you can squeeze me in between the stars.'

'That shouldn't be a problem. I do have a two-hour gap each day when I see ordinary people. I have Mick Lally in first thing tomorrow – sorry, I shouldn't really disclose clients' names – but I can probably squeeze you in at eleven.'

'Eleven's fine.'

'I'm on King Street, in Inchicore. D'you know Inchicore at all?' The accent was slipping back to its former glory.

Aoife decided that she would get out her map of Dublin, rather than prolong this conversation. 'Yeah, that's grand; I'll see you in the morning, so. Good luck.'

She put the phone down and shook her head.

King Street was a fairly normal row of houses, with one in the middle that stuck out like a cobbler's thumb. The outside was whitewashed and there were various crustaceans stuck into the plasterwork. There were several chimney-pots scattered randomly around the front garden, and the pièce de résistance was two toilet bowls sitting on either side of the front door, with a crop of dandelions in each.

Aoife took a deep breath and rang the doorbell. It was as loud as a car horn, and it chimed a cacophonic version of 'She Moved Through the Fair'.

The door flew open and there stood Micky. He was about forty-five, and, judging by the smell, he could have done with standing a bit closer to a bar of soap. He hadn't shaved for a few days, but he'd seen fit to put his psychic costume on, by the look of things: he was wearing an orange robe with gold trimming, flip-flops and a purple turban.

'Aoife, welcome.' The accent was back in Ballsbridge. He ushered her into the hall with a grand flourish of his arm. On the purple wall were a picture of the Sacred Heart of Jesus, a picture of some Hindu god and a picture of what Aoife could only think was Micky's mother – either that, or it was him wearing a long black wig.

He brought her through into the living-room; it looked like the set from *Rising Damp*. There were three lava lamps, an orange light on a pull-down spring and a table with a manky brown tablecloth on it. There was a smell of must, disguised – not very well – by the smell of cheap joss sticks. Around the room were about thirty pictures of Micky with famous people. They all looked either shocked by or oblivious to his presence.

Micky gesticulated towards the seventies-esque kitchen chair that was next to the table. Aoife sat down, while Micky remained standing. He took a deep breath, shut his eyes and smoothed the manky tablecloth with his hands. As he exhaled he said, 'I can feel your aura, Aoife,' and then opened one eye for a second as if to check that she was still there. He felt around for a chair. He couldn't be much of a psychic, Aoife thought, if he couldn't even find a chair in his own room, just because his eyes were shut. Eventually he felt his way to the chair and sat down. *Jaysus*, she thought, *I'm going to be here all week at this rate.*

Micky looked at her hands and said, 'Can I have the ring on your right hand, please? Jewellery holds a person's vibe.' Aoife handed him the ring. She'd bought it in Oasis three weeks before, and she wasn't sure how much of her 'vibe' a hypoallergenic ring would have soaked up in less than a month, but in for a penny, in for a pound.

Micky Callaghan fiddled with the ring for a good few minutes, breathing in and out like an asthmatic grampus. Aoife took the opportunity to have a better look at his pictures. As she looked more closely, she realised that half of them were superimposed; in the other half, Micky had run up behind the unsuspecting celebrity, scaring them silly, got a friend to take a picture and then promptly run off again.

Then she saw it. In among the pictures of Twink, Brendan O'Carroll, Jackie Healy-Rae and Emer O'Reilly, there was a photograph of Micky shaking hands with Bono. It wasn't like the other pictures. He was actually with him; Micky had his arm around Bono's shoulder, and Bono didn't look like he was about to run off.

So even Micky had a Bono story, Aoife thought. She would have to ask him about it.

Micky announced in a deep, dramatic voice, 'You are not married!' He opened one eye again and Aoife replied by raising an eyebrow. He shut the eye and ploughed on. 'But you do live with someone!' The eye was open again. Aoife nodded, and could have kicked herself: she had decided that she wasn't going to give him any clues.

'But you are not happy with him.' Poor old Micky was barking up the wrong tree completely. He opened both eyes this time, saw a fleeting look of scepticism pass across Aoife's face and changed his tack slightly. 'You are not intimate....' It was more of a question than a statement.

Aoife stared at him blankly, trying not to give anything away, but her natural inclination to give people the benefit of the doubt was allowing her to think, *He's talking about Rory – oh my God, he is psychic after all!*

Micky seemed to realise that he might be on dodgy ground; he changed his tune again. 'You are very close to your mother and your father.'

That did it. Aoife started laughing. She couldn't help herself.

'I'm sorry – it's just that.... Well, no, I'm not especially close to my parents. And I find all of this a bit ... well ... odd.'

'What do you mean, odd? This is how I make my living – and a fair living I make, too.' The accent was back to high-pitched inner-city; it was like having three people in the room.

'I'm sure it is, but you're not really telling me anything, are you? All you've said is that I live with someone and I'm close to my parents. You're hardly Nostradamus, are you?'

'Well, if that's the way you want it, you can leave.'

'Fine!' Aoife snapped. 'And I am not paying for this!' She was expecting a bit of a fight about this one, but she didn't care; as amusing as he was, he was completely wasting her time.

But Micky didn't shout back at her. A look of pure fear had come over his face.

'Oh, Jaysus, Mary and Joseph!' he said, clasping his hands to his mouth and staring at Aoife as if he'd just seen a ghost. She stared back at him; his turban had fallen to the side of his head in an almost coquettish fashion.

'What?'

'You're ... you're ... searching for someone. Someone you haven't met before.'

Aoife stopped in her tracks.

'Go on.'

Micky was looking around as if he didn't know where the words were coming from. 'I think it's some-one that everyone knows.... I know I've met them, but I can't place them....'

'It's Bono!' *Bollocks*, Aoife thought; why had she told him? She had wanted to see how far he could get without her help.

'That's it! That's it!' Micky was off his seat now, jumping around the room. 'You want to meet Bono – and you will! I can see it! You're talking to him; you're getting on great guns. Ah, Jaysus, this has never happened me before! I know I shouldn't be telling you that, but it hasn't. My mother was a psychic – they used to come from far and wide to see her; she could tell you the colour of your boxers before she'd even clapped eyes on you, that woman. And she always said I had it – you know, the gift – but I never really did, till now. But I can see it! I can see it!' He had his arms raised, like a Texan who'd just found God.

He was scaring Aoife silly, but she wanted to know what exactly he was seeing.

'What can you see?' she asked.

Micky shut his eyes and breathed in again, but there was something more genuine about it this time.

'You're in a castle somewhere.... There's lots of people there.'

'And that's it? Nothing more?'

'But you're there – I can see you! Don't you understand how important that is? I'm psychic!'

'Well, it's fantastic that I've helped you, someone who I came here to see as a psychic, discover that you actually are psychic. Is there anything else you can see?' Aoife stood up to leave.

'Yes!' Micky nearly fell off the chair with excitement. 'You have a religious vocation! I can see you collecting for charity, and you're a nun.' The facts were getting there, even if his context did need a bit of fine-tuning.

'Anything else?' Aoife asked.

A puzzled frown descended over Micky's face.

'It's going! It's fading! Where's it going?' He was shouting into the room as if he expected an answer. 'It's gone!' He was nearly as close to tears as Aoife was to the door.

'Right ... well, thanks for that; I'd better get going....' Aoife was rummaging around in her pockets. She had changed her mind about not paying him; seeing as he had just had his first psychic revelation, it might be a bit rude to just leg it.

Micky looked at her. 'No, no, no – what are you doing? I don't want any money from you, I swear you've helped me – and, believe me, I've never turned down money before. But you will meet him – you will; and it'll be at a castle, I just don't know where.'

Smashing, thought Aoife; *a fecking castle*. There were hundreds of castles in Ireland and she wasn't a regular guest at any of them. She made her way out into the hall, and Micky followed her. He'd finally given up on the turban and was carrying it in his hand. 'I've met him a few times, you know,' he said.

'What?'

'Bono. I know him. Used to go to the Youth Club with my brother. Didn't see him for years; then all of a sudden he's giving it loads, just 'cause he's in some band. That was at the beginning of the eighties. I saw him in Bruxelles, and I sat him down and said to him, "Paul" – we didn't call him Bono; Paul was good enough for him back then – I said, "Paul, what's the fecking *story*? One minute, you're playing ping-pong at the Youth Club, the next, you're giving it loads all over Dublin, like you own the fecking place!" Well, he was humbled, I tell you. From that moment he stopped acting the gobshite and started behaving himself. I think he saw that conversation as a turning point in his career. I don't think a seminal work like *The Joshua Tree* could have been made if it hadn't been for that little chat.'

Christ, thought Aoife; *he really believes what he's saying*.

'Do you ever see him now?'

'Ah, Jayz, no. Haven't seen him in years. In all fairness, I think he lost it when he started wearing wrap-around glasses and singing through a loudhailer. But he still goes into O'Dwyer's when he's home. Why are you looking to meet him? Are you autograph-hunting?'

'No. This might sound a bit mad' – Aoife decided that, in the circumstances, 'mad' was relative – 'but I win five grand if I can get a Bono story by the end of May.'

'Five grand? That's some money! Why don't you just hang around the airport first thing every morning? The famous ones always come in on the first flight, business class. My nephew, Pat, works there. Says they all come swanning in, pretending they don't want to be recognised, wearing sunglasses even though it's pitch-black and lashing rain. He'll be there some morning, I guarantee it.'

'Yeah, I'll bear it in mind. Thanks,' Aoife said, opening the door to let herself out.

'No bother. Thank *you*,' Micky said, waving his turban. 'And when you do see Paul Hewson, at a castle somewhere, you tell the gobshite he owes me a beer and a word or two of thanks for *The Joshua Tree*.'

'Will do,' said Aoife. She wandered off down the street, a little bit freaked out, and a little bit happier all the same, after her meeting with Micky.

Chapter Twenty-One

Bridie pushed open the door of the pub and surveyed her surroundings sheepishly; then she tucked her handbag under her arm and, taking the bull by the horns, headed for the bar.

'I'll have a rock shandy and a packet of Taytos,' she informed the barman. Bridie had never been in a pub on her own before, but there was a first time for everything. And anyway, she told herself as she took a seat opposite a fella reading a newspaper, this was different; she had been in this pub many years ago and had had a great time.

Bridie was having a ball, if she was truthful with herself. No one knew who she was, and that suited her fine. The barman brought her drink and Taytos over to her, and she watched a few old fellas strike up the beginnings of a tune in a corner. The man opposite her put his paper down and looked appreciatively at them.

'Are they any good?' Bridie asked him, nodding towards the band.

'They're very good. Have you not seen them before?'

'I haven't been in here for years – I was seventeen the last time I came in; so, even if I saw these fellas, I'm not sure I'd recognise them now,' Bridie said, and the man laughed.

She opened her bag of Taytos and offered it to him; he took one, and as he thoughtfully munched on it Bridie inspected him. He had a kind face and a thoughtful way about him, she decided.

'Do you work around here?' she asked him.

The man broke into a broad smile. 'I do, yeah, now and again.'

'Are you a businessman?' Bridie was warming to this fella. She wondered why her daughter never seemed to come home with men with friendly faces and thoughtful ways.

'Well, sort of.' The man looked at his pint. 'That's definitely a Kerry twang there, if you don't mind me saying; what brings you here?'

It had been a very long time since anyone had taken an interest in Bridie. People always asked about Aoife and Michael and Roddy, or asked how she was without really wanting an answer; but this man seemed really interested in her. So she told him all about where she'd grown up, about how she wasn't Dublin's biggest fan, about her horrendous journey in the car with

Roddy and how she had come up on the train this time, and that, all in all, she was enjoying herself. As she spoke, she looked at his wedding finger; it was occupied. *What a shame,* she thought. He was a little bit older than Aoife, but that didn't really matter in this day and age. She could have got his number and introduced them.

The barman came over with another drink for Bridie and one for her new companion. 'This is from the lads.' He nodded at the musicians. 'They were wondering if you'd join them for a song.'

The man turned to Bridie. 'Do you mind?'

'You sing? Go ahead – no bother at all!' *Musical as well,* she thought as the man got up. A musician would have been perfect for Aoife; that would satisfy her flighty side.

The man said, 'This is for my friend over there.' He nodded over to Bridie. '"The Rocky Road to Dublin".' Bridie blushed, very pleased indeed that some young fella was singing to her. Aoife would never believe it, she thought.

Bridie and Aoife settled into a café in Temple Bar. After days of avoiding her mother's incessant phone calls, Aoife had finally caved in and agreed to go for coffee with Bridie after her appointment at the recruitment agency.

'Hi, can we get a coffee and a tea please?' Aoife asked the waitress.

'Who's the tea for?' Bridie demanded.

'You; why? You always drink tea.'

Bridie looked at the waitress. 'Take no notice of her. I'll have a latte, please – and have you any of those cinnamon bagel yokes? Aoife, will you have one? They're lovely.'

'Em, yeah,' Aoife agreed, wondering where her mother had done her crash course in middle-class breakfasting.

'I came in here the other day; I really like it. You see all the backpackers around here, don't you?'

'Yeah, you do,' Aoife said, waiting for her mother to come out with a classic gaffe about 'foreigners'. To her mild embarrassment, it never came.

'So,' Aoife said after a pause, 'how long are you going to stay in Dublin, then?'

'Well, that's gratitude for you! It's not like I've been around at your house every day, breathing down your neck; I haven't even seen this new place you've moved into yet.'

'I only moved in the other day, Ma.'

'I still haven't seen it, though. Except for a few phone calls, I've left you alone. I just wanted to be in the area so that, if you should need me, I could be here for you – that's all.' Someone had booked a violinist to play alongside the burning martyr.

'Well, that's great, Ma, but you've rung me at least five times a day.'

'You want to try picking up that phone of yours

once in a while, and then maybe I won't have to ring you five times a day.'

'So what have you been doing?' Aoife eyed her mother suspiciously as her latte was placed in front of her.

'Oh, you know … just having a look around. Never mind about me – what about you? How did the interview go this morning?'

'Oh, all right. I don't think they're very good.' Aoife sipped her coffee. The interview at the agency hadn't been all right; it had been an unmitigated disaster.

Andrea Powers Recruitment was nowhere near Grafton Street, where it claimed to be. It was off a street that was off a street that was off Grafton Street. It looked more like the entrance to a brothel than a recruitment agency. The building was dilapidated, the plaster peeling off of the walls. Aoife had looked up the stairs and seen a sign in gold italics that said '*APR – Welcome to a World of Work*'. Things hadn't improved from there.

The receptionist carried on with her telephone conversation while passing Aoife a handful of forms. Aoife had dutifully filled them out and then sat looking at the picture above the receptionist's desk. It showed a killer whale jumping out of the sea, with 'What the mind can conceive and believe, it can achieve' written underneath it. The mind that conceived and believed the office environment of APR evidently wasn't setting its sights too high.

Andrea Powers, when she appeared, was visual bombardment on legs. Her skirt was black-and-white checked. Her tights were shimmering gold. Her shirt was a shoulder-padded, ruched affair in green silk. At first glance, she looked a little bit like Farrah Fawcett circa 1974; on closer inspection, years of sunbeds and martinis had taken their toll.

She subjected Aoife to an hour of mind-numbing questions, then announced, 'Here at Andrea Powers Recruitment, we have a philosophy,' and mumbled something about work making you free. Aoife was sure that that had been written above the gates of Nazi death camps, but decided against mentioning this to Andrea. The poor woman had enough on her plate, what with keeping her head upright under the weight of fourteen gallons of hairspray.

Aoife had left the office of APR vowing never to let her mother try to find her a job again.

'Well,' Bridie said, looking round to see where her cinnamon bagel had got to. 'I think you need to have a look at your attitude; she was lovely when I spoke to her on the phone.'

'Look, Ma....' Aoife felt defeated. 'I've worked in offices for ages. I know which the good agencies are, and I just don't think this was one of them, that's all.' Seeing the look on her mother's face, she quickly added, 'So I'm going to ring around the ones I know and get appointments for next week, I promise.'

'Well, you make sure you do. I don't know why you

179

can't just ring companies up yourself; it's beyond me that you have to go to a person in one office to get you a job in another office.' The waitress brought over the bagels. 'Ah, here we are.'

'It's just the way Dublin is. Everyone gets work through agencies; it's just easier. Anyway' – Aoife, seizing her opportunity to change the subject, pointed at the bagel – 'since when do you like bagels? Or coffee, for that matter?'

'Well, I decided I'd try them the other day, that's all,' Bridie said, concentrating on buttering her bagel.

'What, you were just walking through Temple Bar and thought, "I know, I'll just pop in here and try a bagel"?'

'No! I was having a look round – you know, seeing how things were different.'

'From when?' Aoife had a distinct feeling that her mother was being shifty.

'From when I was younger! Sure, you know that I came to Dublin when I was younger than you are now, but I didn't like it and I went back home.'

'Did you come here with Daddy?' Bridie's views on Dublin had always been very vocal, but she had never really talked about her experiences there.

'Oh, it was such a long time ago…. Would you look at the scrappy bit of butter they give you? I'm just going to ask your one for some more.' Bridie got up and went to the counter. Aoife knew that her question was being ignored, but she couldn't figure out why.

When she returned, Bridie launched straight back into conversation. 'That's better – you'd be shot in Kilbane for giving someone a scrappy bit of butter like that.... So anyway, since you've been nowhere to be seen, girleen, I've had to show myself around Dublin. And I thought, when in Rome, do as the Romans do.'

'So you tried a bagel?'

'And a latte. And I took myself off yesterday evening to this old pub that I once ... that I'd heard did live music, and sure enough it was still there.'

'*You* went in a pub?'

'I only had a soda and a packet of Taytos, girl; it's not like I got maggoty drunk.'

'But you, in a pub?'

'Yes, me in a pub.' Bridie took a big swig of her coffee as Aoife gaped at her. 'Shame you weren't with me, actually; I met a lovely fella there. I told him about you. Businessman, he was – and a lovely singer as well.'

'Mother!' Aoife shouted. 'You cannot go around trying to fix me up with strange men that you meet in strange Dublin pubs! He was probably some mad drunk.'

'Well, he seemed nice enough to me. Anyway, I'm sorry to say that he was married.'

'Well, that's a shame.' Aoife dreaded to think what sort of fella her mother would have come up with as her perfect match. 'Anyway, I'm seeing someone.'

'Oh, you are, are you? What does "seeing someone" mean in this day and age?'

'It means … well, I suppose it means he's my boyfriend.'

'That young Dub you had in tow the other day?'

'Yeah, but nothing had happened between us.' Aoife realised that that implied that something *had* happened since. 'Well, not that it has now – you know what I mean….'

'Well, we'll see how you get on with that one,' was all Bridie had to say on the matter. 'I'm going to pay for these, and then I think we should have a wander around town. We can pop into another few agencies and you can put your name down with them, while you're dressed smartly.'

'That's a great idea, Ma,' Aoife said, her spirits sinking through the soles of her office shoes.

Chapter Twenty-Two

Aoife hobbled up the gravel drive to Eoin O'Donnell's house, hanging off Rory's arm, trying to negotiate the rough terrain in her fantastically high-heeled shoes. She had wanted to look good for this evening – she knew how much it meant to Rory – so, especially for the occasion, she had made herself a wrap-around knee-length dress, out of an off-cut of red silk that she had picked up in a shop on Talbot Street. She had gathered her hair back from her face and pinned a lily into it, courtesy of Rory's flower-arranging earlier that week, and had managed to pull off smoky eye make-up without making herself look like a panda.

'Steady, babe; we'll both end up on our arses at this rate.'

'Well, I am almost walking round on stilts,' Aoife said as they wove in between the pricey cars that lined the drive. 'Jaysus, Ror, who's he invited? It's like an ambassador's reception!'

'Oh, you know – overpaid businessmen, ladies who lunch ... the usual.'

'Do you think there'll be anyone famous here? I could get an introduction to Bono.'

'Doubt it. The people here will be just rich and powerful, not famous. My father's too right-wing to have famous dinner-party guests. I think the chances of Bono being seen dead with a bunch of old dinosaurs like this lot are very low.'

Rory rang the doorbell. Aoife was a little taken aback, although she didn't say anything; she couldn't imagine having to ring the doorbell at her mother's house. As they waited for the door to open, Aoife felt her throat dry; she was nervous about meeting Rory's father again, especially as she was now playing the dutiful girlfriend.

Rory was fairly upbeat, considering he was going to be spending the evening in his father's company. During the week, he had called a couple of people he used to DJ with, to sound them out about a possible return to the decks. The response had been overwhelmingly positive – although James Holland, an eminent house DJ who Rory had headlined with, had said, 'Only if you don't puke all over my runners again.'

Eoin's glamorous partner, Mairéad, opened the door. She had been Miss Meath back in 1978. Rory's father had met her at a function at the Shelbourne three years before. She had been with her husband at the time.

'Hello, Rory,' she cooed, air-kissing him. 'And this is?'

'Aoife. Aoife, this is Mairéad, my father's partner.'

'Pleased to meet you,' Aoife said, putting her hand out.

'Likewise, Aoife.' Mairéad shook Aoife's hand warmly. 'Come through, come through. Most of the other guests are here already.' She had an amazing presence; Aoife warmed to her immediately.

The house was a huge Georgian affair, with high ceilings and imposing rooms. It hadn't been Rory's childhood home – he had grown up out in the Wicklow mountains; Eoin had bought the house in Monkstown just after Rory's mother died. He had had a team of interior designers come in to make the place feel like a home, so Rory said. Aoife couldn't help thinking that they'd done a great job. The hallway was beautifully lit with soft orange lighting, and the walls were lined with pictures of Rory, his parents and various members of the extended family, interspersed with pictures of places all over the world.

'Are those places your father's been?' Aoife whispered to Rory.

'No, just what Brown Thomas had in the frame department the day he went shopping.'

Aoife nudged him. 'Will you behave? Let's just have a nice time. We're only here for a couple of hours; it'll be grand.'

Mairéad led them into the lounge, where Eoin was holding court.

'… And he said, "I'll explain the cucumber, if you explain the three children!"' The entire room erupted with laughter. Aoife looked at Rory, who raised an eyebrow.

'Ah, Rory!' Eoin bellowed over to him. 'And this must be Aoife. How do you do?'

'Pleased to meet you, again.'

'Yes, I believe we met years ago, when you were palling around with Rory at college – is that right? You're looking stunning tonight.'

'Thank you,' Aoife said, trying to accept the compliment with grace. 'You've a lovely place here,' she said, and meant it.

'Thanks. Thought if I did the place up, I might get my son to visit me a bit more – hasn't been the case, though!' Eoin burst out laughing and grabbed Rory around the neck; pulling him close, the way Jeremy Beadle used to when he thought some fella was going to deck him for pretending to drive a tank over his car. 'So how are you, son?'

'I'm grand, Dad. And yourself?'

'I'm in great form,' Eoin said, beaming around the room. 'Come on, let me introduce you to some people.'

Rory and Aoife met Dymphna, Rathnait, Saoirse, Cairbre…. The names became a bit much, and Aoife was relieved when she found herself talking to a fella called Brian. At one point, she looked across the room and saw Rory and Eoin, each with a separate captivated audience, both gesticulating in exactly the same way. Watching the two, Aoife couldn't help thinking that maybe a lot of Rory's problems with his father lay in the fact that they were so alike.

Aoife spent half an hour talking about the canal system of Dublin, with a man who looked older than the canal system of Dublin, before Mairéad called everyone through to dinner. Aoife breathed a sigh of relief. She hoped she would be next to someone with a slightly broader range of dinner-party chat.

To her right was a priest who introduced himself as Father Heraghty; Aoife was a little surprised that priests were still dispensing with first names in the twenty-first century. To her left was Mairéad.

Father Heraghty turned to Aoife. 'And are you from Dublin?'

'No, Kerry; Kilbane.'

'Father McGlynn still wreaking havoc down there?'

'Em, no,' Aoife said. 'He's dead.'

'Ah … had no idea. Sure, the old grapevine's not what it used to be.'

'So, have you a parish round here?'

'Up near Whitehall.'

Aoife perked up. 'You don't happen to know Sister Immaculata, do you – Sister Immaculata of the Lamb and Cross? She's my mother's cousin.'

Father Heraghty went pale.

'I do indeed. The woman drove our last curate to a nervous breakdown. He's gone out to the missions now.'

Aoife sat back in her chair, a little taken aback. 'Oh, I'm sorry.'

'No need to be sorry. What is it they say? "You can choose your friends, but you can't choose your family." Very true.'

'Actually, my mother's staying with her at the moment.'

The priest squinted at Aoife as if he were trying to see if he recognised her. 'Your mother's name's not Bridie, is it?'

'Em … yes, it is.'

'Very devout woman, your mother. She's been over at the church every day for the past week. Giving out about electric candles, she was, the other day. I said to her, "Bridie, if we are going to drag the Catholic Church anywhere near the twenty-first century, then I think a little bit of electricity to light the way might not do us any harm." She seemed quite taken with Dublin, actually – said she was here for a while.' The colour drained from Aoife's face.

As she tucked into the starter – Thai-spiced, pan-fried scallops; she knew what they were from the tiny copperplate menu by her place setting – Aoife heard her name being mentioned on the other side of the table. The conversation was between Rory and his father, but was being conducted across four other people.

'So Aoife has an Economics degree, like you? Let's hope she's putting it to better use than you have.' Eoin laughed, but Aoife knew that this must have stung Rory.

'She is, actually.' Aoife caught Rory's eye as he said this; she could sense a lie bubbling up. 'She designs clothes.'

If the table hadn't been so big, Aoife would have kicked Rory under it. She was gobsmacked.

'Brilliant!' Eoin announced, obviously happy that his son was affiliating himself with someone who had a bit of initiative. 'So how's it going, Aoife?'

The table went silent. Aoife looked at Rory; seeing his pleading eyes, she gulped hard and took on her newly assigned role.

'Great. Not too bad at all.'

'She designed what she's wearing now,' Rory informed everyone. There were gasps and coos from the women and nods from the men, while Aoife's face went the same colour as her dress.

'Where do they stock your clothes?' Mairéad asked.

Aoife stared at Rory, mentally berating him for putting her in this situation.

'Oh, it's only a small thing, really,' she said, racking her brains. 'I mostly do one-off commissions, and I have a woman in Blackrock who takes a few things.' This wasn't, strictly speaking, a lie: a girl she had been to college with lived in Blackrock, and she had once borrowed a dress of Aoife's and never returned it.

'Well, Aoife that's great; good for you,' Eoin announced.

Everyone began chatting among themselves again, and Aoife breathed what turned out to be a premature sigh of relief. The woman on Mairéad's right leaned forward.

'Hi, I'm Mari Byrne.' Aoife nodded and smiled; she knew the name but couldn't place it. 'I love your dress; it's fantastic.'

'Thank you,' Aoife said. She was about to explain how embarrassed she was by all the attention, but Mari Byrne carried on.

'I own a boutique in the city centre. I buy in one-off pieces by Dublin designers. Why don't you pop into the shop and we can have a chat? I'll give you my card.' It was a good job that she had to rummage in her bag for it; that gave Aoife enough time to take her jaw off the table.

'That's a great idea,' Mairéad said. 'Do you know Mari's shop?'

Aoife knew the shop, all right. The penny had finally dropped and she was about to hyperventilate. Mari owned Mode Vie in the Powerscourt Centre, and her clothes were worn by anyone who was anyone and were regularly featured in magazines. Aoife had often trawled around Mode Vie, looking for inspiration and trying not to stay too long for fear of being ejected by the supercilious staff.

'Yes, I do,' she said, taking the card. 'I love your clothes.' She hoped she didn't sound too gushing. 'Do

I need to bring a portfolio?' It seemed like the right thing to say.

'Not at all,' Mari told her. 'Just yourself and a few bits that you've made.'

Aoife excused herself and made her way to the toilet. She tried to get Rory's attention on the way, but he seemed to be engrossed in conversation.

Closing the bathroom door, Aoife ran her wrists under the cold tap. When she came out, Rory was waiting for her. She grabbed his arm and dragged him back into the bathroom.

'Easy, tiger! What's wrong with you?'

'You will not believe what has just happened!' Aoife said, propping herself up against the sink.

'What?' Rory asked.

'Things like this just don't happen to me.'

'Come on, spit it out,' Rory said, undoing his fly.

'Rory, you are not having a slash in front of me!'

'Well, turn around, then.' Aoife did. 'Go on, then; tell me.'

Aoife filled Rory in on her introduction to Mari Byrne.

'That is fantastic! And you didn't even want to come tonight,' Rory reminded her, pulling up his zip.

'Not true; I just didn't want to be the other half of your sham relationship. I just can't believe it, Rory – me, with my little bits and pieces, going into Mode Vie!'

'What on earth are you talking about? Your clothes are fantastic; why wouldn't she buy some?' Rory was far better than Aoife at being optimistic.

'Anyway,' Aoife said, remembering that tonight was a big night for Rory as well, 'how's it going with your dad? Have you told him about your plans?'

Rory suddenly looked sheepish. 'Em ... well, I was thinking....'

'What were you thinking?'

'I was just thinking that it might be best if I sort myself out with work first, and then tell my dad I'm doing my own thing. Otherwise I'm just going to look flaky, which he thinks I am already.' Rory had a point, Aoife thought: if he just announced that he was going back to DJ-ing, without having a single gig lined up, his father would be well within his rights to dismiss it.

'And there's another thing.... Dad just slipped into the conversation that he wants a meeting with me next week, to discuss the possibility of my joining the business.'

'What? What do you know about pound shops?'

'It's not really much to do with pound shops any more; he's got his fingers in all sorts of pies. And he wants me to get involved in the marketing side, I think. I don't know – he only mentioned it briefly; I need to see him next week to find out more.'

Aoife was staring in disbelief at Rory, who was avoiding her gaze. 'Do you really think this is a good idea?'

'It's probably suicide, but I might as well hear him out.'

Aoife sighed. She understood the hold that Rory's father had on him, but it still annoyed her to see it in action.

'Come on,' she said.

As they stepped into the corridor, Father Heraghty was waiting outside. The look on his face was a picture. Aoife winced and hoped to God that the fact that she had emerged from a bathroom with a man wouldn't get back to her mother.

Chapter Twenty-Three

'*Story*, Rory?' Rory cringed. He had just walked into the Ground, a bar that was a little bit too up itself, to meet Tem, who was a lot too up himself. He couldn't very well complain, though, as he had organised the meeting himself. Tem greeted Rory in his best Dub accent – a common affliction among the private-school brigade from Dalkey. Rory could guarantee that, when Tem was at the golf club with his father, he didn't say 'story'. He probably said things like 'Froightful' and 'Neo way' and 'I see that Trintech have taken a doive' – but not 'story'. However, when he was being one of the best-connected club promoters in Dublin, he was Tem the Dub. Rory often saw Tem around, at parties and clubs; they usually bid each other a cursory hello, but stopped short of full-length conversations.

Tem was one of those people who had actually made his own nickname up. 'Call me Tem,' he'd said to his girlfriend one day.

'Why, Lorcan?' she had asked.

'Short for Temazepam,' he had said mysteriously.

'OK, Tem,' she had said, shortly before running off with his best friend.

Tem honestly thought it was cool to be named after a drug that he'd never actually taken.

'Hi, Tem. How are you?'

'Great. I am fucking great.' For someone who was self-named after a downer, he was always very upbeat – probably something to do with the amount of coke he stuffed up his nostrils. 'Yourself?'

'Oh, I'm good.' Rory looked over the bar to get the barman's attention. 'Gin and tonic, please – and what can I get you, Tem?'

'Jaegermeister and ginger.' *You can't buy class,* Rory thought. The barman went off to find some ginger to put with the Jaegermeister, and then had to go off to find some Jaegermeister to put with the ginger.

Tem cut to the chase. 'So, rumour has it that you want to get back behind the decks?'

'Rumour has it right for once,' Rory admitted.

'Well, you know, things have moved on a lot since you were DJ-ing. The music, the crowd, the DJs....' Tem took his drink and straddled the bar stool like Daniel O'Donnell about to strike up a song.

'I know that. I do still go out, you know.'

'So what makes you so sure that people want to hear DJ Monkey Business again?' Tem asked in his best world-weary voice.

'Nothing makes me so sure, nothing at all. But if I don't try, I won't know.' Rory was aware that this might descend into a pissing contest if he wasn't very careful.

'Very true,' Tem said, sipping his Jaegermeister and ginger.

'The name would have to go, though.' Rory was playing with the straw in his G&T and looking intently at Tem.

'DJ Monkey Business, you mean? The name is all you have; you can't change the name.'

'It's a bit 1996 hands-in-the-air, don't you think?'

A young woman with blonde hair and breasts that looked as if they had been borrowed from Pamela Anderson for the afternoon came up to them.

'Hi, Tem?'

Tem swivelled around in his chair and grinned the cheesiest smile his smug, bony face would allow. 'It might be. Who's asking?'

'Dervla,' the girl said, looking a little confused. 'We met last week at the Red Box.'

'Sorry – forgive me; it's coming back to me now,' Tem said, mauling her with his eyes. 'Listen, we're just talking business, but can I take your number and give you a call tonight?'

'You took it last week,' the girl said. Tem checked his phone, and Rory read the names upside down: Dervla 1, Dervla 2, Dervla 3....

'Sorry, babe,' Tem told her. 'I've been snowed under

this week, but I'll call you tonight. I'm doing a promotion at the Window; you could come along.' Dervla beamed at him. The Window had been one of the first real dance clubs in Ireland, and it was still one of the places to be seen.

'Yeah, that'd be great!'

Rory couldn't disguise his grimace. He found it hard to take in the fact that women like her were still kicking around post-1962. Then again, there were people like Tem kicking around, so he supposed it stood to reason.

As she sashayed off, Tem turned to Rory and said, 'I know it's not your thing, but did you see the tits on that? I reckon I'm going to ride the arse off that tonight.' He was almost slavering. Rory smiled at him. As much as Tem was getting on his nerves, he needed him.

'So what do you think?' Rory asked.

'About what?'

'The name-change.' Rory bit his tongue; he wanted to say, 'I'd have thought you of all people would have thought that a name-change was a good idea, *Tem*.' Instead he said, 'You don't think it would work?'

Tem was suddenly off the bar stool, arms out-stretched, like a great visionary.

'No, I think it could work; I think it could *really* work.' He looked at the floor of the bar as if the ideas he was having were written on the floorboards. 'I'm remembering your last gig – it was amazing, wasn't it?

The world and his fecking granny were there. But it's been three years, so a re-launch with the same name could be a potential disaster.' Tem's thoughts were coming thick and fast, and he was very convincing. Rory sat there watching him, taking in what he was saying, and thinking to himself that the man might be an out-and-out git but he was very good at his job. 'Say it's DJ Monkey Business, and people will just think you've fallen on hard times and want to cash in.' He looked up briefly. 'You haven't, have you?' he asked, as if he were talking about a contagious terminal disease.

'No,' Rory said. 'I just don't want to work for my father.' He knew Lorcan would understand this one.

'You're dead roight, too. So we set rumours going that the fella who was DJ Monkey Business is playing a small, unconfirmed gig under the name of DJ....'

'Rory?' Rory suggested.

'Brilliant! DJ Rory. And then we let you play – but only for thirty minutes, just before whoever's headlining, when everyone's fucked off their faces and loving it. They'll be crying out for one more tune, and you won't give 'em it. The next day, the word-of-mouth brigade will be out in force, telling each other how brilliant it was that they were there for the birth of DJ Rory.' Tem looked up, utterly convinced that this was going to work.

Rory took a deep breath. 'Well, you've sold it to me. So when are we gigging?'

'Let me get on to some people. The sooner the better, I reckon. I'll call you later this afternoon.' Tem was buzzing, fired up on cocaine and his own thought process.

Rory sculled his drink and put his hand out to Tem. 'I'll talk to you later, then.'

'You will indeed.'

'What's happening at the Window tonight?'

'Ah, not much. Club night I've been dragged in to promote. I just hope Bono's not swanning round like he owns the place.'

'I thought he had a share in it.'

'Yeah, he does, but still. Last time I was down there, I said to him, "Stick to what you know." I'd just had enough of him; you know the way. Telling me which DJs will work and which DJs won't. I said, "Bono, I'm not about to tell you how to perform in front of eighty thousand people, so don't tell me who to put on a line-up for a sell-out club night." You know?'

Rory raised an eyebrow, safe in the knowledge that the best part of this story had never actually happened. 'What are the chances of Bono being there? I thought they were on tour.'

'Yeah, but he turns up like a bad smell. I swear there's more than one of him. He always used be there when I ran anything at the Kitchen, as well. Someone's cloning Bonos, I reckon, just so that he can play all across America and still find time to get on my tits on a dreary Wednesday evening in Dublin. Anyway, I'll sort out when and where we're going to get you back playing, and I'll call you. Listen, why don't you come along tonight? I'll stick you on the guest list.'

'Yeah, I might do that. Thanks, Tem.'

'No worries. But I'll tell you one thing for sure: we need to do something about the nerves. You were a fecking bag of 'em last time you worked for me. There must be something you can take for it.'

Rory wanted to ask him if he could get him some Temazepam, but he thought better of it. Things were going well; he wasn't going to mess it up just to get in a cheap dig at Lorcan.

Chapter Twenty-Four

Aoife contacted Mari Byrne a few days after the dinner party, and Mari agreed to see her the following Thursday, which now gave Aoife three days to get some samples together. She decided to head into town in search of materials and inspiration.

It was a lovely day, so Aoife threw on her long denim skirt, her Indian sandals (which had probably never been near India, as she had bought them in a craft shop in Kerry) and a vest trimmed with sari material. Not wanting to wreck her Mother India look, she decided against a coat, and threw a cardigan over the vest.

Walking into town, Aoife felt great – and she probably would have kept feeling great, if the heavens hadn't opened and dumped a week's worth of rain on her head. By the time she reached St Stephen's Green shopping centre, she looked a lot less like Mother India and a lot more like the wreck of the *Hesperus*. Glad to be in the warmth, she shook her hair like a dog jumping out of a river, drawing disapproving glances. Aoife was past caring.

She headed upstairs to the toilets. Just as she was wringing her cardigan out into the sink, she heard her mobile ringing in her bag; she pondered momentarily the possibility and the shame of being electrocuted by her own phone, but decided to answer it anyway.

'Hello.'

'Aoife, it's Carmel. Where are you?'

'In Stephen's Green shopping centre; I'm soaked to the ...'

'Great. I'm in Proteus. I just popped in for lunch with a friend and noticed there's someone here who I believe you want to meet.'

Aoife felt her heart race. 'Bono?'

'The very same,' Carmel confirmed in hushed tones.

'Where's Proteus?' Aoife asked.

'Kildare Street. Get here as quickly as you can.'

'I will.' Once she had dried her top and reapplied some make-up, it would take her only five minutes to get there.

'Oh, and Aoife,' Carmel added. 'Make sure you look presentable; they're fuckers about the dress code here.'

Aoife felt her heart sink. She looked a complete baggage and no mistake. How was she ever going to get past the maître d', let alone approach Bono, in the state she was in? She decided that all she could do was wash her face, comb her hair and put on fresh make-up; after that, if the downpour slowed for just two minutes, she might not look too bad.

But the weather wasn't on Aoife's side. As she stepped outside, the rain lashed down and the wind blew in her face. Aoife cursed as she flip-flopped her way through the puddles, feeling more and more fed up; each step she took made her take onboard more muddy water. By the time she arrived outside the particularly ornate and especially menacing doors of Proteus, she looked like a drowned rat who'd been washing up and down the sewers for a good few weeks.

She ran up the steps and dragged the door open, throwing herself into the warmth of the restaurant. The maître d' looked at her, and his top lip drew back in a grimace. 'Yes?'

'I'm meeting a friend here for lunch.'

He dragged his gaze critically over Aoife. 'We have a strict dress policy here.'

'What's wrong with what I'm wearing?' Aoife asked indignantly; she wasn't used to being told that her clothes were unsuitable. The maître d' didn't answer; he just sniffed and let her draw her own conclusions. If she had looked in a mirror, she would have been mortified, but at that moment Aoife didn't care; she was wet, she was cold, and the key to five grand was just beyond the doors that this obnoxious man was obstructing.

'Look....' She lowered her voice, trying a different

tack. 'I work at Blues.' She waited for a reaction; the man just looked at her. 'On the Green?' She was trying to play the 'we're all in this catering lark together' card, but the maître d' was having none of it.

'Madam.' Aoife winced and felt her blood run even colder than it already was. He made her feel like a brothel owner. 'I am asking you to leave.'

'You cheeky, jumped-up little man!' Aoife wanted to call him every name under the sun, but she knew that was how he wanted her to react.

'And I'll call the guards if you don't,' he said, giving a fixed-grin goodbye to two guests who looked at Aoife as if she were a bag lady.

'Call them,' Aoife said indignantly.

'If you insist.' The maître d' picked up the phone.

'I do,' she said, calling his bluff.

The maître d's bluff was as good as his word. He dialled the number; the colour drained from Aoife's face – not that anyone would have noticed, as she was covered in mascara and clotted foundation. 'Police?' he said. 'Proteus Restaurant, Kildare Street.' There was a pause, and Aoife began to feel her resolve waver. 'We have a young woman here who is causing a public disturbance, being verbally abusive and refusing to leave the premises when requested to do so.' He arched a well-plucked eyebrow at Aoife, daring her to stay.

Aoife was stubborn, but she wasn't that stubborn. She reeled around and, flinging open the door, ran out into the street. It was still lashing rain.

By the time she got to a taxi rank, she was completely out of breath and miserable. She jumped into a taxi and said, 'Ballsbridge,' to the driver.

'Lovely weather for it, wha'?' he said. Aoife narrowed her eyes at him and fished out her phone, which had been ringing constantly in her bag.

'Aoife, it's Carmel. He's just left. Where are you?'

Aoife had been supposed to meet Paul for dinner the previous evening, but he'd rung her to say he had a seven o'clock meeting the next morning and needed an early night. They had rescheduled for that evening – so now Aoife had to try and find something to wear that was better suited to the Dublin climes. *Maybe a pair of salopettes and a Pac-a-mac,* she thought.

She was busy throwing all her clothes onto her bed when she got a text from Rory.

'Not a door, not a roof, not a wall, but part of a house. Someone famous will b there 2nite. Contract prohibits me from saying more. Rx'

Aoife looked at it with her face scrunched up in confusion. 'What the feck is he on about?' she wondered aloud. Then the penny dropped. She called him.

'Bono, in the Window,' she said.

'Is he? Well, give him a wave from me.'

'Ror, you dope! The Window nightclub. Is that where he's going to be?'

'I can say no more,' Rory said with mock solemnity.

'Gobshite! Is he or isn't he?'

'I don't know, but a little dicky-bird told me that it

might be in the affirmative. Must dash, I fear I may have already said too much.' The phone went dead and Aoife looked at it, shaking her head. Then she rang Paul.

'Got any ideas about what to do tonight?' she asked him.

'Not really; I hadn't –'

'Well, I do,' she told him.

Aoife met Paul at eight outside the Central Bank. 'How was the meeting this morning?' she asked.

'Meeting?' Paul asked, a look of confusion on his face.

'The seven o'clock one – the reason you wanted an early night, remember?' Aoife laughed.

'Oh, yeah – that…. Sorry, we had about seventy fecking meetings today and I don't know whether I'm coming or going. It went fine.' He hugged her. 'You make that?' he asked, nodding at Aoife's cream Victorian lace tunic and tailored brown trousers.

'Yes; you like?' Paul nodded his approval. 'It hasn't seen the light of day for a year, but I've been getting some stuff together to show Mari. I can't believe I'm going to see her on Thursday.' Aoife had told Paul so much about Mari Byrne that she was sure he must feel like he knew the woman personally at this stage.

'*Mari* now, is it?' Paul laughed.

'Oh, God, would you listen to me? Mari this, Bono that … I'm full of it, amn't I?'

'Not at all. You're dead right.'

'I'm so nervous.'

'You'll be great,' Paul said, grabbing her hand and kissing her before pulling her in the direction of the Window.

Rory had finally buckled: he had told Aoife about his conversation with Tem and, after protesting that it wasn't part of the bet, had got her and Paul onto the guest list for that evening. She had pointed out that the contract said that he couldn't get her on the guest list for Lillie's; nothing was said about the Window. Rory was going to meet them at the club; he had decided that it would do no harm to go along, see who was DJ-ing and generally get himself out and about.

There was a queue the length of the North Wall, and Aoife got the cheap thrill that comes with walking to the front of a queue of people and announcing that you are on the guest list.

'This is deadly!' Paul said as they walked in.

'Yep. Rory has his uses. Keep your eyes peeled for him; I said I'd meet him by the back bar, but I'm sure he won't be here yet.' Aoife looked around as the bar began to fill up. There were a few people she recognised; she had met them through Rory. *Liggers,* she thought disparagingly, and then remembered that there wasn't much to differentiate her from anyone else who had blagged their way onto the guest list for the first night of Disestablishment, as this particular club night was called. The music was break beats and hip-hop, or so the flyer said; it could have been ballroom and country and western, for all it meant to Aoife.

She and Paul got a drink and sat down. Aoife sat looking at Paul, and he smiled back at her. 'What you looking at?' he finally asked, eyeing her over his beer bottle.

'Nothing. It's just....' Aoife trailed off.

'It's just what?' Paul coaxed.

'Well, just that I'd like to stay at your place tonight, if that's OK.' Aoife blurted.

Paul looked slightly taken aback. 'That would be no problem, but the place is still in shite, Aoife. I'd rather you came down when the builders are finished, that's all.'

'OK,' she said, a little crestfallen. She had been planning to say this all day. As mad about Paul as she was, she felt that something didn't sit right about the fact that she still didn't even know where he lived. A moment later, she dismissed this thought as ridiculous. He stayed with her only because she lived so near to town; it was more convenient than getting taxis to and from Killiney, only to stay in a building site. Aoife decided she was being petty and a little bit paranoid.

Her over-analysis was interrupted by Rory.

'Where is he, then – the lovely Bono?' he asked, scanning the club.

'How am I meant to know? I'm not U2's bodyguard, am I? And anyway, he probably never even comes in here,' Aoife said.

Paul squeezed her knee. 'He'll be here. I can feel it in my water.'

'You can, can you?' Aoife asked sceptically, raising an eyebrow.

As the night wore on, there was no sign of Bono, but Aoife and Paul were having a great time. Rory seemed to be too; he flitted around the club, checking in every half an hour or so. He was back at the table when Tem wandered over to the three of them, at about one o'clock, with Pseudo-Pammy on his arm. She was grinning like a cat that, after weeks of living on soya milk, had finally got the cream.

Rory introduced Tem to Aoife and Paul. Tem took Aoife's hand and kissed the back of it; looking her in the eye with a heavy-lidded gaze, he said, 'Rory, you didn't tell me you had any friends as beautiful as this.'

Pseudo-Pammy looked crestfallen, and Aoife, who couldn't believe that the cheese level had just hit Gorgonzola, said, 'Rory, you didn't tell me you had any friends as cheesy as this.' The words were out of her mouth before she had a chance to think that this guy could salvage Rory's career as a DJ. Paul stifled a laugh by shoving his beer bottle into his mouth. But Tem seemed unabashed; he was obviously so thick-skinned that a put-down meant nothing to him.

'Rory, just need to have a word in your shell-like re: the whole getting-you-back-to-spinning-the-wheels-of-steel thing.'

Rory wondered why he felt the need to use thirty

words when five would do. 'Great. Come on – let me get you and Dervla a drink.'

Tem looked a little confused, and then looked down at his arm as if Rory had just pointed out a cancerous cyst on his elbow. 'Oh, yeah ... nice one. Good to meet you.' He winked at Aoife and put his finger to his temple for Paul's benefit.

'Back in a bit,' Rory told them, rolling his eyes in the direction of Tem. Aoife and Paul both put their fingers to their temples and then collapsed in giggles. Rory wandered off, and Paul and Aoife recovered from their own comic genius.

Paul was looking intently at Aoife. 'Aoife, there's something I have to tell you.'

Aoife thought for a brief second about Rory's constant warnings to play it cool and calm; but that all went out the window when she was with Paul. *Fuck it*, she thought; now felt like the right time, if there was ever going to be a right time. Aoife had thought about nothing else for days; she was head over heels about him, and she wasn't ashamed of the fact. 'I know there is; I can tell,' she said.

'Right,' Paul began tentatively. 'The thing is –'

'I love you,' Aoife interrupted. The words slipped gently out of her mouth. Tears welled up in Paul's eyes, and he leant forward and pulled her close to him.

'You do?' He seemed genuinely floored. 'Oh, God ... I love you too.' The look in his eyes went deep inside Aoife and wrenched at her stomach. There they were, in the Window; the place was full of skate-boarders, or at least people who were trying to look like they might have owned skateboards once; it was mobbed; the music was pumping out, sounding like someone smacking a stick against a coal scuttle. But Paul and Aoife could have been anywhere. He held her as if he never wanted to let her go. Then he pulled her back so that he could study her face. 'I really do. And I also need to tell you something else.'

'Go on,' Aoife urged him, looking into his wet eyes.

'Lads, lads! Over here!' Rory came flying over so fast that he nearly banged into them.

'What? What's wrong with you?'

'Bono's just walked in!'

'He has not!' Aoife said in disbelief.

'He has! Look – he's over there!'

Sure enough, there was Bono, having a conversation with some fella at the bar, with Tem standing nearby and trying to look like he was with him.

'Go, on, Aoife; go talk to him,' Paul said, turning her round by the shoulders and pointing her in the right direction.

'I can't.' Aoife was standing stock-still; she was utterly and inexplicably petrified.

'What do you mean, you can't?' Rory demanded. 'For fuck's sake, do I have to actually hand you five grand on a plate?'

'I can't!' Aoife said. She was getting annoyed, more with herself than with Rory. 'I just can't!'

'Come on, Aoife,' Paul cajoled her. 'What's the matter? Are you just a bit star-struck?'

'I am not star-struck!' Aoife said through gritted teeth. Paul looked at Rory for help.

'Well, why don't we just stay here, and when you feel like it, you can wander over to the bar and have a chat with him – no big deal.'

'Oh, and what am I meant to say exactly?' Aoife said.

'I don't know; do I have to script you as well as everything else?' Rory asked, exasperated, and then added, 'Sweet mother of God', for good measure.

Paul tried to calm her down. 'Aoife, this is what the bet's about, isn't it? You go and talk to him; that's it. You could even explain the bet – tell him that you think everyone's got a story about him, and that you want one to win a five-grand bet. I'd say he'd go along with it.'

'Ah, that's cheating!' Rory protested.

'No, it's not,' Aoife argued. 'There's nothing in the agreement that says I can't explain to him what I'm trying to pull, is there?'

'Well, all right,' Rory agreed. 'Maybe there isn't; but it's not very sporting, is it?'

'Right!' Aoife announced, standing up. 'I'm going to get my five grand.' She marched across the floor towards where Bono stood, having a pint, minding his own business – as much as he could mind his own business anywhere in the world – but, about five feet behind him, she stopped dead in her tracks. Seeing him sitting there, chatting to a friend and sipping his pint, she felt utterly intrusive. She turned on her heel and headed back to the table, where Rory and Paul were staring at her.

'Five grand, babe – five fecking grand!' Rory reminded her.

'The psychic never said anything about a nightclub.'

'Your psychic was wearing a purple turban, Aoife, and was mad as a brush; don't start quoting him now.'

'Just go, Aoife; it'll be fine,' Paul said encouragingly.

'But I'd feel like such a gobshite going up and saying to him, "Hiya, I'm just trying to win five grand."'

Rory rolled his eyes and threw himself back in his chair. 'I give up! This was meant to be entertaining; instead it's like pulling bleeding teeth!'

'Aoife, you dressed up as a nun to meet him, but when he's standing opposite you in a bar, you can't even go and talk to him. What's that about?' Paul asked.

'OK! OK!' Aoife said. 'I'm going; I'm going. You could do with five grand; you could do with five grand,' she repeated to herself, like a mantra.

She turned around, only to see Tem and Pammy sitting next to two empty barstools. 'Shite! Where is he; where did he go?' she pleaded with Rory and Paul.

'I don't know, I was too busy looking at you,' Rory said.

'Same here,' Paul agreed.

'Shite!' Aoife shouted. She hared back over to the bar.

'Where's Bono?' she asked Tem.

'Gone, I think.'

'Gone where?'

'I've no idea, sweetheart,' Tem said, eyeing her up and down with as much enthusiasm as his weary eyes could muster.

'Great!' Aoife slapped her hand on the bar in frustration. 'That's just fucking great.' She stormed back to Paul and Rory. 'He's only after fecking well leaving!'

Paul and Rory looked at each other.

'Why don't we go after him?'

'What, outside?'

'Yeah, come on.' Rory hopped to his feet. 'Back in a bit,' he told Tem as they piled past him. They ran out of the club, and Rory said to one of the bouncers, 'Any idea which way Bono went?'

'Think he was heading over to the Clarence, boss.'

They ran down the street like their lives depended on it. Aoife was the first to come to her senses.

'Lads, lads, lads … what are we doing?' The two boys stopped running and looked around. 'I mean, even if we go to the Clarence, what are we going to do? Book a room? They're not going to let us in at this time, are they? This is just a wild-goose chase.'

'Well, if you'd gone up and talked to him in the first place, then we wouldn't be running round like a set of fecking eejits, would we?' Rory said, doubled over and out of breath.

'All right! And what's all the amateur dramatics for? We only ran about a hundred yards.'

Rory stood up, still panting. 'That's more exercise than I've done in a year.'

'Well, look, at least you know he's in Dublin,' Paul said, trying to keep the peace.

'Yeah, that's true,' Aoife said.

'I've got an idea!' Rory said. 'Why don't we stay at your house tonight, Paul, and get up early in the morning and try his gaff again?'

'We can't,' Aoife said. 'The builders are still there.'

'Making a meal of it, those builders of yours, aren't they?' Rory said, throwing Paul a look. Aoife missed it – she was still looking up and down the street for Bono – but Paul didn't.

'Em, yeah ... but it's better to get the job done right than have to get it done again....'

Rory's phone rang, and he answered it. 'That was Tem,' he said, pocketing his mobile. 'He says Bono *is* staying at the Clarence tonight and getting the first flight to the States in the morning. Why don't you just come down to the Clarence first thing tomorrow morning?'

Aoife thought about the logistics of it. 'No ... I probably wouldn't get a chance to talk to him, would I? He'll be bundled into a waiting car and that'll be that. But ...' She remembered what Micky Callaghan

215

had told her about his cousin who worked at the airport. '... I could go to the airport in the morning. I could talk to him as he checked in – everyone's got to check in the same, I assume, even rock stars. What do you reckon?' she asked Paul.

'That's not a bad idea at all. Do you know what time the first flight to the US is?'

'It's around eight,' Rory said.

'Will you come with me, Ror?'

'Can't, sorry. Just told Tem I'd see him in the bar for more drinks and a chat. He's disposed of the lovely lady he was with; she was too dim even for him, and that's some achievement. I'll be out till all hours. I'll be fecked.'

'OK, then,' Aoife said, trying to affect a sulk, 'I'll go myself.'

Rory rolled his eyes. 'If you hadn't spent so much time fannying around, you might have saved yourself the bother.' Aoife stuck her tongue out at him. 'Anyway, I'm off back to the club; are you coming, or are you going home?'

'We're going back to the flat. We'll go to see Paul's palace in Killiney some other time.'

'Yeah, can we come round and see it this weekend?' Rory asked, fixing Paul with a stare.

'Yeah, not a bother.' Paul smiled and shuffled his feet.

'Come on.' Aoife pulled on Paul's hand. 'I need to go to bed.' Paul hugged her.

'See you over the weekend, Rory,' he said.

'Yeah; good luck,' Rory said, and winked at Aoife.

Paul and Aoife walked hand in hand along the cobbled streets of Temple Bar as Rory headed back to the club. In all the excitement, Aoife had completely forgotten that Paul had been trying to tell her something.

Chapter Twenty-Five

'I'm just going to see her now, Father,' Bridie said, collecting her cleaning implements. She was in Father Heraghty's house; she had told Mrs Reagan that she'd have a tidy round for her, so that she could have the morning off.

'Will you tell her I said hello?'

'I will, Father, I will.' Bridie cringed, remembering that the priest had seen her daughter and that feckless young fella she was living with coming out of the toilet together. 'Well, I'd better be going; I don't want to be late.'

The truth was, Bridie wasn't meeting Aoife at all. She didn't feel she had to follow her daughter around every hour of the day; she now felt, in her heart of hearts, that Aoife was going to be fine. She didn't like to tell her this – didn't want her getting complacent – but she had found out that the place where she was living was actually in a lovely area, and the girl did seem to want to get herself a proper job, so all in all things were nowhere near as bad as Bridie had first suspected. Also, in her brief stay in Dublin, Bridie had noticed the number of young people; they were everywhere, and they all seemed to be having a great time – not that she'd ever admit this to Aoife.

The strange thing was that, every time she left the convent, she found herself justifying her departure by pretending that she was going to see Aoife – whereas, more often than not, she was just having a wander around Dublin. She loved it – the anonymity of it all; in Kilbane she couldn't walk down the street without the entire town knowing about it, but here hardly anyone knew Bridie Collins, and it felt great. In the last week, she had been on an open-topped bus, visited the Guinness brewery, seen the Book of Kells – which was a lot of fuss over nothing, in her opinion – and been to see a play, which had been entertaining enough if you were into that sort of thing.

But Bridie had been putting something off. There was someone she wanted to see in Dublin, but she hadn't quite managed to pluck up the courage to make contact. Today, she had decided, was going to be different. She wasn't here for much longer, and she was going to make the most of her time.

The first time she had seen the name had been on the riverside. Something was being built or developed or demolished, and the banner along the hoarding said, 'Jimmy Grogan Construction.' Bridie had stood and stared at the name. *It couldn't be the same Jimmy Grogan*, she had thought to herself. But the more she thought about it, the more she realised that it might be. So, in the end, she had got the number for Jimmy Grogan Construction from Directory Enquiries, rung their offices and asked to speak to Jimmy Grogan himself. The receptionist had asked who was calling; Bridie, somehow unable to give her own name, had stuttered, 'Mary Fitzgerald.'

To her amazement, she had been put straight through. As the slow Kerry accent said, 'Jimmy Grogan speaking,' Bridie had felt an unexpected lump rising in her throat and tears stinging her eyes. She had put the phone down, unable to speak. There was no mistaking the voice that she hadn't heard in over thirty-five years. And she had decided that, before she returned to Kerry, she was going to see him again.

As Bridie entered the building where the offices of Jimmy Grogan Construction were housed, she felt so nervous that she actually mistook the feeling for being sick. Then she remembered that she was going to present herself to someone she hadn't seen since she was seventeen years old, and she was allowed to be a bit nervous.

A man in a military-type outfit, the sort that was usually reserved for tin-pot dictators, was sitting at the reception desk. 'Em, hello – em....' Bridie stammered.

'Yes!' the man barked. The tassels on his epaulettes shook.

'I ... I was looking for Jimmy Grogan Construction.'
Bridie was scared that the man actually had some
military affiliation and might do something drastic to
her if she wasn't polite to him.

'Have you an appointment?' he snapped.

This time his shouting annoyed Bridie. She didn't
think it was necessary.

'No,' she began slowly. 'I don't have an
appointment. But I am here to see an old friend, Jimmy
Grogan. I can show you some identification if needs
be, but I would like to go up and surprise him if
possible.'

'That's all well and good, but I have a job to do.
How am I to know you've not got a bomb in your
bag?'

Bridie, who was getting exasperated, emptied her
bag out onto the counter. There was half a packet of
Polos, a picture of the Sacred Heart of Jesus, her purse,
a set of rosary beads that had seen better days, and
three Lotto tickets that made her think that she really
must remember to check them.

'Does it look like there's a bomb in there to you?'
she asked.

'Not on first inspection, but–'

'But what? Do I look like the sort of person that
joins the Provos? Or do you think I'm the sort of
person that holds a grudge against a construction
company and brings in a bomb in my handbag to blow
up the office?'

'I'm only doing my job, that's all. I can't be letting every Tom, Dick and Harriet into the place. What'd be the point in having me sitting here?'

'I don't really see what the point is in having you sitting there anyway.' Bridie realised that the man had reduced her to juvenile sniping, but she didn't care. 'So you won't let me in?'

'Not without an appointment.'

'Is there a problem here?' a voice asked from behind Bridie.

'Ah, Mr Grogan, this lady was just trying to gain access to your floor, and I said not without an appointment, and she was…' The doorman carried on, but neither Bridie nor Jimmy Grogan heard a word he said. They were too busy staring at each other.

Jimmy was the first to speak.

'Bridget?' Bridie nodded, still lost for words. 'My God – Bridget!' He moved towards her as if he wanted to sweep her up in his arms. But the distance of years had made him unsure what to do, and finally he grabbed her hand and kissed her on the cheek. 'My God, Bridget, what are you doing here?'

'Well, I came to see you, I suppose.'

'So you know her, then?' the tin-pot dictator interrupted.

'I do, Michael, I do. And I know you were only doing your job. Thank you,' Jimmy said diplomatically, before turning his attention back to Bridie. 'Do you want to come up to the office? No, that's a mad idea,' he said, floundering like a bashful teenager. 'What would you want to come up to the office for? We'll go get some lunch – is that all right? Are you all right for a spot of lunch?'

'I am; I'll just get my stuff together,' Bridie said. Jimmy and the doorman looked on in bemusement as she swept the contents of her bag back off of the counter.

'Good luck!' said the doorman, as if he and Bridie had just been passing the time of day together, rather than nearly coming to blows.

'Yeah, good luck, Michael,' Jimmy said, waving over his shoulder. Bridie managed to throw a look of disdain over her shoulder at the doorman as they stepped out onto the street.

'I can't believe you're here,' Jimmy said.

Bridie suddenly got all her words back at once. 'I'm up here seeing my daughter. She was having a fierce wicked time of things, but that all seems to have calmed itself down now – she's twenty-six, Aoife. And I've a son, Michael. He's over in Australia at the moment – and I married Tommy Collins, I know you probably know, but he died about sixteen years ago. He was a good man – and Roddy still helps around the farm, you remember Roddy? – and there's not much on it now in the way of cattle, but we sold a fair bit of the land – and so anyway Aoife was up here – she's been living here years now, and I came up the other week and she had no house – some story about the landlord selling it – and then she lost her job, and she had a very good job – and I thought to myself, "Jesus, Mary and Joseph, Bridie, sure the girl needs you up there, even if it's just to know you're around" – so up I come – I'm staying with Mary – you remember Mary, the nun? well, she's up in Whitehall – so I base myself there, so's not to get under Aoife's feet, and I just thought, "Let her know you're here and leave her to it" – so I've been around the city, and I went to the park, and that old pub that we went to – and then I saw "Jimmy Grogan Construction" on the side of something by the river, and I thought it might be you, and then I thought, "You can't be up here for two weeks and not try and find Jimmy, just to say hello," so here I am.' Bridie finally drew breath.

Jimmy was still looking at her, mesmerised. 'Come on,' he said finally. 'Let's go to this little place down here; it's quiet and we can have a good chat.'

He brought Bridie down a small side street to a little Italian café. He was all nerves. 'So, then, what would you like?'

'I'll have a latte.'

'Would you not have something stronger?'

'I took the pledge.'

'And you've kept to it?'

'I have Bailey's on special occasions, but that doesn't really count, does it?'

'Well, I'd like to order a bottle of champagne, to

toast the fact that you're sitting opposite me after all these years. Would you join me in a glass?'

'Ooh, I don't know if I should.' Bridie giggled like a naughty schoolgirl.

'Ah, go on – one glass to celebrate.'

'I had champagne at Aoife's graduation, I think. It was very nice but I was a bit tipsy.' Bridie thought back. She had sat giggling at Aoife's house for a good hour and then had fallen asleep in the car on the way home.

'There's nothing wrong with getting a bit tipsy every now and again, so there's not,' Jimmy urged.

'Go on, then,' said Bridie. 'You've twisted my arm.'

Chapter Twenty-Six

Aoife had set the alarm on her mobile phone to go off at five o'clock in the morning, so that she could head to the airport. So it came as something of a surprise to her to realise that it was seven-thirty and Paul was getting up to go to work.

'I don't think your alarm went off,' he told her, kissing her on the forehead.

'Bollocks,' Aoife said, sitting up and throwing back the covers. 'I'll have to get Tem's number off Rory; if I've missed U2 on the way out, I want to get them on the way back in, and I reckon he'll know when they'll be back in town. I just hope he hasn't got so buckled with Rory that he can't think straight.'

She wasn't too concerned by the fact that her alarm hadn't gone off. Looking at it, she realised that she had set it for the evening rather than the morning. But at least she could now prepare for her meeting with Mari Byrne, rather than rushing off to the airport.

Aoife spent the day panicking. She pulled every item of clothing she had ever made out of her wardrobe, and threw them around the living-room. She chose three things to show Mari and had them dry-cleaned. Then she decided to make something new with some old bits of material that she had, so she spent the afternoon up to her eyeballs in pins, satin and corduroy.

Half an hour before she was due to meet Mari, she had four garments hanging, perfectly presented, in her bedroom. The first was a long, sleeveless evening dress in deep silver satin, with a plunging neckline. Aoife loved that dress. She had made it a year before, for a black-tie event that she had organised for Join the Dots. It was very simple; the only trimming was a dark-grey lace rose on the neckline. Alongside it hung a red kimono dress. Aoife had found the material while rummaging around a shop on Camden Street and had edged it with a broad, deep-red band. It was similar to the dress that Mari had seen her in, and, as she had liked that one so much, Aoife thought this would be a good item to take.

The other two garments were less dressy. The first was a simple vest made of pink cotton; Aoife had stitched bands of rough pink lace around the bottom and across the neckline. She had worn this a number of times with her jeans and high heels, and she knew it looked good. The last piece was a knee-length skirt that Aoife had made by cutting up a pair of brown cords and inserting panels of cream floral satin. This was the one she had made that afternoon; it had taken an age, but, as she looked at it, she knew it had been worth the effort.

Aoife pushed open the door to Mode Vie with one hand; the other was holding four coat-hangers. She smiled hopefully at the shop assistant.

'Can I help?' In the nanosecond that it had taken the woman to look Aoife up and down, she had affected a look that was simultaneously sneering and simpering.

'Hi, I'm here to see Mari Byrne.'

The assistant's face froze and then worked itself into a begrudging smile. 'Oh … I'll just see if she's free; won't be a moment.' She climbed up the spiral staircase in the middle of the shop.

Aoife looked around at the items of clothing that were hanging sparsely around her. On an ornate dressing table was a copy of *Irish Tatler*, open to a large photograph of Mari throwing her head back and laughing as if she didn't have a care in the world. The article was entitled 'Talent to Byrne'. Aoife gulped and, hearing noises at the top of the stairs, moved away from the magazine and over towards the shoes.

'Aoife, how are you?' Mari asked warmly, descending the stairs. 'Would you look at this thing? The designer was a great man for ideas, but it didn't occur to him that we might get dizzy running up and down a spiral staircase.' She reached the bottom step and shook Aoife's hand. 'Rhianna is going to make a cup of tea for us. Would you like sugar?'

'No, thanks, just milk.'

'Just milk for Aoife,' Mari shouted up the stairs, much to Aoife's amusement. 'So then,' she said, turning her attention back to Aoife, 'what have you got for me?'

Aoife felt the butterflies in her stomach flapping furiously as she unzipped the covers that housed her creations. She laid them carefully, one beside the other, along a velvet chaise longue.

'They're beautiful,' Mari said, feeling the stitching on the kimono dress.

Aoife was taken aback. 'Do you really think so?'

'I do – I really do.' Mari seemed very impressed. She stood back and admired the garments again. 'Now then, I need to think what the best way of doing this is.'

Aoife was waiting to hear her say, 'Actually, no … what am I saying? It's a bad idea.' But the words didn't come.

'I will be honest and tell you that I don't think that the cord skirt will be particularly popular with our clientèle, but I'd like to try it out all the same.' She took the tea tray from Rhianna, who had spent the last two minutes negotiating the stairs. 'Now then, let's sit down and have a chat,' Mari said, clearing a space for Aoife on the chaise longue and handing her a cup of tea.

Rory was squeezing oranges faster than the man from Del Monte when Aoife burst through the door. 'Mari Byrne's going to take some of my designs!' she shouted, running over and hugging him. Rory winced. When he spoke, his voice was practically inaudible.

'My head's in bits, Aoife. Quiet down, will you?'

'Sorry – I'm just excited! She's going to put the designs in her shop and see what sort of response she gets. How amazing is that?'

A smile broke across Rory's unshaven face. 'That is fecking brilliant, babe,' he croaked.

'I know!' Aoife said, beaming from ear to ear. 'She's going to call me to let me know the level of interest, and she's going to tell anyone who's interested that at the moment it's not off-the-peg stuff and that they have to order it.'

'Do you have to make any other stuff for her?' Rory asked, sipping his orange juice.

'Not yet; I've just got to see how it goes.' Aoife hunted around for her mobile. 'I need to ring Paul; he's going to be so excited for me.'

'I hope he is,' Rory said. 'Listen, I got your note; I sent Tem a text and he rang just there. He's all over the place today. He had me drinking tequila at seven o'clock this morning.' Aoife winced at the thought. 'Bono et al. are going to be coming back into the airport first thing in the morning, and you are not going to miss them.'

'Why not? I managed to today.'

'Because I'm coming with you,' Rory told her. 'Now, I really must retire; this day has been too much for me already.' He shuffled towards his bedroom. 'I'll see you in the morning.'

'You're getting old, Ror,' Aoife shouted after him. 'What kind of reputable DJ goes to bed at five in the afternoon?'

'One who's had no sleep.' He winked. As his door opened, Aoife saw an Adonis sitting up in bed, waiting for his orange juice. 'Nighty-night. I'll get you up at five for the airport,' Rory said, closing his door. Aoife shook her head and smiled.

Chapter Twenty-Seven

There was a mobile phone ringing, but Aoife couldn't connect it to anything to do with her. The ring tone was different from hers. Then, through the muggy haze in her head, she realised that it was playing 'Elevation' by U2. Rory, in his infinite wit, had obviously been messing about with it. She just managed to get to the phone before it rang off.

'Hello, Ms Collins,' said a camp American voice. 'This is your early-morning wake-up call.'

'Jaysus, what time is it?' Aoife said, looking around the room, disoriented.

'Four a.m., Ms Collins.' Rory gave up on the sing-song voice. 'Come on, get your arse out of bed; we've jet-setting celebrities to meet and greet.'

'Morning, babe, how are you this fine hour?' he chirped two minutes later, standing at Aoife's bedroom door and holding out a croissant.

'No, thanks – I couldn't face food yet,' she said,

sitting up in bed. 'What I don't get is why you woke me up so early. The plane doesn't get in until half-six, according to Tem.'

'Oh, didn't I tell you?' Rory asked, biting into the croissant. 'I haven't got the car.'

'What?' Aoife was in shock. Rory had done this once when he'd made her get the DART to Killiney, but this was unforgivable. 'Where is it? It's not in the garage again, is it?'

'Its second home.' Rory nodded.

'What a shit-heap, Rory! Get another fecking car!'

'Ooh, excuse me, Jeremy fecking Clarkson; I don't see you driving us anywhere in your lovely – now what type of car is it? Oh, that's right: you haven't got one. And it's not a shit-heap; it's a 1964 Jaguar E-type.'

'Like that means anything to me,' Aoife grumbled.

'Come on. There's a bus at a quarter past five outside the Four Seasons.'

'A bus! Have you ever even been on a bus?' Aoife was tired and indignant.

'Have I ever been on a bus?' Rory pondered for a second. 'Do you know, I don't think I have – not in Dublin, anyway. But I thought it might be fun.'

'Fun? At this time in the morning? Are you out of your mind?'

'Come, come, now, babycakes – that's just not the spirit.'

As Aoife walked out of the door into the cold spring air, she cursed herself for having been roped into

233

celebrity-badgering. Waiting at the bus stop, she turned to Rory. 'Who was the Greek god you had in your bed last night?'

'Fred. He's a male model from Sweden. Perfect English, perfect teeth, and, by ten o'clock last night, perfectly boring. I kicked him out so I could get some sleep.'

'You are so fickle, Rory.'

'I am not. I just know when not to flog a dead horse.'

The bus was on time and deserted, but for a lone businessman who looked like Frank Stapleton had just had a long word in his ear. Aoife and Rory paid and sat down. The bus swung around Stephen's Green; it was still dark. Aoife felt sick from lack of sleep.

'Oh my God, I forgot to tell you!' Rory said suddenly.

'Tell me what?' Aoife asked, bleary-eyed, staring out of the window.

'I'm DJ-ing tonight!'

'Whereabouts?' Aoife spun round so quickly that she nearly gave herself whiplash.

'It's a night called Doggie Bag, at the Fab Café on South William Street.'

'Oh my God, Ror, that's mad! When Leonardo Di Caprio was here the other month, that's the night he went to. How the fuck is Tem sneaking you in there?'

'Thanks for the vote of confidence.'

'No, I just meant – won't the other DJs be pissed off?'

'No; two of them worked with me when they were first starting out, and the other one is Sam Le Strange, who I've known for years.'

'Oh, yeah – the one who fancies himself?'

'They all fancy themselves; you have to fancy yourself to be a DJ. Anyway, Tem's running the entire evening, so what he says goes.'

'He's some man for one man, isn't he?'

'He's some gobshite for one gobshite, but he knows his DJ-ing onions.'

'So how are the nerves?' Aoife asked.

'I've decided that I'm going to have a few beers before the gig, and when I feel the rush of nerves, I'm going to go with it. I'll bring a bucket behind the decks with me, just in case I feel like chucking my ring up. New philosophy: don't fight it, go with it.'

Aoife screwed her face up. 'You're going to puke behind the decks?'

'I am. Are you coming?'

'Deffo. I'm meeting Paul for a drink, and then we'll come along. What time's your set?'

'Ten o'clock, for an hour or so. The launch of DJ Rory. You can't miss it, babe, or I'll never forgive you.'

'I wouldn't miss it for the world,' Aoife said, putting her head on his shoulder. 'As long as you keep your slop bucket away from me.'

The bus finally pulled into the airport at a quarter to six, and Aoife and Rory headed for the Arrivals hall.

'Six-thirty – EI419,' Rory said, scouring the Arrivals board. 'Fuck!'

'What?'

'It's delayed. It's not expected in till eight.'

'Marvellous.' Aoife sighed. 'Shall we go get a coffee, then?'

'I think we need to wait by Arrivals all the same. Sometimes, when they say there's a delay, the plane comes in earlier than the time they estimate. Now that you've bothered your pretty little head with all of this, you don't want to miss them because you're necking coffee upstairs, do you?'

Aoife and Rory found seats in front of the arrival doors. Every few seconds, the sliding doors opened to reveal people from all walks of life. There were bored businessmen and women, who looked as if the entrance of Dublin Airport were the bowels of hell. There were excited young travellers who ran squealing over to their families or friends; they were easy to spot, because they had dressed appropriately for the Thai climate twelve hours before, but were now doing a nice line in goose pimples, erect nipples and plaited hair that looked great on Bo Derek but not so great on fellas who had to go back to their mammies in Mitchelstown. There were also several priests and nuns. 'There's one of your lot there,' said Rory, pointing at a confused old nun who couldn't seem to find anyone she knew.

Out of the corner of her eye, Aoife saw a small man

pacing up and down like an expectant father. He was wearing a shell-suit jacket, flecked suit trousers and a cap that said, 'I suppose a Rock's Out of the Question? Def Leppard.' Aoife glanced across at Rory, nudged him and nodded over in the man's direction. Rory raised an eyebrow. 'Mad as a bike, babe; mad as a bike.'

The man caught them looking over at him and headed in their direction. *Shit,* thought Aoife; *not good.*

'How're you?' he asked, in what Aoife assumed was a thick Mancunian accent; he sounded like Liam Gallagher. The man proffered his hand for Rory to shake. Rory obliged; any excuse to talk to someone mad.

'I'm grand. Yourself?'

'I'm great. And you?' He grabbed Aoife's hand.

'Yeah, I'm good as well. Waiting for someone, are you?'

The man knelt down in front of them and looked around as if someone might be listening in.

'Yeah. But I need to keep it hush-hush.'

'It's not U2, is it?' Rory asked. He realised that he was talking to the Def Leppard hat rather than the man. *Probably get more sense out of it*, he thought.

'Yes!' The man was visibly gutted that Rory had seen through his covert operations. 'How did you know?'

'That's who we're waiting for as well,' Rory admitted.

'Why are you waiting for them?' For a split second there was a possessive note of desperation in the man's voice; then he composed himself. 'Are you autograph-hunters?'

'No, not exactly,' Aoife said.

'I didn't think so; I haven't seen you on the circuit before,' he said, sitting down next to Rory and fixing his gaze on the sliding doors.

'What circuit's that, then?' Rory asked the hat.

'Autograph-hunting.' The man followed Rory's gaze. 'Oh, you noticed my hat. I met them back in '92, when they played the Sheffield Arena. Very emotional, it was. Put Sheffield back on the map, Def Leppard did. The place was on its arse after the collapse of the steel industry. Thatcher forgot about places like Sheffield, but she didn't bargain for people like Joe Elliott to remind her, did she?'

Aoife shook her head in agreement. She had no idea what he was talking about.

'Do you have many autographs?'

'Three thousand, four hundred and eighty-two. I'm aiming for three thousand five hundred by the end of the month, but if I get U2 today, I'll be more than happy for the rest of the week.' The man was fidgeting in his chair; he looked excited and anxious at the same time.

'Who was the nicest person you've met?' Aoife asked.

'Why?' the man snapped defensively.

'No reason; I was only asking.' *Christ,* Aoife

thought, *paranoid autograph-hunters; that's all I need at six-thirty in the morning.*

'Sorry, sorry....' The man took a deep breath. 'I get a bit edgy when I'm about to meet a new star. I'm Lee Edmonds, by the way; pleased to meet you.' He shook their hands again. *Get me out of here,* Aoife thought. 'The nicest person I've met is Baby Spice, Emma Bunton. But she's more of a friend than a star, really.'

'What, do you go out for drinks with her?' Rory asked in mock innocence.

'No.' The agitation was back in Lee's voice. 'Of course not; she's famous, I'm not. But she always talks to me.'

'OK,' Rory said, hoping he hadn't riled the man too much. 'So who else have you met?'

Lee had met all of the cast of *Coronation Street*, the cast of *EastEnders*, Geri Haliwell, Steps, Tony Blair, Liam Gallagher (who had told him to fuck off), Jimmy Tarbuck … the list went on. He began telling them about the dog-eat-dog world of autograph-hunting, but then clammed up; Aoife wondered if he thought that they were invading his territory.

'Do you have a mobile phone on you?' Lee asked them.

'Yeah; why?' Rory asked suspiciously.

'Oh, nothing.... I was just thinking – you two could go grab a coffee, and I'll call you when they get here. You know, just so you don't have to hang around waiting for them.'

Rory eyed him sceptically. 'No, we're fine, thanks; we'll wait here, if it's all the same to you.'

Lee took a deep breath. 'Well, I could do with a coffee. Can I get you one?'

Aoife felt a bit embarrassed about the way Rory had spoken to Lee. God love him, this was his life, to all intents and purposes, and they were intruding upon it. He was within his rights to get a bit agitated as his next autograph opportunity neared.

'Thanks, Lee; that'd be great. Rory, you'll have a coffee, won't you?'

Rory shrugged. 'Might as well. We'll be here for another hour; I need something to keep me awake.' He rummaged in his pocket for some change, handed it to Lee and said, 'White, no sugar; same for Aoife. And get yourself one.' Lee wandered off to the coffee shop at the other side of the hall. Rory and Aoife smirked at each other as their barmy new acquaintance moved away.

'Have you worked out what you're going to say to Bono?' Rory asked.

'I might pretend I work for *In Dublin*. What d'you think?'

Rory shrugged. 'Can't do any harm.'

Lee returned with three coffees and a look of concentration on his face. 'Right, white coffee …' He handed one to Aoife. 'White coffee …' He handed another to Rory. 'I don't drink white coffee; I only ever take it black,' he explained.

'Good for you,' Rory said, taking a sip of his drink. He really wasn't that interested in seeing much more of Lee. They all sat in silence for a while, drinking their coffee. Lee was beginning to unnerve Aoife; he kept staring at her and Rory.

'Lee, are you all right?' she asked. She was beginning to get agitated herself. It was too early in the morning for this, as far as she was concerned.

'Yeah – yeah, fine. Why, what makes you ask?'

'Well, it's just that you keep staring at us.'

'I'm not. Anyway, I've told you: I'm a bit on edge. I mean, come on – any minute now, U2 are going to walk through that door over there. Well, in about fifteen minutes.'

Aoife slumped back in her chair, too wrecked to argue; she wasn't really a morning person. She looked over at Rory. He had his head back and his eyes closed; he was obviously fed up with talking to Lee. Suddenly she felt very drowsy, as if someone had turned up the gravitational pull around her. She looked over at Lee, who had stood up and seemed to be hopping from one foot to the other, looking down at her and Rory. Then her field of vision began to narrow; it got slimmer and slimmer, until it was just the backs of her eyelids. Then she fell asleep.

Aoife could feel her whole body being rocked. Then she heard Rory's voice: 'Wake up – wake up, Aoife, for fuck's sake.' Her mind felt as if it were trying to swim

241

through mud. It took a few minutes for her to register where she was and what she was doing there.

'What time is it?' she croaked to Rory. He wasn't looking too hot either.

'It's … three o'clock.' He looked at Aoife in complete confusion. 'Three o'clock?'

'No way!' she said, pushing herself up in the chair.

They both looked around, utterly bewildered. Eventually Rory stood up and put his hands out to Aoife to help her up. They stumbled over to the information desk.

'Hi, can I help you?' the young man behind the desk said, shuffling papers like a newsreader.

'Em, yeah…. Bit of a weird one, this,' Rory said distractedly, 'but is it three o'clock in the afternoon?'

'Yes, it is.' The guy was looking at them as if they were mad.

'Thanks….' Rory said, his voice trailing off. 'Yeah … em … thanks.' He started to walk away from the counter, but then, remembering something, he turned back. 'Did U2 come through here this morning?'

'Apparently, yeah. I wasn't in at the time, but the fella on the other shift said they did. There was mayhem, apparently. Some fella told Bono that he'd been sent to save him from all the people who constantly want a piece of his celebrity. He ended up getting carted off by the guards.'

Aoife and Rory stared at each other.

'Thanks,' Rory said again. 'Thanks a million.'

They walked slowly, in silence, out of the building.

'Rory,' Aoife asked tentatively, 'do you think we were drugged?'

'Well, I know you like your bed, but I don't think either of us could manage a seven-hour catnap in the middle of an international airport, do you? Come on, we'd better get a taxi.' Rory checked his phone; he had a list of missed calls. 'Tem's going to kick my arse if I don't make an appearance soon.'

Chapter Twenty-Eight

Rory felt awful. Whatever Lee the autograph-hunter had stuck in the coffee had had a terrible effect on his head. He felt like he had a marching army in there.

He arrived at the Fab Café at seven o'clock, with his record bag slung over his shoulder. 'Howya?' He greeted Tem and looked around. 'Well, this is a cool enough place.'

'It fecking is, all right, so don't go ballsing it up by puking your ring up on stage.'

'I'm not about to.' Rory's head was not in the mood for Tem, but he had enough cop-on to realise that he shouldn't be abrupt with him; Tem was, after all, doing him a huge favour.

'Where's Sam? He said he'd be here by now to sort out his set!' Tem shouted at no one in particular. No one in particular answered, much to his annoyance. He pulled his mobile phone from his pocket and angrily located Sam LeStrange's number.

'Sam? Tem. Where the fuck are you? … Well, what the fuck are you doing there? … I don't care if you're getting a blow job off the Pope. Get your fucking maggoty arse down to Dublin *now*, or I'll make sure that the only place you'll be playing from now on is Rody Bolands!' Tem slammed the phone down. 'Prick!'

'Problem?' Rory asked, stating the obvious.

'Yeah, the fucking tool went and got himself wankered and had no sleep, and is currently in the process of riding some Page Three girl in Belfast. Pilled-up fuckwit. I mean, if he's going to do anything, why doesn't he just do coke? He gets it for free, for fuck's sake. But no, he goes and eats a bucketful of Es and then can't work out why I'm shouting at him. Jesus.' Tem's veins were ready to burst out of the sides of his head.

Rory looked at him, feeling helpless and out of it. It seemed such a long time since he had been in this world that he felt like a new boy again.

'Give us a look at what you've brought,' Tem said, nodding at Rory's record bag. He opened it. 'Right, you'll have to go home and get some more; you might be headlining after all.'

Back at his apartment, Rory took a deep breath. He felt terrible – and it had less to do with the fact that he had been drugged earlier than with the fact that he was bricking it about the evening that lay ahead of him.

As he ransacked his record collection, he took deep breaths and muttered to himself that it was going to be fine; he wasn't performing open-heart surgery; he was just going to play a few records. This didn't stop him scrabbling to his feet, charging to the bathroom and heaving the contents of his stomach into the toilet bowl. Rory voyeuristically stared at what he had just produced, spitting into the bowl, trying to regain his composure, and realising that it was predominantly coffee. 'Little autograph-hunting bollix,' he muttered to himself.

He finally got it together enough to stand up straight, and stared at himself in the bathroom mirror. Pushing his shoulders back, Rory drew himself up to his full height, eyeballed himself in the mirror and said simply, 'Cop on.'

He decided to give himself half an hour in the flat to go through his set. He looked at the twelve-inch records in front of him and decided to start off with something slow and funky. Rory had a fairly basic policy when DJ-ing. Start off with something danceable that no one has heard of; add in a few tracks that have been played around clubs for a while; bring it back down with something funky, preferably with no words; then slowly up the pace, throwing in the odd tune that every clubber would know; as the pace picks up, slide in an all-time classic – but just one line, or sometimes just a few notes, sliced through the previous tunes – and then give the crowd the tune of the night. This strategy had never failed in the past. Tonight, he decided, required a little bit of Michael Jackson. Even the coolest clubber in Dublin couldn't help losing the head when Billy Jean got thrown in with an eclectic mix of underground house.

Rory packed up his records and called a taxi, hoping the modicum of composure he had managed to achieve was something he could maintain for the rest of the evening.

Rory was nodding his head, nonchalantly discussing his role as DJ with a young man who was hanging onto his every word and frankly boring the arse off him. *Where the hell is Aoife?* he thought. As he scanned the room, he saw Aoife and Paul come in. Paul went to the bar, and Aoife pushed through the crowds towards Rory.

'I'm headlining!' Rory shouted.

'You are not!' Aoife shrieked. 'That is fecking brilliant!' She gave him a huge hug.

'I know; I can't believe it. I just hope I can keep it together. I can do without making an eejit of myself in one of the best clubs in Dublin.'

'You'll be great,' Aoife said, hugging him again. 'What you having to drink? Paul's at the bar.'

Rory wasn't due to play until midnight. At eleven-thirty, he checked his watch for the fiftieth time and felt a familiar feeling of dread building up in his stomach. He knew he needed to get to the toilet as quickly as his legs could carry him.

Rory threw up three times in quick succession. He clung to the side of the toilet, praying that, if his nerves wanted to eject anything else from his body, they would do it within the next half-hour. He flushed the toilet and stood up straight, trying to gauge whether he was in any fit state to emerge from the cubicle. As he gave himself the all-clear, he heard the door to the toilets open and a familiar voice talking on a mobile phone.

'I can't get away right now. I just can't.... Ah, come on, don't be like that; that's not fair. You know I love you.... I know that! Jesus, don't I know that? ... Well, why don't you meet me tomorrow and we can go home together?' Rory stood stock-still, eyes wide. 'I'm not abandoning you; I just have something to do tonight. We'll talk about this tomorrow.' There was a pause, and Rory held his breath. 'Please don't be like this; I'll explain – just meet me tomorrow at the arch by Stephen's Green, at one o'clock.... Don't put the phone dow– Shit!'

There was a dull thud as he kicked the door open, and then Rory was alone again. He wasn't sure what that conversation had been about, but one thing he was sure of: the person speaking had been Paul.

Rory emerged from the toilet a few minutes later. He saw Aoife and Paul laughing together, and tried to marry this image with what he had just heard. He thought about saying something to Paul, but he realised that ten minutes before he was due to re-launch his career as a DJ wasn't exactly the best time.

'Where've you been? Are you all right? We've been looking for you, haven't we?' Aoife said to Paul, who nodded and smiled at Rory.

'Well, you're here now,' Paul said. 'Fancy another drink before you have to go on?'

'No, thanks,' Rory said curtly. 'I'm fine.' He turned to Aoife and smiled. 'Well, better get up there and do my worst.' He kissed her on the cheek. 'Wish me luck.'

'Good luck!' she said, winking at him.

'Yeah, good luck,' Paul said, putting his hand out to Rory.

Rory waited a split second longer than was comfortable to shake it.

'Thanks,' he said, and headed over to the DJ booth.

Looking down into the crowd, Rory saw that they were going bananas. It was nearly two in the morning; He had gone down a storm – and he had managed not to let his nerves get the better of him. As the final notes of his set hung in the air, the crowd applauded and cheered; people were hugging each other, and grown men with tears in their eyes were trying to shake Rory's hand. He knew better than to get big-headed and think it was all his doing; drugs had an amazing way of making people act like the most mundane night was on a par with seeing the Beatles live at the Hollywood Bowl.

Aoife was in the crowd with Paul, waving up at Rory; he made his way over to greet her. 'You were brilliant!' she said, hugging him. 'Look – everyone loved you!'

'You were fantastic,' Paul said. 'Fair play; the place was hopping.'

'Thanks,' Rory said, smiling cautiously at Paul.

'Listen, Rory, we're going to head back; I'm knackered,' Aoife said.

'No problem. I'll be here for a while, I imagine.' Rory looked at the queue of people who were politely, if a little spacily, waiting to get his attention. 'But I won't be too late,' he told her; 'I've got stuff to do tomorrow. Night, babe. Night, Paul; I'll probably see you in the morning.'

The truth was, Rory would see Paul the following day either way. He was going to find out who he was meeting at Stephen's Green, and what exactly he was playing at.

Chapter Twenty-Nine

Aoife and Paul awoke the next morning to Rory presenting them with breakfast in bed, along with the *Sun* and the *Mirror* – both of which carried pictures of Lee Edmonds, of no fixed abode, being dragged away from a bewildered-looking Bono at Dublin Airport. In the background, the feet of a sleeping Aoife could be seen next to the slumped body of Rory.

'Oh, God!' Aoife moaned. 'Can you believe it?'

'You can't really tell it's us, can you? You can only see your feet, and my head's out of shot,' Rory said, holding one of the papers at arm's length to get a proper look. 'At least they got my good side. I'll be in the lounge, lovebirds.'

'You could've got yourself in a load of shit yesterday,' Paul said, throwing the paper down and looking at Aoife seriously.

'What do you mean?'

'What I say. You put yourselves in a dangerous situation; the man was a madman.'

Aoife didn't like being told what to do. 'Well, I was with Rory, so I was fine.' Paul rolled his eyes. 'What's that supposed to mean?'

'Sorry – I didn't mean to look so despairing. It's just that – well...' He paused. 'I don't know ... it's just that, from what I can gather, it's never you who gets yourself into stupid situations; it's always Rory. So I don't think having him there means that everything was OK and that you were safe, that's all.'

Aoife pushed herself up in the bed, annoyed. 'How was this Rory's fault? It was my idea to go to the airport!'

'Yeah, but you wouldn't have had any reason to think of it if he hadn't made that bet with you, would you?'

'Rory would do anything for me; he'd never put me in a situation where I wasn't safe. He went with me to the airport early in the morning; it's not like he sat me in the middle of a minefield, is it?'

'No, I suppose not.' Paul pulled Aoife into a hug, and they left it at that.

Paul, with perfect timing, managed to leave five minutes before Bridie arrived.

'Jesus, Mary and Joseph, girl! You look like you've been sleeping rough. What's he been doing to you?' she demanded, gesturing towards Rory.

'Nothing, Ma. I'm fine. I just got up, that's all.'

'Up? You don't even look like you've been to bed!' Bridie sat herself down in an armchair. 'I've been trying that walkie-talkie of yours, but the little fella inside keeps telling me it's full up.'

'Yeah, sorry; I forgot to clear the in-box.' Aoife ignored her mother's technophobia; she was sure she only said things like that to wind her up.

'Well, get it fixed; it'd be easier to contact the dead, so it would.'

Bridie looked around the room, taking in the huge David Hockney print that hung on the wall, the wide-screen TV, the large black leather settee and the distressed brickwork. Aoife expected her to hate all of them, but instead she announced, 'Well, this is a nice place you've got yourself – for Dublin, anyway.'

'It is. See, I told you I wouldn't be destitute.'

'Didn't doubt you for a second, girl.' Aoife threw her mother a look; who was she was kidding?

'Well, it's like a palace. I hope you've thanked your friend Rory for letting you come and live with him.'

'Of course I've thanked him.'

'Good. Because he's being very generous.' Bridie turned her attention to Rory as if he hadn't been in the room. 'I said you're being very generous.' Rory nodded and smiled.

'So what have you been up to? Been helping out at the church, have you?' Aoife asked.

'Oh, you know the way – I help out when they need me, but I don't like to get in the way.' Aoife couldn't help noticing that her mother wasn't looking her in the eye. Bridie squinted and regained an interest in the David Hockney painting. 'Is that art, then?' she asked.

'Yes,' Aoife said wearily, waiting for her mother to say a four-year-old could have done better.

'It's lovely. Makes a change from pictures of flowers in baskets.' Aoife was beginning to think that her mother had suffered some kind of personality-altering trauma.

'Well, Mammy, if you don't mind me saying, Dublin seems to be doing you some good.'

'Oh, I wouldn't go that far,' Bridie said dismissively. 'Anyway, I was wondering if you'd like to go to the nice cake shop I just saw on the way here. We could have a good old chat. What do you say?'

Aoife arched an eyebrow; Bridie wasn't the sort who sat down for good old chats. 'Yeah,' she agreed slowly, eyeing her mother suspiciously. 'I'll get dressed and we'll head down there.' She was just getting up when Rory turned the sound up on a news report on the TV.

'... The man is believed to have been an autograph collector. In a statement issued by his lawyer, Mr Edmonds said, "I did not intend to harm Bono in any way; on the contrary, I was merely protecting him from others who wished to do harm."' Aoife wanted to howl laughing, but she knew that if she did, her mother would want to know what on God's earth was going on.

There was some footage of Bono leaving a dinner he had attended the previous evening. The newsreader was asking him what he thought of being launched upon by an autograph hunter when Bridie shrieked, 'That's him!' Aoife and Rory both spun around to look at her. 'That's yer man!'

'Who?' Aoife asked. 'What are you talking about?'

'The fella – remember, I said I was talking to a fella in that pub, and I thought that he was married, but he was very nice all the same, and he got up for a song?' Aoife hoped she was hearing things. 'Well, that's him. The one with the sun-yokes on his face even though it's pitch-dark. Now, what does he need them for?'

'Bono, Mammy; it's Bono.' Her mother, who'd only been in Dublin for two minutes, had met Bono.

'Bone-o; who's Bone-o?' Bridie asked.

'The lead singer of U2, Ma,' Aoife said wearily.

'You don't know who U2 are?' Rory asked.

'Of course I do.' Bridie began to sing 'With or Without You'. 'But I wouldn't *know* them if they were playing in our back field. Unless, of course, they played a couple of the ones I know – you know the way you pick them up from the radio.'

Aoife put a cushion over her face and shook her head.

'What's wrong with you?' her mother demanded. 'What's wrong with her?' She asked Rory, who shrugged his shoulders and gave Bridie an enigmatic smile. 'Come on now, Aoife,' Bridie instructed, 'I haven't got all day if we're going to go for this chat.'

Aoife and her mother settled down at a corner table in the Bridge Café, and Bridie ordered them coffee while mulling over the menu. 'I was sure this place was a cake shop; I saw a woman eating a cake as I went past.'

Aoife rubbed her forehead. 'They sell cakes, Mammy; they're over there,' she said, pointing to the counter.

Bridie wandered over to the cake-stand. 'I've got myself the carrot cake, and I've got you the lemon cheesecake because I know you like cheesecake,' she informed her daughter upon her return.

Aoife noticed that her mother was acting fairly strangely, even for her; she seemed very distracted. 'What's all this about, Mam?' she asked.

Bridie looked at her daughter and then looked away again. 'Em,' she began nervously, 'I've got something to tell you.' Aoife was alarmed; the tone of her mother's voice suddenly made her afraid that something might be really wrong. Seeing her daughter's expression, Bridie said, 'Good God, girl, don't look like that – I'm not on my last legs or anything. It's just that …' Bridie paused and smoothed her napkin against her lap. 'I've met someone,' she said finally, sheepishly, looking at her daughter to gauge her reaction.

'You've met someone?' Aoife almost shouted. 'What, a *man*?'

'No, a goat! Of course, a man,' Bridie stage-whispered through gritted teeth as the waitress brought over their coffee and cakes.

Aoife sat back in her chair. She was speechless. Her mother didn't meet men. Her mother was her mother, for God's sake. She huffed and puffed and cleaned up after Roddy; she did not come to Dublin and develop a social life.

Finally she asked, 'Who is he?'

'His name is Jimmy, Jimmy Grogan.'

'I know that name,' Aoife said, almost accusingly.

'He has a construction business in town,' Bridie said, taking a sip of her coffee.

'That's right.' Aoife was almost mesmerised.

'Anyway,' Bridie went on, 'he's not some strange fella that I just bumped into; I've known him for years.'

Aoife looked at her as if she had gone mad. 'How could you have known him for years? I know everyone you know.'

'Well, now, that's where you're wrong.' Bridie played with the handle of her coffee mug.

'Well, then, who is he?' Aoife demanded.

'He was a friend of mine when we were younger.'

'A *friend*? I thought all your friends were women.' Aoife sat back with her arms folded, petulance scrawled all over her. 'He was your boyfriend, wasn't he?' she asked finally, shocking herself with the suggestion.

'We didn't call it that back then,' Bridie said defiantly, trying to ignore her daughter's huffiness.

'So how long were you and this fella *friends* for?' Aoife asked.

'A good few years, until we came to Dublin.'

'*We?*' Aoife leapt at her mother.

Bridie's face blushed purple and she stammered, '"He" – I said "he", not "we".'

'No, Mammy, you definitely said "we". I'm not deaf. And look at the cut of you. You're mortified, for some reason.' Bridie couldn't look Aoife in the eye. Knowing that she was on to something, Aoife persevered. 'So what does "we came to Dublin" mean, exactly?'

Bridie had picked up her napkin and was shredding it into fifty bits. 'It just means that...' She took a deep breath.

'Go on,' Aoife urged.

'It just means what I said.' She finally exhaled. 'That the two of us came to Dublin. But I didn't like it, and that was that.' Bridie still couldn't manage to look at her daughter.

'You!' Aoife exclaimed, really giving the table next to them something to talk about. 'You came to Dublin when you were younger? And with some fella?'

'I went straight back home to Kerry. And anyway, you make it sound so dirty. We were just friends. It wasn't like it is now, everyone hopping in and out of bed with each other.'

'Firstly, my friends and I don't hop in and out of bed with each other,' Aoife said indignantly, mentally omitting her flatmate from this assertion. 'And, secondly, how have you had the nerve to go on and on about Dublin if you ran away here?'

'That's why I have the nerve. Because I remember what an unholy kip the place was.'

'What, all those years ago? It hardly makes you an expert, does it? And what about Daddy?' Aoife demanded, changing tack. She had never thought of her mother having had any interest in any man but her father, and she found that she couldn't be anything but annoyed and disgusted by it.

'Your father and I got together a long while after I came here with Jimmy – and, anyway, your father knew about him. But Jimmy wasn't going to come back from Dublin, the same way I wasn't going to come back here, so in the end everyone quietened down about the whole thing, and your father never really mentioned it.'

'So why have you decided to meet up with this fella after all these years?' Aoife nearly wailed.

'Because,' Bridie snapped, 'I have often wondered how he was getting on.'

'And how is he getting on?' Aoife mimicked.

'He's getting on fine, and I want you to meet him because I hope you'll like him too.'

Aoife huffed a sigh.

'You don't have to – I'm not forcing you – and I don't mean this very minute, either, but I would like you to meet him. I was thinking of next Saturday. I'll book a table at a nice restaurant in town and we can all sit down and have a chat.' Bridie looked at her daughter for her reaction. There wasn't one; she was too busy sulking.

'Aoife….' Bridie softened her tone and leant forward, putting her hand on her daughter's knee. Her proximity shocked Aoife; they weren't exactly the most huggy of families. 'I'm not going to elope to Nova Scotia with the man. I just wanted to meet up with him, that's all.'

'Is he married?' Aoife asked, childishly hoping to score Catholic points off her mother.

'He was, but his wife died.'

'Handy,' Aoife muttered.

'What was that?' Her mother snapped.

'Nothing.' Aoife sighed wearily. 'I didn't say anything.' She signalled to the waitress for the bill and realised that she was acting like a child for two reasons. Firstly, she felt left out. Secondly, and perhaps more importantly, if her mother had a boyfriend – the thought alone made Aoife cringe – she might stay in Dublin for longer, or for good.

She tried to force a smile as she took her money from her coat pocket. 'I'll get these, Ma,' she said, trying to sound amicable. 'I'm sorry if I've overreacted. It was just a bit of a shock; you know the way.'

Aoife's mind raced. How was she going to get her mother to see sense? There was only one thing for it, she concluded: she would call Roddy and get him to come and get Bridie. Once her mother saw the poor man, she would surely realise that she was behaving like a teenager and that what she really wanted was to go home to Kerry. Bridie obviously didn't know her own mind at the moment. Aoife decided, surveying the high ground from her wobbly perch on the back of an extremely high horse, that she would make this a nice surprise.

Chapter Thirty

Rory walked up the stairs to the coffee shop opposite the archway to St Stephen's Green and took a place in the window, with a double espresso, waiting to see who exactly it was that Paul was meeting.

Just after one o'clock, a beautiful young woman with auburn hair walked out of the park and stood by the railings, obviously waiting for someone. Rory was positive that it was the woman that he had seen with Paul – or someone who looked very like Paul – before.

A moment later she waved over at a man crossing the road. Rory felt his heart race. Paul ran across the road and put his hands up questioningly to the woman, before taking her in his arms. He grabbed her hand and spoke intently to her; she spoke quickly back. The exchange, from where Rory was sitting, looked intense and fraught.

Rory grabbed his coat and headed down the stairs. He hid behind the large stone pillar at the entrance to the coffee shop, peering after the two, as they headed across the road towards Grafton Street. People walked past and looked at him, wondering what he was playing at, and he felt like a complete prat.

Once Paul and his companion were a respectable distance in front of him, Rory put on his shades and followed them. They walked quickly past Trinity, through the Saturday crowds. Rory, who wasn't used to walking at the best of times, had to concentrate on not losing them, while at the same time not letting himself be seen.

They crossed over the bridge and carried on along O'Connell Street, with Rory following suit. The place was mobbed. Rory very rarely came to this end of town, and, seeing the number of people trying to squeeze themselves in and out of Penney's, he knew why. He followed the bobbing auburn hair and felt his gut lurch as Paul put his arm round the woman's shoulders and kissed her on the forehead.

Hundreds of thoughts were flying around Rory's head. Why didn't he just approach them? Because he didn't have the bottle, and also because he wanted to see where they were going. Why didn't he ring Aoife? Because she was with her mother and he didn't want to upset her over the phone. He would follow them to wherever they were going and then decide what to do next.

Ten minutes later, Rory found himself crouching behind a dilapidated Peugeot 205 outside some flats by

Mountjoy Square. He put his hand up to steady himself on the wing mirror, and it came off in his hand. 'Bollocks,' he said, quickly looking around to check that the owner wasn't behind him, ready to insert the broken mirror somewhere painful, but there was no one around.

Paul put his hand in his pocket and produced a key. The woman was still talking animatedly as he unlocked the door of a house. Rory's mind raced. Why did Paul have a key to some place by Mountjoy Square when he allegedly lived in Killiney? Who was the woman – and what was he going to tell Aoife?

Just as he was standing up and dusting himself down, the door of the house opened again and an angry-looking Paul stormed out. Rory dived back behind the Peugeot and watched Paul get into his car, which was parked down the road, and drive off.

Rory stood up and strode across to the house. He was going to find out what Paul was playing at, and he was going to find out from the other woman.

He put his hand up to knock on the door, and then stopped. He was nervous, he realised, and he wasn't sure what exactly he was going to say. Biting the bullet, he knocked.

The door opened slightly, and a craggy-faced woman who looked like she'd had a very hard go in goals peered out.

'Yeah?' she asked.

'Em, I was just looking to speak to the woman with

the long red hair,' Rory stammered; this woman made him uncomfortable.

'Why?'

'I'm a friend of Paul's.' Rory hoped that might make her warm to him.

'That eejit?' the woman asked, still not opening the door any further.

'Well, I'm actually a friend of his girlfriend.'

'Girlfriend!' she snorted. 'Is he at that again?'

Oh, God, Rory thought. This was worse than he had imagined.

'Well, yeah, he has been seeing my friend, but only for a short while.' He found that he was explaining himself to the woman. 'And I saw him today with the red-headed woman, and I thought I'd better find out what the story was – I don't want my friend going out with someone who's already got a girlfriend....' he finished lamely.

The woman came out to stand on the step, pulling the door gently closed behind her.

'She's more than a girlfriend,' she said, her craggy face wrinkling and her hard eyes boring into Rory.

'She's his wife?' Rory gasped. 'Oh my God – he's married?'

The woman shook her head as if she feared she had said too much. 'He's my son, and I love him no matter what – that's all I'm saying.' So this was Paul's mother, Rory thought.

'I just can't believe it,' he said, almost to himself.

'I never said anything,' the woman announced, grabbing the door handle.

'No, no, of course not.... Can I speak with – with...' Rory couldn't bring himself to say 'Paul's wife'. 'The other woman?'

'The other woman?' Paul's mother cackled. 'That's a good one.' Rory flushed red: if anyone was the 'other woman', it was Aoife. 'Sorry, love, she's gone out. Went out the back to see a friend.'

The woman opened the door, and Rory knew he only had a few more seconds.

'Just one more thing,' he said. The woman was back in her hallway and the door was already closing.

'What?'

'Does Paul live in Killiney?'

The woman's craggy face creased up, and she laughed so hard that she began to cough. *Obviously not*, thought Rory.

'Killiney? It's far from Killiney he was reared!' she said. 'That boy has some notion of himself. He lives here.'

She shut the door on Rory and left him, bewildered, out of his territory and wondering how he was going to tell Aoife without wrecking her head or, worse, breaking her heart.

Chapter Thirty-One

There was a pause, and Aoife heard the receiver at the other end of the line falling on the floor, and Roddy shouting obscenities until he finally managed to get the thing to his ear.

'Hello! Hello! Who's this?'

'Roddy, it's Aoife. How are you?'

'Half-starved. Your mother didn't leave enough food in the freezer. I've got the number for the Chinese chipper stuck on the phone at this stage. Terrible shambles altogether.'

Aoife couldn't have cared less about Roddy and his rumbling stomach. 'I'm just ringing to ask you to come up here and get Mammy. Next Saturday would be good. We'll go for a decent meal and you can stay the night here – you know, to break the trip.'

'I don't know about that, now. The woman's barely been in touch since she's been up there.'

'She's missing home, though, Roddy.' Aoife had her fingers crossed. 'You know how stubborn she is; she's not about to just ring you up and ask you to come and get her. She's not going to admit that's she wants to go home, because you didn't want her to come here in the first place.'

There was a pause, and Aoife hoped that she had convinced him. She didn't think it would take much; Roddy's basic needs were obviously getting the better of him.

'Well, I suppose so, but I'll need to set off early; I don't want to get caught in traffic.'

'You'll be fine, Roddy. Call me if you have any problems.'

'Good luck,' Roddy said, and put the phone down. *Well, that's that sorted,* Aoife thought. It was for the best. Her mother would be better off back at home, not having some mid-life crisis in Dublin.

Just as she was congratulating herself, she heard the door open, and Rory came in. 'What's up?' Aoife asked; he didn't look well at all.

'Listen, Aoife, there's something I have to tell you. I don't want to freak you out or anything' – Aoife felt every muscle in her body tighten – 'but I really think you should sit down.'

'He can't be! You've got it wrong,' Aoife said angrily, tears springing to her eyes.

'Aoife, it was his mother who told me – his own

mother. She's not going to say her son is married when he's not.'

'Why didn't you tell me that you thought you'd seen him hugging some woman?'

'Because I wasn't one hundred per cent sure, and I needed to be. You were so happy with him that I didn't want to stick my nose in.' Rory sat beside Aoife and stroked her hair. 'Look, I just want you to know the truth, that's all.'

Aoife's mind was racing. 'He kept having weird phone conversations,' she said, almost to herself. The awful truth was slowly sinking in.

'And?' Rory asked.

'Well, they were just strange – you know, really secretive – and he just used to say they were family stuff and he didn't want to talk about it....' Aoife pulled her hands down her face, wiping away the streaming tears. 'He can't be married, Rory – he told me that he loves me, and he's so genuine....' She broke off. 'Oh, God, Ror, what sort of fool have I been?'

'You haven't.' Rory took her hand. 'You haven't at all. You had no way of knowing.'

'And he doesn't even live in Killiney; he lives by Mountjoy Square in some kippy hole – is that right?'

'Well, I don't know if it's kippy, it was just –'

'Ror, you know what I mean; he pretended he lived in fecking Killiney! "Got the builders in" – the lying bastard....' Tears began to topple down her cheeks again.

'I did think they were taking their time, those builders,' Rory observed. 'I thought they were connecting his house to the Luas, the way he went on about it.' Aoife laughed despite her tears. 'That's better, babe,' Rory said, squeezing her knee.

Her misery was being replaced by rage. 'I want to kill him! What a complete fucking arsehole!'

'Look, why don't you ring him and clear the air?' Rory suggested.

Aoife shook her head adamantly. 'No way. There is no way I am giving that bastard one more second of my time. I don't want to hear him trying to come up with pathetic explanations. Not a chance.'

'OK, but he'll ring you, won't he? He doesn't know that you know, sure he doesn't?'

'Well, he can try, but there's no way I'm answering my phone,' Aoife said defiantly. Rory put his arms around her.

Aoife was working at five, and it was the last thing she felt like doing. She had spent most of the afternoon crying and felt like she couldn't cry any more. Now she was just angry and hurt.

Paul had tried to call her three times, and each time she had switched her phone off. On the third call, she had felt herself wavering. Maybe Rory was somehow wrong; maybe, if she spoke to Paul, she would realise that it was all a mistake.... But then her rational mind kicked in. She thought back over the telephone conversations he had had with his 'flatmate', and the appointments he'd cancelled at the last minute. Once they had been out and, just after a shrouded telephone conversation, Paul had gone home, saying that he had to be up very early.... She had assumed that Paul was a private person and didn't want to burden her with his family problems; in fact, he had been leading a double life.

He didn't have the telephone number of the flat, so he couldn't call her there. The only way he could get hold of her was to come to the flat or to her work. She would have to be prepared for that eventuality, but until then she didn't want to talk to him. She removed the SIM card from her phone and threw it down a drain on Leeson Street. She regretted it two seconds later; Paul wouldn't be able to contact her, but neither would anyone else.

As she neared work, she felt physically sick. This wasn't just some crush that had come to nothing. Aoife realised that what she was experiencing, for the first time in her life, was a broken heart – and she didn't like it one little bit.

She looked at the door of Blues and took a long, deep breath. She was going to have to put on her bravest face just to stop herself from bawling into the first dish she had to carry.

Chapter Thirty-Two

'You all right, Niamh?' Rory asked. Niamh looked awful. There were large dark circles under her eyes and her hair looked as if it hadn't seen a brush for a good week. It was Monday morning; Rory wondered if she hadn't had any sleep over the weekend, dreading the prospect of coming into work.

'I'm grand, yeah – I'm grand,' she said distractedly, hunting for something on her desk.

'I think you need a holiday.'

'Oh, God, no – I couldn't take a holiday now.' Her voice trembled. 'I just couldn't. Your father is way too busy; he'd have me shot, and –'

'Niamh!' the intercom barked. Niamh seemed to jump a good foot in the air.

'Yes, Eoin?' She was shaking.

'Send Rory in, will you? Oh, and Niamh?'

'Yes, Eoin.'

'Put an old brush through your hair, would you?

You are, after all – what is it they call it? – first point of contact for the company.'

'Yes, Eoin,' Niamh said, looking utterly broken. Rory felt a rush of guilt at having a blood association with Eoin O'Donnell.

'Rory!' Eoin greeted him like the proud father he wasn't. 'Glad you could make it.'

'No problem,' Rory said, taking a seat.

'Right, I have an offer that I think you'll find fairly hard to refuse.' Rory shuffled in his chair. Eoin paused for effect. 'I want you to head up the think tank on where O'Donnell Properties goes next.'

As Rory sat pinned to his seat with shock, Eoin pressed a button on his laptop and a PowerPoint display lit the wall.

'Now then, as you can see from this, sales to tourists have buoyed our growth for the past few years – silly hats, shillelaghs, leprechaun snowstorms, that sort of thing.' Eoin saw the confused look on his son's face and looked at the display. It read, 'Have You Got the Vision to Spot the Next Pokemon?'

'Aagh, for fuck's sake, it's the wrong bloody slide. Niamh!' he shouted through the intercom. 'Will you come and fix this thing!' Niamh scurried into the room and hurriedly changed the documents on the laptop so that the display read, 'Sustained growth 1998–2003'.

'That's better,' Eoin went on. 'Anyway, now we've had some fella in to have a look at where we can diversify, and I think that's where you come in.'

Rory said nothing; he just nodded and waited for his father to fill him in on his fate.

'Well, you hang around with the young crowd; the ones with the high disposable income. I want to know what they're spending their money on and why. I don't mean designer labels and the like; I mean things that we could easily diversify into.'

Eoin changed the slide, and Rory felt his gut lurch. 'And this is the biggest area of growth spending.' Eoin gesticulated at the slide. It read, 'The Pink Pound.' Rory felt sure his father's eyes were burning through him. 'Do you know what that means?'

Rory nodded weakly. 'I think so,' he said, and was immediately ashamed of his tacit denial.

'It means,' Eoin went on, 'what the gays are spending.' Rory fidgeted in his seat. He hated people who said, 'the gays'. It was like people who said, 'the blacks'.

'So,' Eoin went on, 'I thought that you might have a few fairy friends who you could ask, in the name of research and' – Eoin paused for effect – 'in the name of becoming a partner of O'Donnell Properties.'

He broke into a huge smile, as if he had just arranged for all Rory's birthdays to come at once. He put his arm around Rory and looked up at his display. 'What do you say?'

'So, what did you say?' Aoife asked, presenting Rory with the tuna salad she had made for lunch.

'What could I say?' Rory said sheepishly.

'"No,"' Aoife offered. '"Fuck off." Or maybe even, "You wreck my head and I've decided to look after myself from now on."'

Rory sighed. 'Look, I know I give out stink about my dad all the time, but this time he seems really genuine.'

Aoife played with her food. In her opinion, Eoin O'Donnell would never be genuine; he always did what was best for him. 'It would appear so.'

'I said I'll get back to him by next Monday with a market-research report. That should keep him happy.'

'I've got a few questions about this.' Aoife put her plate down on the coffee table. 'Firstly, I didn't think you were bothered about making your father happy; I thought you wanted to try and break away from him. Secondly, you know that company that suggested he should go after the Pink Pound? Why didn't he get them to do the market research? Thirdly, what on earth do you know about think tanks and marketing? Fourthly – and I was going to say finally, but something else will probably come to me – won't this interfere with the DJ-ing?'

'Look, I know what you're saying. It's a bit odd that he's drafted me in to do something I have no experience of, but I think he's trying to show that he trusts me....' Rory trailed off. Aoife knew he didn't really think that at all; he was as suspicious of his father's motives as she was. But he was obviously strangely

flattered that, after all this time, his father was showing an interest in him.

'Well, answer my question: what's going to happen
with the DJ-ing?'

'I can do it alongside and see what happens.'

'You need to take control of your life, Rory. You
have options. Use them.'

'Don't get your knickers in a twist. Just because
you're upset about Paul, it doesn't mean you have to
snap at me.'

The truth was, Aoife wasn't getting her knickers in
a twist; she was just glad of the opportunity to think
and talk about something other than Paul.

'I'm not,' she told Rory. 'Far from it. I just think
that, if you want things to happen in life, you can't just
sit around moping, that's all.'

'That's great coming from you! You're hardly Miss
Decision, are you?'

'Well, that's where you're wrong. Since you told me
about Paul, I've had an epiphany.'

'You've had three wise men? Dirty girl!'

Aoife threw a cushion at Rory's head. 'Don't be so
puerile. I've had a good think about myself, and I need
something constructive to help me get over Paul.
Otherwise I'll crumble and ring him.'

'The only way to get over one man is to get under
another, that's what I've always said,' Rory said,
throwing the cushion back at Aoife.

She gave him a look of disdain. 'Anyway, I've made

a list.' She retrieved the piece of paper she had been scrawling on and handed it to Rory.

Rory raised an eyebrow. 'Is this like the last list you made, where what you weren't going to do to find Bono wasn't worth knowing about?'

'Shut up, Rory. I've been busy.' The truth was that Aoife hadn't been particularly proactive in her search; every time she had gone to call U2's management company, she had lost her nerve. 'Anyway, this list is different; I'm going to follow this one.'

Aoife really had been thinking long and hard about the way her life was going. She was realising that it was a fairly static lump, very susceptible to being launched in any direction by events. And her reaction was usually just to let this happen. Once launched, her life would finish up somewhere random and wait, with its defences down, for another shunt from whatever circumstances were hurtling towards it. But that was all going to change, Aoife had decided – starting today.

The list said:

1. *Paul: Forget him. You thought you knew him, but you obviously didn't, so forget about him.*
2. *Buy new mobile phone. Not just a SIM card. The other one was like a calculator from 1985 anyway, and you could do with treating yourself.*
3. *Work: It is not your vocation to be a waitress. You have given samples to Mari Byrne. She was interested. Follow it up and contact other people.*

4. *Mother: Tell her that she needs to go home. She is behaving like a teenager. All will be fine when she sees Roddy and realises that she is missing home.*
5. *Home: Pay Rory rent.*
6. *Bono: Find him, talk to him, claim five grand; use the money to buy materials to make more clothes.*
7. *Thank Rory.*

Rory read over the list. 'Very good, babe; I like it, especially the bit about thanking me. What for, incidentally?'

'Everything,' Aoife said. 'You've just been brilliant about everything, and I want you to know that I appreciate it. But from now on I have to stand on my own two feet – with one tiny exception: the bet. I was going to say we should forget it altogether, but then I thought that I've come fairly far with it, and I could put the money to good use. And if my mother can meet him, anyone can.'

Rory was still looking at the piece of paper. 'You don't have to pay me rent.'

'I do,' Aoife said, getting up and heading for her room. 'You don't appreciate something fully if you get it for free,' she shouted over her shoulder; then she winced, realising that Rory probably wasn't the best person to say that to.

She came back with five hundred euro and handed the notes to Rory. 'There you go.'

'No.' Rory shook his head.

'Take it!'

Rory could see that Aoife was adamant, and he didn't want to put a spanner in the works of her positive-thinking list. 'OK, OK.' He reluctantly pocketed the money. 'What are you going to do about your ma? She seems to be quite enjoying herself.'

Aoife scowled at him. 'She's behaving like a child!'

'And so are you. You just want to get rid of her because you're annoyed that she's got a boyfriend and you haven't.'

'No, I'm not!' Rory had hit a very sore nerve. 'She's far happier in Kerry, that's all – and he's not her boyfriend.' Rory raised an eyebrow. Aoife went on, 'She's just playing the martyr. "Look at me,"' she mimicked, '"standing by my poor wayward daughter...." Well, she can feck off out of that. She needs to go home, where she's happy.'

'Well, this is the last time I'll mention this, but I think you're thinking more about you than about your poor mammy. Maybe she really likes Dublin, and the thought of going home and looking after Roddy strikes the fear of God into her after a few weeks of freedom.'

'Not at all! She's Kerry through and through, Mammy is,' Aoife said dismissively.

'OK, whatever you say.' Rory stood up. 'I'm going to make a cup of tea to celebrate the new and decisive Aoife Collins.'

As he went off to make the tea, Aoife thought about

the first point on her list. Even though she had known Paul for only a few weeks, she had let him get very close to her – and, despite the fact that she felt like an awful fool, a tiny bit of her wanted to hear his side of events.

No; she had to be firm. She had been a complete eejit about Paul. Aoife had always thought that women who got involved with married men were deluding themselves. And if someone had tried to tell her that they had been seeing a married man and hadn't known, she would have taken them for an awful fool – but now she was that person, and she could have died of shame. No, she realised; she was just going to have to get over him.

Chapter Thirty-Three

Two days later, Aoife found herself waiting patiently by the phone until one minute past nine, when she dialled the number she had been given.

The previous evening, she had been curled up in front of the telly when Carmel had rung her. Aoife had bought herself a fancy new mobile phone that afternoon, and had mentally thanked God that the only place she had Paul's number was on her old SIM card.

Carmel had told Aoife that Paul McGuinness was in Blues, and that she had just plucked up the courage to go over to him and tell him that her friend was Bono's biggest fan and was wondering where she could possibly meet him. He had been very polite – and he had given Carmel his PA's number.

Aoife had nearly hopped off the chair. 'Carmel, you're a genius! Thank you – thanks a million. I owe you for this one.'

To Aoife's complete surprise and delight, Paul McGuinness's PA informed her that she had been expecting her call and that, although there was no guarantee that U2 would be there, part of one of their videos was being filmed by the Grand Canal that week. Aoife got the exact time and location from the woman, thanked her very much and hung up. She was delighted with herself.

As they walked along the banks of the Grand Canal, Rory was pretending to be various members of U2's entourage whom Aoife had to get past in order to reach Bono.

'Go on,' he said impatiently.

'All right.' Aoife sighed. 'Hi,' she said, getting into the role of eager fan, 'I was wondering if I could have a quick word with the band.'

'No, that won't be possible,' Rory said.

'Why not?'

'Because I don't like your hair.'

'Ah, Rory,' Aoife protested. 'They're not going to say they don't like my hair!'

'Well, they would if they were any friends of yours.'

'Well, they're not. What's wrong with it, anyway?' Aoife asked, self-consciously patting her head.

'Nothing a brush couldn't sort out.'

'I did brush it!' Aoife protested.

'All right, babe, whatever.' Rory stopped suddenly.

'Look!' He pointed down at a group of people huddled under lights and surrounded by cameras.

'Oh my God, Rory, it's them – it's actually them.' They could see U2 leaning against a trailer; they had attracted a fair crowd. Aoife looked over at Rory. 'There's quite a lot of people there, but wouldn't you think it'd be mobbed?'

'Oh, you know what Dubliners are like. Everyone'd like to have a good look, but they'll all walk past and pretend they're not bothered.'

Aoife still thought something odd was going on. She ran ahead, leaving Rory sauntering behind. She returned a minute later, a look of resignation on her face.

'What's wrong?'

'It's a fecking cover band, that's what's wrong!' Aoife said, shaking her head.

Rory blurted out a laugh of disbelief. 'A cover band? Honestly?'

'Yes, honestly. I don't know why I thought it would be the real thing – I mean, we haven't had the best success rate so far, have we?'

'Come on,' Rory said, grabbing Aoife by the sleeve. 'Let's go talk to them anyway. I'll give you a tenner if you talk to the pretend Bono.'

The cover band was a Liverpool outfit called YoosTwos. The lead singer was dressed in leather trousers, a see-through blouse and huge plastic shades that nearly covered his entire face. He looked like he was just off to do some welding.

There didn't seem to be too much singing or filming going on. Aoife asked one of the cameramen what the story was. Apparently Paul McGuinness's PA hadn't lied to her just to get rid of her. It was a U2 video, of sorts. For their soon-to-be-released single, they were getting ten different U2 cover bands around the world to perform the song, and then they were going to cut it together with the real U2 singing.

After much pushing and jostling, Aoife managed to make it across to the lead singer, who was sitting on a speaker, trying to look melancholy and mysterious.

'Hi,' she said, offering him a smile. He pulled down his wraparound shades ever so slightly and looked at her as if she had just said something outrageously stupid. 'I was just wondering what it was like pretending to be Bono all the time.' She thought she might as well give him something to warrant the look.

'I don't pretend to be Bono; I *am* Bono.' He paused for dramatic effect. 'Well, as near to Bono as it's possible to be without actually being him.'

'Riiight,' said Aoife. 'And how do you do that, exactly?'

'I just get into his mindset.' He stared at her.

'What does getting into the mindset of Bono entail?'

'Are you a reporter?' the man asked suspiciously.

'Yeah,' Aoife said quickly, 'I work for *Hot Press*.'

'Where's your press pass?'

'Em …' Aoife stammered, rifling round in her bag. She found her out-of-date USIT card, which she kept to remind herself that she was no longer a Young Person and therefore should be doing something about not acting like a Young Person. She ignored its nagging reminder and flashed the card – which had a picture of her looking like an axe murderer – at pseudo-Bono. He seemed satisfied.

'I can be anywhere, and all I have to think is, "How would Bono handle this?" – and I'm transported; I am him again,' the man drawled in a fake mid-Atlantic accent.

'What, even when you're at the supermarket, like?' Aoife knew she was being flippant, but she wasn't too bothered.

'Look, are you going to ask me something sensible?'

Aoife pulled an embarrassed face and said, 'No, that'll do for now.' Faux Bono pushed his glasses up and got back to looking melancholy and serene. Aoife pushed her way back to Rory.

'Gobshite!' she said.

'Who, me or him?' Rory asked.

'Him, of course.'

'Why?'

'Thinks he's Bono.'

'Under the circumstances, that seems fair enough.'

'Come on; I can't be bothered hanging around here,' Aoife said. 'Let's head back. I've got loads to do today.'

'Such as calling Mari Byrne?' Rory asked.

'I was thinking about that.'

'Well?' Rory persisted.

'Well, she's a very busy woman and I'm sure she sees dress designers all the time – and I don't want to hound the poor woman till she's sick of hearing from me. I'm just going to wait until next week, and then, if she hasn't called me, I'll give her a call. I want to concentrate on getting my mother out of Dublin first; then I'll think about Mari.'

'Pathetic excuse.'

'Shut up, Rory.' Secretly, Aoife would have loved to call Mari up casually and ask how it was going, but the idea sent the fear of rejection flying through her at a rate of knots.

Rory took one last look over his shoulder at the pretenders to the U2 throne. 'Sure you don't want to stay and watch your friend perform?'

'Not really. I think I'll wait for the real thing.'

'Maybe they're "even better than the real thing" – d'you get it?' Rory said, pushing Aoife.

'God, Rory, shut the feck up, will you?' she groaned, nudging him affectionately up the street.

Chapter Thirty-Four

Rory pulled the back of his hand across his forehead, wiping the sweat away before it ran into his eyes. He looked out onto the sea of people crammed into Spy, applauding him as he finished his set, and smiled in bashful disbelief. He felt fantastic.

He stepped back from the decks as Billy Wilde took the stage. Billy slapped Rory on the back. 'You brought the house down,' he told him with a wink. Rory nearly turned inside out with pride.

He wasn't under any illusion that everyone there was there for him. Billy Wilde was a top New York DJ; he could play anywhere in the world and pack the place out. But Rory was thrilled to be his warm-up act, and he knew the applause he was receiving was genuine. As he stepped onto the floor of the bar, he was besieged by people slapping his back and shaking his hand. *I must have done something right,* he thought.

His nerves were gradually improving, too: he had been sick only twice before he went on. Aoife wasn't there to provide moral support – she was working – but two old friends of Rory's, Gavin and Dave, had been at the front of the crowd, yelling encouragement. Rory, Gavin and Dave had been in school together, and they had all faced the difficult realisation that they were gay, and the struggle to come out, around the same time. Gavin had been Rory's first boyfriend.

Gavin stood with Dave and Neil, Dave's boyfriend, holding up a fresh bottle of beer for the triumphant DJ. He squeezed Rory's shoulder. 'That went well enough, didn't it?'

'Not bad at all, even if I say so myself,' Rory agreed, gratefully accepting the beer.

'You were brilliant, Rory,' Neil said.

'Yeah, Rory,' Dave joined in. 'I don't know why you want to go and work for your dad when you know that you can do this for a living.'

There was an uncomfortable silence before Rory replied.

'This is great, Dave, but it's not forever. People are fickle. Unless you're a really big name, it's hard to keep making a living at it.'

'But it'll do for now, sure,' Gavin said, trying to lighten the mood.

'It will indeed,' Rory said.

He thought about the work he had done for his father over the past few days. He had decided to present his father with four categories: necessities, labour-saving devices, luxuries and leisure-related spending. He reckoned that, from there, he would be able to gather some statistics that his father might find useful. He had taken Gavin and Dave out for lunch, and together they had drawn up a list of things that they believed fitted the spending pattern of the average gay man in Dublin.

But Rory wasn't under any illusion. He realised that the information he gave his father would, in all probability, never be used. Eoin O'Donnell was both market-savvy himself and too conservative to throw caution to the wind and make a crucial business move on the basis of a few charts and a PowerPoint display delivered by his son. What this was, Rory realised, was a test. He had to demonstrate to his father that he was capable of the task, and then Eoin would let him tackle something bigger.

But the truth was, he didn't really want to work with his father. DJ-ing was what he really wanted to do. He would have to work hard, and he wouldn't be guaranteed an income; but at least he knew, by the reaction of the people who heard him, whether his work was genuinely good or bad. However, Rory also knew that he was, as he had always been, desperate to live up to his father's ever-changing expectations.... He dismissed the thoughts; he wanted to enjoy the rest of the evening and not worry about his dad.

Rory enjoyed his newly revived status, while the

other three proudly basked in his reflected glory. Dave came back from the bar with a round of drinks and asked Rory, 'Where's Aoife this evening?'

'She's working.' Thinking of Aoife, Rory suddenly asked, 'None of you would happen to have a way of meeting Bono, would you?'

There was a burst of laughter from the others.

'He's always round at my house.'

'I'll just give him a ring.'

'He hasn't been in touch for a while; I think he's fallen out with me.'

Rory rolled his eyes. 'All right, I know it sounds like a bit of a stupid question. But I wanted to lend that stubborn wagon Aoife some money, and she won't let me, so – as always – I'm having to wrap it up as something else.'

'Not another bet!' Gavin laughed.

Rory nodded wryly. The lads had heard all the bet stories before. 'Yeah, but this time it's serious: it's for five thousand euros.'

'What?' Dave nearly choked on his pint. 'Five grand? Are you mad?'

'The thing is, she's up to her eyeballs in debt. I've worked it out, and if she had five grand she'd be sorted, rather than constantly being broke,' Rory explained. 'And I want her to have it. She's my best mate; she'd do anything for me.' The others nodded. All three knew how much Aoife meant to him.

'So what's Bono got to do with it?' Gavin asked.

Rory grinned and told them about the bet.

'I love it!' Gavin exclaimed. 'It's so true! Don't you remember when I worked in Four Star Pizza, when we were at school, and I had to deliver the pizza to his house? There I was, waiting for someone to come to the gate of this big fuck-off house in Killiney – and when they finally do, it's fecking Bono! Takes the pepperoni pizza, pockets the two Cokes and gives me a tenner tip. God bless him. I nearly wet myself, 'cause I was just after queuing up outside Virgin to buy *Achtung Baby*.'

'Oh yeah!' Rory said. 'I'd forgotten about that.'

'I've never met him,' Neil admitted. 'But you know Tommy Calver?' The others shook their heads. 'You do; he used to go out with that fella – you know, the playwright.' Still no recognition. 'Used to own the music shop on Camden Street?' The others nodded at last. 'Well, he sold Bono his first microphone, back in the seventies.'

'Go 'way,' Dave said.

'He did, too.' Neil nodded solemnly, pleased with himself.

'Well, I'm sorry to disappoint you, but my Bono story is shite,' Dave admitted.

'That's not the point,' Rory told him. 'The point is that you've got one. Go on, tell us.'

'He drove past me with a Christmas tree hanging out of the back of his car. It was definitely him, though.'

'Is that it?' Gavin asked disparagingly.

'I said it was shite. What did you expect? "Actually, lads, that reminds me, I forgot to mention that I once sang a duet with Bono at Radio City"? He just drove past me with a Christmas tree.'

As Rory was laughing, he felt a tap on his shoulder. It was Billy Wilde, who had finished his set and had, predictably, been brilliant. Rory introduced him to the lads, who did little to hide the fact that they were impressed to be hobnobbing with the DJ-ing élite.

'Rory, great set,' Billy said.

'Thanks. You weren't too bad yourself.' Rory offered Billy a spare seat next to him.

'No, I won't; can't stop for long. Going to a party at a place called Shallow – do you know it?'

'Yeah, I do.' Rory nodded nonchalantly. Shallow was a new VIP club. You were allowed through the door only if you'd been nominated for an Oscar at least twice or had at least three chart-topping albums under your belt.

'Are you and your friends coming? I want to talk to you about the possibility of doing a few gigs in New York. You know how the Americans are suckers for the Irish. I think you'd go down great.'

'Em … that'd be brilliant,' Rory said, trying to control his excitement enough that he wouldn't sound like a fourteen-year-old whose voice was breaking. 'I'd need to talk to Tem about it; he's got some things lined up for me.'

'No need; it was Tem who suggested it to me. He says you're the hottest DJ on the Irish club circuit.'

Rory stifled a laugh of disbelief: he'd done only two gigs, and Tem was working his magic already. 'He did, did he?' he asked, as casually as he could under the circumstances. The other three, sensing something was up, had stopped their own conversations and turned their attention to Rory's.

'He did,' Billy confirmed. He looked at the other three and said, 'Might see you down there. Nice to meet you.' And he went on his way.

'So what was all that about?' Gavin asked.

Rory shook his head in disbelief. 'He wants me to play in New York,' he told them simply, his face breaking into a huge grin.

Chapter Thirty-Five

Aoife had spent the last few days on autopilot. She had loathed the fact that she had to go to work when she felt so desperate, but now she was thankful for it: if she had been at home, she thought, she might have gone mad.

As she scribbled down an order (from two women who, after putting away huge main courses, were now ordering *crème brûlée* with all the self-beration of lapsed crack addicts), she saw someone trying to get her attention outside the window of the restaurant.

She felt her throat dry up and her heart began to pound. Quickly pocketing her pad and pen, she headed to the door.

Paul reached out to hug her, but she pulled back. 'I've been trying to get hold of you,' he said, 'but there's been no answer. What's wrong? Has something happened? I went to the flat, but there was no one there, so I thought I might catch you here….' His voice trailed off as he saw the look on Aoife's face.

'On your way home to Mountjoy Square?'

Confusion flashed across Paul's face, and was instantly replaced by realisation. 'Oh, God.' He rubbed his temple. 'Who told you?'

'Never mind who told me. Is it true?'

'Yeah ... yeah, it is,' Paul said, his head bowed. 'Look, Aoife ... I'm sorry I lied about that. It's just that I am moving soon, and things have been rough at home –'

'So I believe,' Aoife said coldly.

'How did you know, though?' Paul asked again.

'If you must know, Rory followed you the other day.'

'He did *what*? Who the fuck is he to be following me around?' Paul shouted.

'He's my best friend,' Aoife spat back. 'And anyway, it was your mother who told him.'

'My mother?' Paul shook his head. 'And what exactly did she have to say, the stirring old bitch?'

'Old bitch? Paul, I had a right to know you were lying to me.'

The door of the restaurant opened and Martin popped his head out. 'Everything all right here?' he asked, looking sternly at Aoife.

'Yes, fine, Martin – sorry. I'm just coming in.'

'Aoife, look.... I'm sorry I lied, but you shouldn't have your friends following me.' Paul ran his fingers through his hair. 'Can we just meet up tomorrow and have a chat about it?'

'No, Paul, we cannot. I don't want to see you again. You're a liar and I don't want anything more to do with you.'

'This is ridiculous. You're completely overreacting.'

'Overreacting?' Aoife spat at him, opening the door of the restaurant. 'If you think I'm *overreacting*, then I think you need to ask yourself a few questions.'

She shut the door behind her and felt her knees go weak. She heard Paul shout, 'What the hell is that supposed to mean?' She was going to have to be strong enough to get through this. People split up all the time, Aoife told herself, nodding to a table who were signalling for the bill. And people got through it.

She glanced back at the door and caught a glimpse of Paul, still staring angrily at the door of the restaurant. She had thought she was starting to get over him, but she suddenly realised, as the weight of her feelings hit her like a ton of bricks in the stomach, that she was just as hurt and angry as she had been when Rory first told her the truth. She wanted to vomit; she wanted to hide. She certainly didn't want to bring customers their bill with a nice happy 'Thank you!' As she tried to compose herself on her way to the till, Aoife knew that she didn't know the first thing about getting over a broken heart.

Chapter Thirty-Six

Jimmy wove his way back from the counter of the National Gallery's coffee shop with two cups of coffee and two scones.

'There you go, missus,' he said, smiling at Bridie with a twinkle in his eye.

'Thank you; ooh, currant scones, my favourite!'

'So did you like the pictures?' Jimmy asked, pouring milk into his coffee.

'I like the one of the fellas swimming down the Liffey; it reminds me of the summer swim back home.'

Jimmy laughed. 'Do you remember when I won that?'

'I do indeed. How could I forget? My father kept saying, "The bloody Grogans, I tell you they're up to no good," as if you'd somehow fixed it to be the strongest swimmer. I remember having to sneak away to meet you later; if I had come up and congratulated you, God forbid, like everyone else was doing, my father would have had me shot. Ridiculous, how he used to look down on your family just because you didn't have a farm.'

'He wasn't the only one, Bridget. Nearly everyone in Kilbane thought my family was a set of knackers.'

'Ah, now, I wouldn't go that far –' Bridie began, but Jimmy didn't let her finish.

'They did, and well you know it. Your father was just more outspoken than most, that's all. He was some man for one man, your father.'

'The man was an old eejit, most of the time,' Bridie said. The words were as much of a shock to her as to Jimmy. Jimmy looked at her, stunned. Bridie blessed herself. She felt terrible that she had just said something bad about a man who could not defend himself, but she still thought that her father had played a large role in keeping her and Jimmy apart. She decided to change the subject.

'I'm looking forward to this evening.' They were meeting Aoife at Eden in Temple Bar.

Jimmy looked up from his scone. 'Actually, I'm very nervous about the whole thing.'

'Not at all,' Bridie said. 'She'll think you're great. She was always on at me about looking after Roddy all the time and not getting out more myself. Anyway, what's there to be nervous about?'

'Oh, nothing – I'm just meeting the daughter of the woman I once thought I'd be spending my life with, that's all.' Jimmy tried to make light of it, but what he said prompted Bridie to put her hand across the table and touch his wrist.

'Come on, you big yoke,' she cajoled. 'You'll get on great. She's a lovely girl.' Bridie was deliberately avoiding the meaning of what Jimmy had said. In meeting Aoife, he was being confronted with what might have been, and it was something he was right to be nervous about.

Rory sat at the kitchen table, surrounded by bits of paper, a laptop, notes that he had made at his lunch with Dave and Gavin, and print-outs of web pages about the 'Pink Pound' and the 'Dorothy Dollar' around the globe. He was just getting his teeth into his presentation when the intercom buzzed.

'Hello?'

'Ah ... hello there! Hello there! Are you there? Hello there!' *Fuck*, thought Rory; *it's Aoife's bloody Roddy.*

'Roddy, is that you?' he asked, hoping to God he was mistaken.

'That's right, that's right – is this thing an answering machine? If so, I'm looking for Aoife Collins....'

'Christ!' Rory said, slamming down the receiver and heading to the door.

Roddy was standing outside, looking like a fish out of water. 'Hello there ... I was ... I was looking for Aoife Collins,' he stammered.

'She's upstairs. I'm her friend, Rory. We've met before; I came down to Kerry a couple of times.' Rory watched, with a mixture of annoyance and pleasure, as the realisation dawned on Roddy that he was talking to a bona fide homosexual.

'Oh … yes, I remember now. I think I saw you all right.'

'You did.' Rory decided that he was going to enjoy this. 'You told Aoife I had a funny way with me.'

He took a good look at Roddy, just to unnerve him. He had always been very well presented, the couple of times Rory had had the pleasure of meeting him, but now he looked like a wreck. He had bits of beard shooting out all over the place, giving him the look of a small woodland creature, and his shirt looked like it and its owner had been dragged through a hedge backwards.

'I suppose you'd better come on up,' Rory said.

'Well, Roddy, you found the place all right,' Aoife said as they entered the apartment. She gave him a less-than-enthusiastic kiss on the cheek.

'I did.' 'He did.' Rory and Roddy said simultaneously.

Looking at Roddy, Aoife realised that she couldn't think of a time when she had seen him without her mother. There must have been times, of course, when she had bumped into him on the way to the shop, or when her mother was out and he had come to the house; but they hadn't stuck in her mind. As odd as they seemed together, Aoife saw her mother and Roddy as a couple. Without Bridie, Roddy looked abandoned. He definitely wasn't as full of himself as he usually was.

Aoife checked her watch; it was five o'clock. 'Roddy, are you going to be all right if I leave you to it while I have a shower and stuff? We'll get a taxi about a quarter past seven.'

'Fine, not a bother. You have told your mother I'm here, haven't you?' Roddy said.

'No … I thought it might be a nice surprise – show her how much you care,' Aoife said, catching Rory's eye.

'Ah, here now,' Roddy complained. 'Don't you be letting her think that I've come running up here after her because I … I…'

'Care?' Rory offered.

Roddy nodded at him as if he'd hit the nail on the head. '… About her,' he finished.

'So you don't *care* about her?' Rory goaded. 'Then what are you doing here?'

Roddy gave him a venomous stare. 'I'm here because I think the woman needs to come to her senses and come home.' To Aoife, this was as near as he was ever going to get to an admission that he cared about her mother. But Rory obviously didn't think it was good enough.

'What makes you so sure she wants to go home?' he asked.

'Rory!' Aoife stage-whispered through clenched teeth. It wasn't only Roddy who didn't want to hear this.

301

'What?' He stared blankly at her. 'I just think that, if your mother's enjoying a taste of freedom, the last thing she needs is Roddy coming up here and telling her to go home and wash and iron for him.'

'Now you listen here, young fella –' Roddy wagged his finger at Rory.

Rory, who had had his fill of fun with Roddy for the time being, gave him his sweetest smile. 'I'm sure you'll get on grand, Roddy,' he said. 'Bridie will be delighted to see you, I'm sure.'

Chapter Thirty-Seven

Eden was hopping. All of the tables were full, and there were people crowded around the bar waiting to be seated. Aoife was finding it difficult to maintain small talk with Roddy, who was getting increasingly agitated as it got nearer to the time that they had arranged to meet Bridie.

'Table for Collins,' Aoife told the waiter who greeted them.

He looked down his list. 'Ah, yeah – table for four, is that right?'

'Yeah,' Aoife said, as Roddy shuffled behind her.

'Who else is coming with your mother?' Roddy asked, as he wriggled into his seat

'Might be Sister Immaculata, although I can't really see her in here,' Aoife said, thinking on her feet. Looking around at the trendy interior, she didn't think this was exactly Roddy's scene either; the fact that women were allowed in and that it had tablecloths

were making him twitch nervously. 'Or Mrs Reagan –
she's the housekeeper at the convent; she and Mammy
seem to get on very well. Will you have a drink?'

'A Guinness.'

'A Guinness and a dry white wine, thanks,' Aoife
told the waitress. 'You all right, Roddy?'

'Fine, fine; this place is like a swimming bath.' Aoife
shook her head; there was no helping some people.
Roddy was referring to the little white tiles that
decorated the walls.

They sat in silence, pretending to read the menu,
and keeping an eye on the door. It was then that Aoife
was struck with panic. She realised that she really had
to brief Roddy on who her mother was bringing;
otherwise he would feel foolish. Up until that moment,
Aoife hadn't considered Roddy's feelings, ever. She'd
never even thought about his having any.

'Look, Roddy, there's something I need to tell you –'

Roddy was busy throwing his tie over his shoulder
and tucking his napkin into the collar of his shirt.
'What's that, then?'

But it was too late. Aoife saw Bridie first; she was
giving her name to the waiter at the door. 'It doesn't
matter. She's here now; she can tell you herself.'

Roddy stood up, nearly sending the table flying, and
tried to get out and go over to Bridie.

'They'll show her to the table, Roddy; sit yourself
down,' Aoife instructed him. She could have sworn,

from his behaviour, that the man had never been out in public before.

Aoife had expected to feel a glow of self-congratulation at this moment. *Wait until she sees Roddy sitting there*, she had thought virtuously to herself during the week; *she'll be over the moon that I've arranged this for her.* But, suddenly, she had an overwhelming feeling of dread that she had done the wrong thing entirely. As Bridie turned to face them, with a man in tow who was obviously Jimmy, time, for Aoife, seemed to stop. For an eternal moment, she felt as if she had stepped outside of herself and was looking at the stunned faces of her mother, her companion, Roddy and herself.

Then she was flung back into her body, shocked into saying something. 'Ma, I ... I brought Roddy to Dublin ... as a surprise.'

'I can see that,' Bridie said quietly, glancing at her companion.

He stuck out his hand. 'Roddy, long time no see. How are you?'

Roddy slowly wiped his right hand on his trouser leg and put it out to shake the other man's. 'Well, Jimmy; and yourself?' he asked, visibly shaken.

'Oh, can't complain.' The man turned his attention to Aoife. 'You must be Aoife,' he said. 'I'm Jimmy – an old friend of your mother's.'

Aoife managed a weak, 'Pleased to meet you.' As

Jimmy's huge hand took hers and shook it gently, she noticed how he towered over Roddy.

'Likewise,' Jimmy said.

They all sat down uncomfortably. When someone eventually spoke, it was Bridie. 'Well, Roddy, did you get here all right? The traffic all right, was it?' she asked, tight-lipped.

Roddy nodded meekly. 'Oh, you know the way this country is – sure, the roads are ridiculous; someone in the government wants to take a drive down the country one day and see how it is, rather than flying down there in helicopters.' His voice was almost inaudible and the feistiness was gone from his signature traffic speech.

'You're right there, Roddy,' Jimmy agreed. 'Sure, if the roads are the spine of a country, then Ireland's in traction with a broken back.' They all laughed uncomfortably.

'It was bad coming up through Littleton today,' Roddy said, looking back at his menu for the eightieth time.

Aoife was eyeing her mother. She hadn't said a word about Roddy's unexpected presence, and Aoife was hoping that she might have got away with it. But the way Bridie was pursing her lips indicated that this might not be the case.

'It's just the one road, and you've had it if you get stuck behind a tractor,' Roddy continued his soliloquy. Bridie glanced up abruptly from her menu, and Aoife saw anger in her eyes.

'Right,' Bridie announced. 'I've had enough of this.'
Aoife felt the colour drain from her face. 'What in the
hell is going on here, my girl, if you don't mind me
asking?'

'What do you mean?' Aoife asked, barely able to
meet her mother's eyes.

'I mean you dragging Roddy all the way here
without even telling me. And, as far as I can tell, you
didn't tell him Jimmy was coming, either. Is that right,
Roddy?'

'No,' he said quietly, 'I didn't have a clue.'

Aoife was beginning to feel a complete fool; but,
rather than giving in gracefully, she tried to turn the
tables.

'I just wanted you to see sense – to see that you're
running around like a teenager up here, when you
belong in Kerry.' The words were out of Aoife's mouth
before she had time to consider what a child she was
being.

'I belong in Kerry?' Bridie asked, her voice almost
inaudible with rage. 'Is that what you think?' She
turned to Jimmy and Roddy. 'Will you excuse us,
gentlemen? I think I need to have a conversation in
private with this girl of mine.' Without waiting for
Aoife, Bridie got up from the table and headed out of
the restaurant.

Aoife couldn't see where her mother had gone, but
as she stepped out into the cool night, a hand grabbed
her elbow and pulled her across the square outside the

restaurant. 'Sit there,' Bridie instructed her daughter, forcing her onto a bench by the Arts Centre.

'Ow, Mammy, you're hurting me!' Aoife complained.

'I'll give you "Ow, Mammy, you're hurting me" if you don't quiet down. Now you stay there and listen to me, my girl.'

Aoife was scared. She could not remember a time in her life when she had been scared of her mother. Bridie had shouted at her, made her stay in for being naughty, taken away her spending money, even clipped her round the ear on a good few occasions; but nothing she had done in the past had ever made Aoife feel really scared. Now, though, Bridie obviously meant business, and Aoife was petrified.

'I have always done what was right for you. I've always put you and Michael – and, to a great extent, Roddy – before myself.' Aoife was thinking, *Especially Roddy*, but she decided not to voice this opinion. 'But I am a person, you know. I don't exist just through my connection with you, or Michael, or Roddy – despite what you might think, my girl.'

Aoife felt tears well up in her eyes. Bridie was right: she never treated her as an individual – she was always just her ma. She felt foolish and ashamed; but, at the same time, her argumentative streak was thinking that Bridie had never demanded to be treated as anything other than an extension of her family.

'Mam, I'm sorry. I'm sorry you feel like that. I know

308

I always treated you as my mammy, but you *are* my mammy.' Aoife tried to keep the whine out of her voice.

'I am, but I'm also Bridie Devoy, and that's something I have to remember now and again.

Hearing her mother use her maiden name made Aoife balk. 'Is that it, then? Are you just going to abandon Roddy to look after himself while you go off with your new boyfriend?'

Bridie's eyes narrowed. She said in a low, measured, angry rasp, 'How dare you?'

Aoife knew she'd overstepped the mark.

'How dare you? I have looked after Roddy since I was married to your father – washed for him, cooked for him, cleaned for him, peeled his spuds for him, even poured his bloody tea for him.' She drew breath. 'And you!' Aoife sat up as if the words had pinned her back to the bench. 'You are the one who always said I shouldn't. And I knew that, girl. I knew that all right; but it was just the way that things happened over time, and I couldn't very well just stop.' Aoife opened her mouth to say something, but her mother ploughed on. 'And yet now you sit here and tell me that I'm abandoning him, like he's a child who can't look after himself. Well, I'll tell you who's got the problem, Aoife Collins, and it's not Roddy; it's you.'

Aoife felt a lump rise in her throat.

'What have I done? I just brought him up here because I thought it would make you happy.' She could definitely hear herself whining, and it sounded pathetic.

'The problem is that you have never once thought that I was – and am – someone other than your mother.'

Aoife, unable to argue with this, fell silent. She couldn't believe all this was happening. Half of her wanted to apologise, but the other half wanted a fight.

'Well, who is this Jimmy, anyway?' she demanded. 'Just because you shifted him once doesn't mean that you can just forget who you are.'

Bridie shook her head. It was as if she had used up all her anger and just wanted to get through to her daughter in the quickest and simplest way she could. 'Aoife,' she said slowly. 'Are you listening to what I'm saying, or are you just listening to what you want to hear?'

'Yes, I'm listening.' Aoife sniffed.

'You say I'm forgetting who I am. Well, do you want me to set the record straight and tell you about me and Jimmy, or are you just going to sit there bawling like a baby?'

At the suggestion that Aoife was crying, she began to do just that. Bridie exhaled sharply and got to her feet.

'Mammy?' Aoife said, rubbing her nose. 'Will you tell me?'

Bridie sighed, sitting down again, and started to talk. She and Jimmy had been childhood sweethearts for two years, but they had never been able to tell anyone. Jimmy was from a family that was looked down upon in Kilbane. His mother had died in labour at the birth of her tenth child, and his father was a terrible alcoholic. The kids were left to bring themselves up – and a fine job they did of it, under the circumstances; the eldest sister, Theresa, was mother enough for all of them. This, however, didn't stop people like Bridie's father looking down their noses at Jimmy's family. He would happily have the Grogan boys work for him on the farm when he needed cheap labour, but he always kept a suspicious eye on them and would barely acknowledge them in the street.

While Jimmy was working for the Devoys, he and Bridie had struck up a romance. For two years, they had carried on a clandestine relationship, meeting on the beach and going for cycles. But, as Bridie told Aoife, 'There's only so many times you can cycle round the Ring of Kerry with some fella your father doesn't like before word gets back to him.' They knew they could never be together in Kilbane, so they decided to run away.

Jimmy was eighteen by this time, and he wanted to leave Kilbane, as most of his brothers and sisters had before him. But he didn't want to go abroad; he wanted to work in his own country. He wanted to head for Dublin. And, through much cajoling, he managed to persuade the seventeen-year-old Bridie to accompany him.

They had left in the early hours of the morning; a friend of Jimmy's had driven them up. Bridie had been terrified.

When they arrived in Dublin, she had naïvely thought that it was the start of a new, exciting life; but things weren't as they should have been. They had been promised lodgings, which turned out to be non-existent. One of Jimmy's friends said that they could share his place, an unholy one-room kip on Harcourt Street.

Bridie had hated the place instantly. But it was more than that: she felt terribly guilty – guilty because she'd left her family; guilty because she knew they would have to cope with the shame of her running away, and with a Grogan, no less; guilty that she hadn't told anyone where she was going or what she was doing. She lasted five days.

Aoife, who had been listening quietly, felt as if she was, for the first time in her life, thinking seriously about the time before she was born. Of course, she had thought about life before she had come along – when she was in History class, or when her mother had talked about what Kilbane used to be like; but it had never really meant much to her. She realised that she had the Year of Aoife etched into her consciousness as the beginning of time. She felt an overwhelming sense of remorse as she looked at Bridie, for the first time, as someone other than her mammy.

'Ma, I'm sorry,' she sobbed. 'I really am.'

Bridie's eyes were glistening. 'Don't be sorry,' she said, shaking her head. 'Just don't tell me what I can and can't do.' She rummaged around in her handbag and produced a tissue, licked it and wiped it under Aoife's eyes. Aoife started laughing through her tears.

'What happened when you got back home?' she asked tentatively, once she had composed herself.

'Well, my name was mud, as I'm sure you can imagine. My father didn't speak to me for a good few years, and there were whispers in the town every time I went anywhere. It was a terrible time.'

'What about Daddy? Did he know about all of this?'

'He did, of course. He was a great man, your father. He asked me to the dance in the church hall a few weeks after I got back from Dublin; he said that everyone else should mind their own business. I didn't go, of course. It was another few years before I went anywhere with him; I was too heartbroken about the whole other business.

'It took a good while, but once it was official that your father and I were walking out together, the gossiping stopped, and your grandfather stopped threatening to send me away to the Sisters. People got bored of the story – although I do get the odd comment even now. Patricia Cleary, your one in the hairdresser's, mentioned Dublin to me only the other year, and nearly died the minute she realised what she'd said; tripping over herself with apologies, she was. I told her to stop being so ridiculous. But I suppose no one would ever have mentioned it around you or your brother.'

'Didn't you want to contact Jimmy before now?' Aoife asked.

'I did, of course, but it wasn't like nowadays where you have mobile phones and computers and the like. All for the best, really. It would have done neither of us any good. I couldn't live away from Kilbane and Jimmy couldn't live there, and no amount of letter-writing in the world would have changed that.'

'And you've never seen him since?' Aoife asked.

'I have not!' Bridie said indignantly. 'I was a married woman. He came home for his daddy's funeral but I didn't go – unlike the rest of the hypocrites in Kilbane.' She laughed. 'Anyway, I was heavily pregnant with you.'

'And did you love Jimmy more than Daddy?' Aoife asked, curiosity getting the better of her. As soon as she had said it, she was embarrassed.

'That's unfair, Aoife. They were two very different men. But' – Bridie nodded her head slowly – 'I did love the both of them. That's all I can really say.'

Aoife thought that she should have some reaction to this, that she should in some way be defending her father's memory. But she didn't feel anything; what her mother said made perfect sense. Aoife realised that this was probably the first real adult conversation she had ever had with her mother, and the one thing she did feel was relief.

The two women sat in silence for a minute or two. Then Bridie said, 'Come on. Let's get you back in the restaurant.'

They both stood up. 'Aoife,' Bridie said. Aoife turned to face her. 'Come here, girleen; give your mother an old hug.' She pulled her daughter close and squeezed her, then pulled her back and smoothed her hair. 'Come on, now; let's go inside and enjoy the meal. Roddy's probably told Jimmy about every road from here to Killarney by now.'

As they reached the door, Bridie said, as if remembering something, 'Oh, and Aoife – I've no intention of staying in Dublin. I want to go back to Kerry; it's home and Dublin isn't.' She smiled at her daughter. 'If that's what you were worried about.'

'No – no, I just….' Aoife trailed off; there was no point in lying to her mother any more. She changed tack. 'What about Jimmy?'

'Well, I might just have a visitor now and again, that's all.'

'And what are you going to tell that one in the hairdresser's when she starts to gossip?' Aoife enquired.

'I'll tell her to mind her own business. Sure, haven't they enough to be talking about, without concerning themselves with me?' Bridie said. She linked arms with her daughter and marched proudly back into the restaurant, and Aoife smiled with a mixture of pride and relief.

Chapter Thirty-Eight

Rory arrived at O'Donnell Properties with his head stuffed full of facts, figures and worries. He was worried about what he was going to present to his father, how it would be received, what the implications would be for his burgeoning DJ career; he had nearly got beyond himself and called Tem to say that he might be working for him only for a short time. He had copped himself on in time, realising that he shouldn't burn his bridges; also, Tem was over the moon at the thought of Rory playing in New York.

Niamh was nowhere to be seen. It was Sunday afternoon, but Rory knew that Niamh was often dragged into the office over the weekend, to water the yukka plants or to make sure that Eoin hadn't accidentally put any of his ring binders next to his lever-arch folders. Rory knocked on the door of his father's office.

'Come!' bellowed Eoin.

'How are you, Dad?' Rory asked, self-consciously

proffering his laptop as if to say, 'Look, Daddy, I've got what you wanted!' He caught himself doing this and felt immediately ashamed.

'Good, good. I'd be even better if that secretary of mine could drag her sorry arse into work on time. Ten o'clock, she was meant to be here. Said she has a doctor's appointment. A doctor's appointment on a Sunday, I ask you.... I think she's just making excuses because she's on the rag.' Rory winced. 'So, what have you got for me?'

'Well, I've done a fair bit of research, and I've come up with a presentation for you to look at,' Rory said, setting his laptop down on the desk.

'Fire away, so.' Eoin sat back in his large leather chair. 'Did you have to talk to many fairies?'

Rory gritted his teeth and took a deep breath. 'Dad, could you try not to use words like "fairies"? I don't think it's going to do you any favours if you're trying to get a piece of the gay market.'

'Very touchy there, Rory; they haven't turned you, have they?' Eoin bellowed with laughter and slapped his son on the back. Rory tried to concentrate on setting up his presentation.

Making himself comfortable, Eoin put his feet up on the desk. He had a new executive toy to play with; it was a bouncy rubber ball with a tiny strobe light in it, and he was firing it at the wall and catching it, occasionally missing and nearly knocking the head off himself, much to his own amusement. By the time

Rory had his presentation set up, he felt tense and agitated, like a teacher trying to get the attention of the one unruly child who was disrupting the entire class.

'Right,' Rory said, putting up a slide that read, 'The Might of the Pink Pound.'

The change in the social climate in Ireland, Rory explained, meant that more people were willing to come out and admit that they were gay. The irony of what he was saying wasn't lost on him. He went on to explain that most gay people do not have children, and that, statistically, they have better-paid jobs than heterosexuals; so it stands to reason that they have more disposable income.

Rory was just displaying a slide that said, 'Areas of Growth Spending', when Eoin said, 'So did they all tell you about rent boys, going to saunas, buying dildos and the like?' Rory looked at him; he seemed to have developed some form of Tourette's syndrome.

'No,' Rory said. He was rapidly losing patience. 'I didn't realise you were thinking of going into the sex industry.'

'I'm not, but that's what they're all into, isn't it?'

Rory was sure that his father wasn't having a go at him personally, but it felt that way. His face burned bright red.

'I don't know what you mean, Dad. You asked me to do some research, and that's what I've –'

'Like you don't know.' Eoin was holding the strobing sphere up to his eyeball for inspection.

Rory felt his gut clench. 'Do you want to explain what you mean by that?'

Eoin set the ball down carefully, so it wouldn't roll off the desk, and looked up at his son. 'I mean,' he said, 'that I don't think you're too far off spending the "Pink Pound" yourself, are you?' His face twisted as he said 'Pink Pound', and he used his fingers to indicate inverted commas.

The fog of confusion in Rory's brain began to clear, and, as it did, he felt something inside him snap. He slammed down the lid of the laptop and shouted, 'All right – I'm gay! I admit it. I'm fucking gay! Are you happy now, are you?' He leant over the desk, his face nearly touching his father's. Eoin didn't flinch.

'Oh, yeah, I'm delighted that my son's a queer. Can't wait to tell the fellas down at the golf club.' He stood up, raising himself to his full six foot four. 'What the fuck do you think?'

'Is that what all this was about?' Rory asked, pointing at the laptop. 'This Pink Pound bullshit – was that all just to get me to say, "Yeah, actually, Dad, I'm gay"? Is that it?'

'For fuck's sake, boy, I've known for years! Do you take me for some kind of fool? But I thought if I left you to your own devices, you'd realise it was just a phase. But that doesn't seem to be happening, from what I've been told.' Eoin moved away from Rory, as if he couldn't bear to be in the same space as his son.

'From what you've been told?' Rory shouted in disbelief. 'Have you got someone watching me?'

'I know a lot of people in Dublin, and I don't want you out there making a fool of me.' Eoin's voice was menacing. It would usually have thrown Rory into submission, but not now.

'You don't need any help making a fool of yourself. And what do you mean, you've known for years?'

'I knew when you were at school. You and that Gavin fella that you used to pal around with – you weren't exactly football-team material, were you?'

Rory was staring at his father with utter disbelief and contempt. 'You knew?' He shook his head, unable to grasp what his father was saying. 'You knew, and you never said anything.'

'Ah, for feck's sake!' Eoin was evidently becoming exasperated. 'What was I going to say? "I think you're going through a queer phase"?'

'It's not a phase!' Rory shouted. 'Pink hair is a phase, skateboarding is a phase; listening to fucking Abba is a phase. But being gay is definitely, definitely not a fucking phase, Dad!'

A look of disdain came over Eoin's face; shaking his head, he snorted a laugh. 'No, it wouldn't be with you, would it? Always do what's right for Rory. Fuck the consequences. You don't give a rat's arse about anyone or anything other than yourself. You flaunt it round the place like the biggest fecking nancy-boy since Liberace, and I'm meant to sit back and let you do it, am I?'

Rory was incensed. 'I have never flaunted it! I'm not some mincy queen who shoves being gay in everyone's face.' He realised that he sounded as if he was trying to get his father on his side – something he was way past caring about. 'Not that it should matter if I did. And you … who the hell do you think you are? Dublin and his fucking granny knows about you and your affairs. You couldn't keep your straight fucking dick in your straight fucking trousers, all the time I was growing up. I was the one who had to listen to Mum crying because you were out on the town with some fucking floozy or other –'

'Out!' Eoin bellowed, from the bottom of his lungs. 'Get out of my sight, you ungrateful little bastard – out, now!' He stabbed the air with his finger. 'I've fed you, clothed you and all but wiped your arse for you, all of your life, and this is how you repay me. Get the fuck out of here!'

'I'm going, don't you worry.' Rory gathered his belongings up as quickly as he could.

'You could have been a part of all this!' Eoin shouted, waving his arms at the office as if it were the Kingdom of Heaven. 'But you just won't toe the line, will you?'

'And by toeing the line you mean being straight, don't you?' Rory's face was scrunched into an angry grimace.

'Is it too much to ask?' Eoin spat.

'What?' Rory yelled. He took a deep breath and lowered his voice. 'This is it, Dad; this is me. If you can't accept me as I am, then I'm sorry.'

Eoin stuffed his hands into his trouser pockets. 'Right, so, if that's the way you want it. I'll give you a month to find yourself a place, but I want your credit card and cash card now.' He held out his hand.

Rory fought hard to disguise his shock. 'Fine,' he said, rummaging in his pocket for his wallet. He fumbled to get the cards out and pressed them, hard, into his father's waiting palm.

Then he turned around and walked out, trying to hold his head up, slamming the door satisfactorily behind him. But it wasn't fine. It wasn't fine at all.

Chapter Thirty-Nine

When Aoife awoke on Sunday morning, she sat up in bed, mulling over the events of the previous evening. It was funny, she thought: at the end of it, it was Roddy she had felt sorry for. The man had annoyed her for as long as she could remember; and yet, as they sat there eating their meal, he had seemed like a child. They had all tried to include him in the conversation, but his responses had been stilted and flustered. He had even allowed himself to be press-ganged into staying at Jimmy's. *The face on Roddy,* Aoife thought; he would rather have sat on top of the Spike in the middle of O'Connell Street all night, but he couldn't seem to come up with a reason to refuse.

As she watched how happy Bridie and Jimmy were in each other's company, Aoife had thought she might feel a twinge of jealousy in support of her father's memory. Strangely, though, she hadn't. For all her sulking and performing, Aoife found that, now that her mother had been truthful with her, she was actually happy for her and Jimmy.

Roddy had gone off with Bridie and Jimmy, at the end of the evening, looking utterly bewildered. Jimmy had said that he would drop him at Aoife's the following day, to get his car, and Roddy had nodded in agreement. Bridie had said, 'Roddy, you'll be grand driving back on your own, won't you? I'll come back down at the beginning of next week.' Aoife had looked at the crestfallen Roddy and cringed for him all over again.

But, as she thought about it, Aoife realised that Roddy had made his own bed. His relationship with her mother had largely been one of convenience. And now, Bridie was over the moon with herself and Jimmy, and there wasn't much room for Roddy.

Aoife decided to get out of bed. Standing in the kitchen, she looked around, wondering what to have for breakfast. Rory had offered her some scrambled eggs earlier, but she hadn't been in the mood. He had been pacing nervously around, getting himself together for his meeting with his father.

As she pulled out some packets of cereal, the phone rang. Presuming it was Rory, she demanded, 'Well?'

'Hi, Aoife; it's Mari, Mari Byrne.' Aoife dropped the packet of Coco Pops.

'Mari, hi, how are you?'

'I'm sorry to ring you on a Sunday, but it's a good day for me to talk. I've had a fair bit of interest in your designs; I was wondering if you could come into the shop and we could have a chat,' Mari said.

'Yeah, that'd be fine,' Aoife said. She was trying to seem calm, but she sounded as if she had been sucking helium balloons.

'Great. How does two o'clock sound?'

'No problem,' Aoife said. 'I'll see you then.'

She checked that her phone was properly turned off; then she jumped onto an armchair and bounced up and down, shouting, 'Yes! Yes! Yes!'

By the time she had calmed down, about five minutes later, it occurred to her that she should probably go and apologise to the people in the apartments around her. But then she decided not to bother. If she was going to be a designer about town, she needed a reckless, avant-garde image.

'Glad you could come down at such short notice.' Mari greeted Aoife with a kiss on the cheek that surprised her and gave her a feeling of embarrassed glee.

'No problem; I wasn't doing much.' Aoife said, and then immediately regretted it: she wished she'd said that she'd been up all night, knocking out dresses by the truckload.

Mari gestured at the kimono dress, hanging on a rail. 'I have to tell you, Aoife, everyone who walks into the shop has asked about this piece.' Aoife felt butterflies of pure excitement wheeling in her stomach.

'One woman who came in yesterday nearly got down on her knees, trying to get me to sell it to her for a gala dinner.'

'Jaysus!' Aoife heard the word slip out before she realised she had said it. 'Sorry – I mean, that's great.'

'I know. I told her that this piece wasn't for direct sale, that we were just getting a feel for what people wanted; but she tried it on and it fitted her perfectly, so she asked me if you would consider selling it.'

'That's not a problem at all, except for the fact that it's been worn. I mean, I've worn it before. I don't know how she feels about second-hand clothes.' Aoife gave a nervous laugh.

'Oh, I told her that the designer had worn it; but you often find, with one-off pieces, that as long as it's not in rags, it doesn't matter.' Aoife had goosebumps of excitement. Mari went on, 'Desperate, she was. Going to that charity thing at Dublin Castle, with Bono and Bertie and Bob Geldof and the rest of them. There's nearly been fist-fights between women trying to get the most exclusive designs to wear; it'll be in all the glossy magazines, and they don't want to turn up wearing the same thing as someone else, God forbid.' Mari laughed; she'd seen it all before. But Aoife's mind was elsewhere.

'Bono?' she asked, trying to be as casual as possible. 'He's hosting some charity dinner, then?'

'He's not hosting it; he's just attending it, so I believe. It's for the Drop the Debt campaign that he's involved in. It's great, though, isn't it? He can get all those people to pay a thousand euro a ticket, and they'll all turn up and eat dry bits of duck because he's there. He's some man,' Mari said absentmindedly, fingering the hem of the kimono dress.

Aoife felt her heart sink slightly. Even though she now knew well in advance exactly where Bono would be on a particular evening, there was no way she could come up with a thousand euro, even if it meant getting five thousand in return. She couldn't get her hands on that sort of money – not unless she asked Rory, and that would defeat the whole purpose of the bet. Anyway, even if she had had the money, the chances were slim that someone as lowly as her would be allowed to obtain a ticket.

Then something struck her. Micky Callaghan, the deranged psychic, had said that she would meet Bono in a castle!

'Have you met him?' Aoife asked, even though she didn't really doubt what the answer would be.

'I have, a couple of times.' Mari nodded. 'He came in here looking for something for his wife, and walked out with a dress that he finished up wearing himself in one of their videos – I forget the name of the song. Imagine! You don't see many Irish fellas with enough courage to wear a frock, now, do you?'

Typical, Aoife thought. *Why can't he just walk through the door now and buy his wife something nice? Because I'm here,* she concluded.

327

'Now then,' Mari said, 'here's what I'd like you to do – if it fits in with your schedule.' Aoife suppressed a laugh. She didn't have a *schedule*. Liz Hurley had a *schedule*; what Aoife had was more like a winter timetable for a country bus. 'I think I need to put an order in with you.'

Mari told Aoife that she would take ten more dresses, in a variety of sizes and colours, and see how they sold. On the first garments, she would give her twenty-five per cent of the shop price. Aoife's heart sank – it didn't sound like much – but she perked up when Mari told her that the dresses would retail at five hundred euro each.

Mari pulled out some papers and passed them to Aoife. 'Once I see how the first stuff sells, then we should be able to draw up a contract. Here's an example – it's nothing fancy. It won't be a huge amount that I'll want from you, but it should be enough to get people talking.' She smiled at Aoife, who was still trying to take everything in. 'What do you think?'

'I think it's fantastic,' Aoife said, the enthusiasm in her voice bouncing off all four walls of the boutique. 'Thanks.' She beamed.

'Don't mention it. Would you be able to have the order ready by the end of the month?'

'I can have it done by the end of next week,' Aoife said immediately. She didn't care if she looked eager; she *was* eager.

'Well, don't kill yourself, but the sooner the better for me.' Mari stood up, and Aoife took this as her cue to leave. 'And I'll let the woman buy the dress for the gala dinner, will I?'

'Yeah, do; that'd be brilliant. It might even get a mention in *IT* or *VIP*,' Aoife joked.

Mari looked at her. 'I'd say that goes without saying. The woman who wanted the dress is Dervla Cannon.'

Aoife's legs nearly went from under her. Dervla Cannon was the daughter of an Irish racehorse-owner, and she was a favourite with the tabloids and broadsheets alike; she could barely stick her head out of her front door without someone sticking a camera up her nose and hoping to get her bad side. 'No!' Aoife gasped.

'Yes, but I don't want that to panic you. That's why I wanted to get the business stuff out of the way first. She's a lovely young woman, and she was very interested in your designs. And the beauty of it all is that you don't have to make any alterations. The dress fits her like a glove. But,' Mari added gently, 'don't think that this has made your career and you'll be opening Dublin Fashion Week next year; it's still just a start.'

'No, of course not! I realise that,' Aoife agreed.

'Good; that's good. Now then, anything else you need to ask me before I head off?'

'Yes,' Aoife said tentatively. 'This charity thing – what day and time is it, exactly?'

'It's Tuesday week, at eight, I think. Going to go to

the Castle and get a glimpse of her in the dress, are you?'

'Something like that,' Aoife said evasively.

'Not a snowball's chance in hell of getting a ticket; my other half was trying, through a friend of his in the Dáil, and they were like gold dust. But you might be able to see her if you wait outside.'

'Not a bad idea,' Aoife said. 'Look, Mari, thanks a million for this opportunity – and I promise to have the pieces to you by the end of next week.'

'Good luck, Aoife. I'll ring Dervla and tell her you said yes.'

As she left the boutique, Aoife felt a huge wave of euphoria wash over her. *Dervla fecking Cannon!* she wanted to yelp. She wanted to rush up to people in the street and tell them that, next time they were reading the *Sunday Independent* and saw Dervla Cannon staring out at them, looking gorgeous as always, the frock that she would be wearing would have been made by her, Aoife Collins.

Aoife drew a couple of stares from passers-by. Realising that she was actually skipping down the street, she slowed herself to a pace that was less likely to lead to a straitjacket, and headed towards Blues.

She wasn't working that evening, but she needed some help. She was almost sure she had a way of getting into Dublin Castle the following Tuesday.

'So all I have to do is go and sign up at this place on Wednesday, and they security-check me, and then I can work as a waitress for this out-catering place that does all the official functions! They're always desperate for staff, apparently.' Aoife hadn't drawn breath since she walked through the door. In the fifteen minutes she'd been home, she had told Rory, in animated, arm-waving detail, about her afternoon.

After her meeting with Mari, she had gone to Blues and talked to Martin; he had given her the number of a firm that organised outside catering events, and told her to give him as a reference. She had rung them and spoken to some woman called Róisín, who had told her that she needed to sign up at the Cellar Bar on Merrion Row. It was a formality, she told Aoife; with a reference from Blues, there was no way they wouldn't take her.

Aoife was delighted with herself – so delighted, in fact, that she had failed to notice the look on Rory's face. But, as she passed him a glass of kir royale (or, strictly speaking, a glass of sparkling wine with some Ribena in it) to celebrate her afternoon, she realised that he hadn't said a word since she had got in.

'What's up with you?' she demanded.

Rory placed his pretend champagne cocktail on the table, untouched. 'Aoife,' he said, 'I'm delighted for you, really I am.'

'Well, good; I'm glad to hear it.'

'But I've had the single most shit day of my life, and I really don't have anything to be celebrating.'

Aoife suddenly realised that he was close to tears.

'God, Rory....' She sat down next to him. 'Are you OK?'

'No, Aoife, I'm not OK. We're fucked,' he said simply. Then he began to tell her about his afternoon.

Chapter Forty

Aoife had been gutted when Rory told her about his meeting with his father – not because she was again going to have nowhere to live, but because Rory was so upset. For her, it was a pain in the backside to have to move out of the lovely apartment in Ballsbridge, but it had always felt a little too good to be true; she was probably better off in Dublin's less elegant post-codes (and price ranges). Anyway, she had been too busy with her sewing machine to panic about moving; she would cross that bridge when she came to it.

But she knew that Rory, on the other hand, was going to struggle. He had never had to support himself before. His bravado was keeping him aloft at the moment, but Aoife knew that the day he started a job – a proper job – it would all come crashing down. A very tiny bit of her was glad, in a way, that he was going to get a taste of what it was like to be a normal person; but this was far outweighed by the huge amount of sympathy she had for him.

It was Wednesday, and Aoife and Carmel were heading for the Cellar Bar, to sign up as catering staff for the charity dinner.

'Are you seriously going ahead with this bet?' Carmel asked. 'Now that Rory's penniless?'

'God, no – I'm not doing it for money any more. But, after all this, I'm not going to let the opportunity of a real Bono story pass me by. Anyway, if nothing else, it'll give Rory a bit of a laugh.' Aoife followed Carmel down the steps into the bar. 'Where to?'

'We're in here – first on the right. Some events company's doing all the organising, so this should only take a minute or two.'

'Great; I've got to get back to my sewing.' Aoife laughed. 'D'you hear that? I'd make someone a great wife.'

Standing in front of her, handing out forms to applicants, was Paul. Aoife wanted to run, to hide, to retract the word 'wife' from the air around her, but it was too late: he'd seen her, and heard her.

'Aoife!' he gasped, and a red flush crept up his neck from under his shirt.

'Paul,' she said; she wanted to sound cool and in-different, but she was too shocked to pull it off convincingly.

'What are you doing…?' they asked simultaneously.

Carmel was looking alarmed; she had heard all about Paul's misdemeanours.

'... here?' Aoife finished lamely.

'I'm organising the catering for Dublin Castle next week. Are you here for that?' Paul said, almost formally.

'Yeah ... yeah, I am.' There was a silence; Aoife couldn't bear it, so she broke it by saying, 'Bono's going to be there.'

'He is,' Paul agreed. 'I was going to ring you and tell you, but after the way...' He took a breath. 'Well, after the way you spoke to me, I decided not to bother.'

Carmel took this as her cue to make herself scarce. Spotting a woman taking people's details, she headed across to the other side of the room.

'After the way I spoke to you? And don't you think that maybe' – Aoife dispensed with politeness – 'maybe you deserved it?'

'What, because I told a white lie?'

'A *white lie*?' Aoife demanded, dumbfounded. 'How is not telling me that you're married a white lie?'

'Married?' Paul's eyes clouded over with confusion. 'I'm not fecking married! Who told you I was?'

'Rory. He said –'

'Rory told you, did he? I might have guessed he'd have something to do with it.' They were drawing stares from the other people in the bar. Paul nodded towards the door, and Aoife followed him out into the corridor.

335

'What's that supposed to mean?'

'It means that I think he's a stirring bastard.'

'Don't call Rory a bastard!' Aoife was seething. 'You lied, Paul, and don't pretend you didn't. And it was your mammy who told him you were married.'

'My fecking mother said I was *married*?'

'I told you this when you came to the restaurant! I said –'

'No, Aoife. I'm not deaf. I would definitely have remembered the word "married".'

'Rory knocked on the door and said he was a friend of your girlfriend's, and your mother asked if you were at that again – and she said you were married....' She trailed off, wondering if Rory had got his facts straight.

'She did what?' Paul was raging. 'I'll kill her, so I will. She's nothing but an old conniving bitch. She'd do anything to see that I'm not happy. The woman thrives on it.'

'Well, if you're not married,' Aoife said, trying to maintain her defiance, 'who the hell is the red-headed woman you've been wandering round Dublin hugging and kissing?'

'The red-headed...?' Realisation dawned in Paul's eyes. 'That,' he almost spat, 'is my sister!'

Aoife's mouth fell open in shock. If that really had been his sister, then she had just made a complete fool of herself.

'Your *sister*?' she asked shakily.

'Yes, my sister. She's been really stressed about … well, about the stuff that's been going on with our mother.' Paul leaned against the wall. 'Look,' he said, running his hand over his face, 'I don't know how this has all happened. I just know that, if my mother has anything to do with it, I'm not one bit surprised.' He took a deep, tired breath. 'She drives me and my sister up the wall. She's a lunatic. Any time we want to move out, she pretends to be ill – she gives it all that "I won't be here this time next year" bollocks – so we stay and look after her, and she makes our lives hell.'

'Yeah, but … saying you were married?' Aoife asked. It seemed very extreme.

'Oh, yeah, she'd definitely be up for that if it meant getting rid of a girlfriend; no bother to her. That's not the half of it.' Paul looked over his shoulder, back into the room they had just abandoned.

'Do you need to go back in?' Aoife said. She had a barrage of questions that she wanted to ask.

'Yeah, I should, really.' Paul looked into the room again, and then back at Aoife.

'You have to believe me.' He touched her gently on the arm, and this small gesture made Aoife want to cry. 'I've missed you, but after the way you spoke to me I just thought there was no way I was going back for more. I thought it was obvious that you'd made your mind up. So I just left it.'

Aoife suddenly felt foolish. She knew that she had been so self-righteous, steaming in, believing every well-meaning, ill-informed word that came out of Rory's mouth. She looked down at her feet; she couldn't hold Paul's gaze any longer. The hurt she had been feeling seemed to melt away. She wanted desperately to believe that Paul was telling her the truth.

'Aoife, I'm sorry that this all got mixed up. I didn't mean to confuse you or mislead you; I just didn't want you to have to hear what a psycho my ma is. You were keeping me sane through all that – and then, when you started bawling at me outside the restaurant, I thought the whole world had gone mad.'

'But I moan about my mammy,' Aoife protested.

'Yeah, but your ma's funny and has your best interests at heart. Mine's just selfish and – well, I hate to say this about my own mother, but she's a horrible woman.' Aoife wanted to say that he didn't mean that, but she could tell from the look on his face that he did.

'I'm sorry,' she said.

'Don't be. I'd just like it if we could sort it out. What do you think?'

Aoife nodded slowly, and Paul leaned forward and kissed her gently. Her mind was racing; she couldn't believe how happy she felt. But there were questions she needed answered in time; and her better judgement, which seemed to have returned after flying south for the winter, was urging caution.

From now on, she wanted honesty – no more going on hearsay and jumping to conclusions. She wanted to meet Paul's sister and make absolutely sure that what he said was true. Also, she wanted to set the record straight with Rory – who seemed to have lost the run of himself altogether on this one.

Chapter Forty-One

Aoife flew through the door like a woman possessed. 'You've got some explaining to do,' she informed Rory, her voice quivering with anger.

He hadn't a clue what she was talking about, and his scrunched-up face said as much.

'Don't look at me like that, Rory.' Aoife took a deep breath, reining herself in slightly. 'Look, I know that you're not having the best time at the moment, but I think this needs saying because I am so bloody *furious* with you.'

'Aoife,' Rory said wearily – the best part of his fight had been knocked out of him by the whole business with his father – 'would you mind explaining what the fuck is the matter with you?'

'Paul is not married! That is what's the matter with me!'

Rory just sighed, a deep, dejected sigh, and put his

head in his hands. 'What do you mean, he's not married?'

'He hasn't got a wife! What bit of "not married" don't you –'

'All right, Aoife, I fucking hear you! Good God,' Rory snapped. 'So if he's so *not* married, how the hell do you explain the woman who looks like something from an advert for holidaying in Connemara?'

'She's his fecking sister!'

Rory paused, slightly taken aback, but he soon rallied. 'Do you kiss your sister? Do you tell her that you love her, like he did on the phone the night before I followed him? Because I'd like an explanation for that.' Rory noticed that Aoife's stare wavered slightly; sensing a chink in her armour, he ploughed on. 'And what about the phone calls? And his own mother looking me in the face and saying that this woman was far more than a girlfriend?'

'Did she say she was his wife?' Aoife retaliated.

'Oh, come on, Aoife. What sob story has he fed you?'

'Did the word "wife" come out of his mother's mouth?'

'Oh, I should have taped the conversation. Sorry that my detective skills are so shoddy, but I wasn't working with a great deal of notice –'

'And it's not a sob story! And I'll know fairly soon what all this means, because I'm going to meet Paul's sister – and don't you worry, I'll expect an explanation for everything that's happened.'

Rory looked at Aoife; whatever Paul had told her, she obviously believed him. Rory didn't know what to think any more; he shook his head and got up, heading for the kitchen.

'Is that it?' Aoife followed him. 'Are you just going to walk away?'

'Aoife, I'm tired –'

'Yeah, so am I. I'm tired of your possessiveness and your suspicion of anyone who shows an interest in me; it's stifling, Rory.' Rory put the kettle on and got a cup from the press; this didn't go down too well. 'And now you're not even listening!'

Rory slammed the cup down and turned to Aoife. 'I'm all fecking ears.'

'Good; listen to this, then, Rory O'Donnell. I am not your girlfriend and I don't need looking after twenty-four hours a day. And I don't want any more bets; I am not here for your amusement.'

Rory resumed making his cup of tea. He didn't offer Aoife a cup; he'd had enough of her for the time being.

'Fine. I was just trying to help. I didn't do anything out of badness or malice; I just wanted you to take some money to sort yourself out. And the Paul thing … to be perfectly frank, Aoife, at this stage I don't care if he's married, divorced, or shacked up with a fecking horse.'

Despite herself, Aoife felt her lips beginning to curl

in a half-smile. She looked away so Rory wouldn't see that she was laughing, but it was too late; the giggles burst out of her. It was the crack in the ice that they needed.

'I know you weren't, if I'm honest,' Aoife admitted, composing herself. 'It just bugs me that all this has come out of you trying to help me. I don't want help, Rory; I want to do things my way, for a change – on my own.'

Rory pulled out another cup, put a tea bag in it and waved it at Aoife. 'Truce?'

Over the tea, Aoife told Rory that, despite everything, she was still going to try to meet Bono. 'I might be fed up with you betting me, but I'm going to win this one. It's more a matter of principle than anything. But I certainly don't want any money for it, especially not now you're in dire straits.'

'I am not!' Rory looked appalled. 'Dire Straits? Sweat bands and mullets and Mark Knopfler making his guitar gently weep next to me? Please! It's not my scene, babe.'

Aoife laughed and shook her head.

Bridie and Jimmy stopped by on their way out of town, and Aoife went down to say goodbye, leaving Rory with his thoughts. It felt good to have cleared the air, but the unresolved business with Paul still niggled at him.

Rory lay on his bed and stared vacantly at the

343

ceiling. *What a fecking terrible week*, he thought. Unless Tem really came through for him, he was going to have to get a proper job, and he was dreading the thought. If he had to work in an office, he'd be a useless embarrassment: he could barely type, he didn't know any of the computer packages that had come out since he left college, and he could only file because he knew the alphabet. And he wouldn't fare any better in a bar or a restaurant: he'd have to get Aoife to show him how to carry three plates and how to take orders and how to be nice to people when he wanted to smack their teeth down their throat. Rory groaned at the thought.

Most of all, he wanted to make it up properly to Aoife. She was right, he realised. He swanned around, doing whatever he pleased, yet he expected her to be at his beck and call – and she had been, for a long time. Other friends had gone by the wayside as Rory and Aoife built up a secure little unit between themselves. Aoife had said that it was stifling, and she was right.

It suddenly dawned on Rory that his best friend was growing up. She was more of a woman about Dublin than he was a man about Dublin; he was just playing at it, whereas she was doing it for real. He was really proud of her for getting Mari Byrne to buy her designs. She was happy and independent, she didn't need Rory or his money, and, whether they had a flat or not, Aoife would be fine; she always had been. And she was mad about Paul – and, if what Aoife was saying was true, Rory had nearly wrecked their chances by jumping the gun with his possessiveness.

He sat up purposefully. From now on, he was going to be as good a friend to Aoife as she was to him. He was going to be supportive and encouraging, and stop treating her like she was his little sister, put there for his entertainment. And there would be no more bets. He was never going to bet her to do anything, ever again.

Well, once they'd got Bono out of the way, of course.

'Well, that's it, girleen; I think I have everything.' Bridie stood by Jimmy's car, on the road outside Rory's apartment. Aoife had offered to come up to the convent and wave her off, but Bridie had been very evasive; she had said something about not worrying the nuns, as if she were talking about sheep.

Reading between the lines, Aoife realised that her mother hadn't mentioned Jimmy to anyone in Whitehall. She had probably pretended that she was off doing charitable work, rather than meeting up with her ex-boyfriend. Aoife decided that, under the circumstances, she would let her mother have that one. If she bumped into Sister Immaculata any time soon, she wasn't about to let the side down by telling her anything different.

'You going to be all right, Mam?' Aoife asked.

'I'll be fine; why wouldn't I be?'

'It's just that' – Aoife smiled over at Jimmy – 'you seem to have become very attached to Dublin, that's all.'

'Not at all!' Bridie protested. Aoife smirked; with Kerry looming on the horizon, her mother was reverting to type.

'Ah, come on, Mammy! The conversation we had the other day, meeting up with Jimmy ... none of that meant anything? Sure, it was just a little visit to see the daughter, wasn't it?'

Bridie broke into a smile. 'All right, so; I might miss it a little bit. But that's all I'm saying.' Aoife gave her a big hug; Bridie hugged her back, pulling her daughter close with such genuine feeling that it made Aoife's eyes well up.

'Will you be all right driving back tonight, Jimmy?' Aoife asked, sniffing and getting out her stiff upper lip.

'I'm staying there for a few days. Going to see how the place has changed.' He winked at Bridie.

'You're staying overnight? Ma, the town gossips'll have a ball.'

Bridie flushed puce. 'Aoife, would you be quiet! It's not like that – and, anyway, Jimmy will probably stay at Roddy's.'

'I'll bet Roddy's over the moon about that,' Aoife said under her breath.

'What was that?' her mother asked.

'Nothing; I was just thinking that Roddy would be glad of the company.'

'I'm sure he will,' Bridie said happily. 'Now then, shall we go, Jimmy?'

'Not a bother,' Jimmy said, opening the passenger door. 'In you get, Bridget.' Bridie climbed in, and Jimmy gave Aoife a kiss on the cheek. 'I'll take good care of her, I promise.' Aoife smiled; she knew that he meant in general, not just on the journey down to Kerry.

'Thanks, Jimmy.' She flashed him a big warm smile.

Before he had a chance to shut the car door, Bridie had her head out of it again. 'It'd be nice to see you in Kilbane soon.' Aoife rolled her eyes, thinking that her mother was being sarcastic, but stopped them mid-roll when she realised that she wasn't. 'But if you can't,' Bridie continued, 'it's not a bother; I'll be back up here in July for Jimmy's birthday.'

Aoife laughed and shook her head in bemusement. 'Good luck!' she shouted, as they drove off. She waved, thinking that it was a good job she hadn't mentioned the fact that she and Rory were being thrown out of the flat at the end of the month. Her mother would probably have unpacked her bags and stayed. Any excuse.

As the car turned the corner, Aoife heard the door open behind her. She turned to see Rory's head sticking out.

'They get off all right?' he asked tentatively.

'They did.' Aoife nodded.

'Good,' Rory said, giving her an awkward smile.

Aoife looked at him and felt an ache of love in the pit of her stomach. Suddenly she felt terrible – terrible for blaming Rory for being intrusive, terrible for giving out to him about the bets. It wasn't as if he had forced her to do anything; she had always been a willing partner in crime. He didn't stop her from going out with other people; the truth was that, on the whole, she preferred going out with him.

'Rory.'

'Yeah?' he said, raising his eyebrows hopefully.

'I'm sorry.'

'For what?'

'For being horrible to you.'

'You weren't horrible to me,' Rory told her. 'You were right. I can't go through my life expecting you to be there all the time.'

'Well, whatever, I'm sorry.' Aoife hung her head. 'I really am. And I just want to say thanks for all your help.'

Rory stepped forward and put his arms around Aoife; giving her a big hug, he kissed her on the head. 'Come here, you mad wagon,' he said. 'You don't have to thank me for anything.'

Chapter Forty-Two

Rory spent the next few days panicking about his future. He had had a resoundingly successful meeting with Billy Wilde's people, and they had invited him to guest-DJ in New York on the last Friday of every month for six months, starting in July. Tem was telling everyone that he was the best thing since Pop Tarts. But Rory still couldn't help thinking that, without his father's assistance, he was nothing. Strangely, though, he was a lot less nervous about DJ-ing now that it wasn't just an amusing distraction; it was the only thing that could potentially pay his bills.

Work aside, Rory still wasn't delighted with the fact that he and Aoife were going to have to move into a grotty flat – or, horror of horrors, shared accommodation. He wasn't even sure if Aoife would want to live with him any more. He might have a few grand left in the bank, but that wouldn't get him a deposit on a tent, let alone a flat; and, considering that he had little credit history and his father wasn't about to guarantee a mortgage for him, there wasn't much chance of him owning anything to live in – not in this lifetime, anyway.

Rory was driving to a garage in Ballsbridge, to discuss selling his car. *My pride and joy*, he thought dismally. Rory adored his car; he loved the roar of the engine underneath him and the looks he got from passers-by. He'd have to do something pretty extravagant to make people look at him on his new mode of transport, namely the DART, he thought. Then he went into a by-panic, realising that he and Aoife might never have the luxury of living within walking distance of a DART station again.

He was slowly slumping into abject despair when his mobile began to ring. He didn't recognise the number. 'Hello?'

'Is that Rory?' a low, timid female voice asked.

'It is, yes. Who's asking?' he said, pulling the car into the forecourt of the garage.

'It's … it's …' The voice became even quieter. 'It's Niamh, your father's PA.' She was nearly whispering.

What the feck does she want? Rory thought. She couldn't be calling on behalf of his father. Rory knew how his dad operated, and he was sure that he wouldn't get in touch. It would be up to Rory to initiate any future reconciliation.

'Well, ex-PA,' Niamh whispered.

'What, you've left?' Rory asked; he couldn't keep the sheer delight out of his voice.

'Don't shout it out, Rory!' she hissed. She was beginning to sound borderline psychotic.

'All right, Niamh,' Rory said calmly. 'What's the story? Why have you left?'

'I need to meet you.'

Rory was puzzled, but he was also intrigued – and he was revelling in the fact that Eoin O'Donnell would be in big trouble without Niamh. 'OK. Where?'

'Meet me at Doheny and Nesbitt's on Baggot Street, at half past twelve. Go to the top floor; there's a room at the back. The place'll be mobbed, but I want somewhere busy so that, if your father has his spies out, I can say that I just bumped into you.'

'Jesus, Niamh, this is all very clandestine.' Rory tried to joke with her.

'Just do it, Rory. I have something for you that I think you'll be very interested in,' Niamh said sternly.

'OK, Niamh. I'll be there.' Rory put the phone down and sat for a moment with his brow furrowed in confusion. What on earth could Niamh have that could possibly interest him? he wondered, getting out of his car and steeling himself for the horrible prospect of being carless by the end of the week.

Niamh was sitting in the room at the back of the pub, clutching a bag and nervously smoking a cigarette. Rory couldn't believe the state she was in.

Her long blond hair was scraped back into a scraggy ponytail; the circles under her eyes were now nearly black, the eyes above them sunken and wild. At O'Donnell Properties she had always been immaculately presented, but now she was wearing what Rory could only describe as a velour jumpsuit that had definitely seen better days, sometime around 1982.

'Niamh, how are you?' Rory asked, kissing her on the cheek. She flicked her cigarette ash into the ashtray.

'Fine, Rory. Yourself?' she asked flatly.

'Good. Do you want a drink?'

'Gin and tonic, thanks.' Niamh did not even attempt a smile. This was the woman who, for years, had bounded around Rory like a bloodhound that had just been thrown a stick; and now she couldn't even manage a smile. It all made Rory slightly nervous, but he was dying to find out what had happened.

He returned from the bar and, setting the drinks down, turned to Niamh. 'Look, Niamh, I need to level with you: you look terrible. What's the story?'

'Thanks a million,' Niamh said curtly; she didn't seem to be in the mood for banter. 'The story is …' She looked around the bar to see if anyone was listening, then brought her voice down to a barely audible whisper. '… I have resigned from my job.'

Rory bent his head towards hers. 'Yeah, you told me that. Good for you; my father's a gobshite.'

'Shhh!' Niamh looked around again. 'We both know that, but keep your voice down; you don't know who's listening.'

'Niamh, you have to stop acting paranoid and tell me what's going on. No one is watching us.'

Niamh laughed bitterly. 'Paranoid? I'm not paranoid. Your father used to have someone watching you all the time. He paid a man twenty-five grand a year just to follow you around – well, you and some associates of his that he didn't trust. You think I don't know you're gay, don't you?' Rory pulled his head back in surprise. 'I didn't when I first started working for your father, but, thanks to him, I soon found out. Your last long-term boyfriend, Alan, married a nurse called Celia in Maynooth; they're expecting their first child, but that hasn't stopped him trying to get back in your pants. You told him to fuck off, am I right?' Niamh was studying Rory's face; he looked like 'The Scream'.

'What else do I know?' she pondered. 'I know you've been trailing Bono with your friend Aoife – but that's been a bit of a fiasco, hasn't it? Your father hit the roof about that one. What was it he said? "Am I paying that good-for-nothing bollix to trail round after singers, am I?" He smashed his fist through his Palm Pilot after that little outburst.'

Rory tried to take in the information. 'How long has this been going on?' he asked finally.

'Oh, I don't know. Over a year.'

'Jesus!' Rory felt suddenly unclean.

'The reason he gave was that he was waiting for the best time to suggest that you change your ways. He thought you were going through a phase, and nothing I or anyone else said could change that.'

'Who else knows?' Rory shouted angrily. Niamh looked around again.

'His partner Mairéad, the fella who was following you, and me.'

'Mairéad knew?'

'Yeah, but she just thought it was one of your father's mad schemes and left him to it.'

'The fucking...' Rory struggled for a word. '... wanker. I'm going to kill him.'

'You're right. He is an utter wanker.'

Rory softened, suddenly realising that he wasn't the only one who had been affected by his father's behaviour. 'What made you leave – in the end, like; what was it that finally made you go?'

'Look at the state of me, Rory. You said it yourself: I'm in bits. I went to the doctor last week and he said I was suffering from nervous exhaustion. So, when Eoin ordered me to come into the office on Sunday, I said I wasn't going in. I told him I had another doctor's appointment. It was Sunday, for fuck's sake; how many office workers have to work weekends? Anyway, after you'd been in and had your argument, Eoin kept leaving messages on my phone –'

'It was more than an argument,' Rory interrupted.

'Whatever it was,' Niamh snapped. 'It had your father pestering me. In the end I went into the office, about two hours after you had left. Eoin was going mad, saying that he'd all but disowned you, that he wanted to make sure I had the keys to your apartment by the end of the month, that he didn't care if you ended up sleeping rough....' Rory was shaking his head in disbelief. 'And when I told him that the doctor said I needed to take time off, he gave me an ultimatum. He was screaming; he scared the shite out of me. He said that if I left O'Donnell Properties, he'd make sure I didn't get a job anywhere else.' Niamh's lip was trembling.

'But you left?' Rory asked gently.

Niamh wiped her nose and tried to hold back the tears. 'I know he's capable of trying to prevent me from getting another job – he has contacts all over Dublin – but I'll take the chance. I just couldn't spend another day in that office.' She sipped her drink and tried to calm herself. 'So I got myself together and cleared my desk out. He was ... well, you know what he's like: he was calling me all the bitches under the sun.' Niamh's eyes welled up again and she took a deep breath. 'Then he slammed his office door, and I walked out. I was shaking like a fecking leaf.'

'You're shaking like a fecking leaf now,' Rory pointed out.

'Anyway, so I left, but not before taking these.' Niamh opened her bag and took out a sheaf of papers.

'What are they?' Rory asked, peering over the top of the papers.

'The deeds to your apartment in Ballsbridge. Your

father kept them in the safe at the office.' Niamh was shaking so violently that she looked as if she were about to have a fit. She passed the papers to Rory.

He stared at them; then he looked up at Niamh, his mouth open in utter disbelief. 'My name's on them,' he said finally, stunned.

'That's because the apartment's yours. It was never Eoin's. Your mother bought that apartment in your name. And you have a share in the other four – a quarter, I think.' Niamh took the documents from Rory and leafed through them. 'There; it says it there. Your father owns the rest. I heard him telling his accountant that your mother wanted you to have all of them, but he talked her out of it: said you'd never "develop character" if you owned a rake of flats. He thought it was hilarious that she'd agreed so easily; said she wasn't much of a businesswoman, your mother.'

'The twisted bastard!'

'Yeah, I know, but I honestly think he believes that everything he does is for the best. Anyway, all of this stuff is in her will as well, but you can get hold of that yourself. As you weren't twenty-five – that's when your mother wanted you to have them – your father got his lawyer to pass the deeds to him. He told me that if I mentioned it to anyone, I'd be finished – but I probably am anyway, so what harm can it do?' Niamh gave Rory a bitter half-smile.

'No, you're not, Niamh – don't say that. How the fuck can he get away with this sort of thing?'

'Your father has a lot of very important people in his pocket, and his lawyer is as dodgy as a nine-pound note. He can stop me from working, and he can prevent you from getting your hands on something that's rightfully yours. Where there's a will, and all that; and your dad has the will of an ox.' Niamh sniffed and gulped some more of her drink. 'Anyway, he did get away with it, until now, didn't he?' She dragged hard on her cigarette.

'Why didn't my mother tell me?' Rory wondered.

'Your father said she wanted you to get your degree and grow up before you got the apartment. Your father knew damn well that you were meant to find out when you turned twenty-five, but he used to say that he'd tell you what was yours when you started behaving yourself.'

'The twat! I suppose by "behaving myself" he meant by not being gay.'

'Exactly.' Niamh nodded. 'The longer I worked for him, the more I realised that he never had any intention of telling you that the apartment was yours.'

Rory shook his head again. Suddenly he realised something. 'So the money he used to give me was essentially mine anyway – what with me having a quarter share and all?'

'Of course it was. He was forever pulling equity out of those flats and making money elsewhere; he wouldn't have had such a free rein if you'd been able to stake your claim to a quarter of it. You don't think

357

he'd be that generous with his own money, do you? He's made a small fortune out of those apartments.'

Rory ran his fingers through his hair in agitation. 'I can't believe this.'

'Yeah, but at least now you know,' Niamh pointed out.

Rory felt humbled. She had put her neck on the line to tell him the truth, and he was griping because he'd found out that he owned his apartment after all. 'Sorry, Niamh. You're completely right: at least now I know.'

'So what are you going to do about it?' Niamh asked, fiddling with the only beer-mat that she hadn't already ripped into a hundred bits.

'I'm going to get myself a lawyer and claim what's mine,' he said. 'But I want you to know that you are going to get a great big thank-you for this – and I don't just mean a box of Quality Street; I mean hard cash.' Rory was thinking on his feet. He didn't want Niamh thinking that she had done all of this for nothing.

'No, you're fine, Rory, honestly,' she protested half-heartedly.

'Would you cop on? You've just given me papers saying I have property worth a small fecking fortune. The very least I can do is see that you get some sort of compensation.'

'I don't want anything from you, Rory; I just want what's right and fair. And your father having the deeds wasn't,' Niamh said, stubbing her cigarette out.

'That's very noble, Niamh, but it's not going to pay

the bills. You're getting some cash for this, whether you like it or not.' Rory leant forward and kissed her on the cheek. 'I can't thank you enough for what you've done. Don't be worrying about getting another job; you'll be getting some cash very soon, I promise.'

Niamh smiled for the first time that day. 'Thanks, Rory. Thanks.'

'Not a bother,' Rory said, getting to his feet and tucking the papers safely inside his jacket. 'And Niamh?'

'Yeah?'

'Go home and get some kip, will you? You've had a long few years, working for that gobshite.' He winked at her and she smiled.

Rory stepped into the bustle of Baggot Street and took a deep breath. He felt like doing cartwheels all the way down to St Stephen's Green, but he decided to go to a solicitor instead and get the deeds verified. After that, he'd call Aoife and tell her the fantastic news.

Chapter Forty-Three

'I feel like a complete and utter gom!' Rory hissed at Aoife, while maintaining a chat-show-host grin as they headed towards the door of Fitzers restaurant in Temple Bar. Standing at the entrance, handing their coats to the waitress, were Paul and the beautiful redhead. Aoife had made Rory come with her, not only for moral support, but so that he could hear the truth for himself.

Aoife nudged Rory to be quiet and said, through her own grin, 'How do you think I feel?' She was slightly embarrassed about all of this, in the cold light of day; but she needed to clear everything up.

She needn't have worried; Fiona was more than happy to talk with Aoife and, it transpired, to handle Rory.

'Hi, Aoife; I'm really pleased to meet you. And this must be Inspector Clouseau, right? I'm Fiona.' Aoife watched Rory redden. Fiona shook his hand, her eyes twinkling with mischief. 'I'm Paul's sister,' she informed him.

Rory smiled charmingly. 'So I believe.'

Paul shook Rory's hand in a very alpha-male way – shoulders back, eyes level, firm handshake. Aoife hoped that everything would be resolved before the two lads started weeing on each other's chairs.

Her first concern was cleared up almost immediately. Despite the difference in colouring, there was no mistaking the fact that Paul and Fiona were related. They had the same defined bone structure, the same sleek nose, the same high cheekbones; they were as alike as bookends. Aoife was dying to say to Rory, 'Do they look like bloody husband and wife?' And what Rory had taken for romantic kissing and hugging wasn't some sort of weird incestuous link, but plain old fraternal affection. They were tactile with each other in a way that Aoife found endearing.

She was looking for ways to quiz Fiona subtly when Fiona leaned forward over her menu and said, 'Shall we order and then I'll put everything straight for you, Aoife? I'd much rather get our nightmare mother out of the way first thing, so I can spend the rest of the evening getting to know you and Rory.'

This allowed Aoife to relax slightly. They ordered their food and a bottle of wine, and over the first course, Fiona told Aoife and Rory all about her and Paul's home life.

'Our mother is ... well, how would you describe her, Paul?'

'An old bitch.'

'Would you agree, Rory?'

'Oh, I don't know; I was only chewing the fat with her for a few minutes. I spent most of my time hiding behind a rusty Peugeot.' Everyone laughed, and the atmosphere around the table relaxed another few notches.

'Well, put it this way: the woman is never, ever going to be happy until everyone who's ever come into contact with her is miserable. She's turned martyrdom into an art form – every time we want to do anything, it's "I've given my health and my life for you, and this is how you repay me...." Her latest is hypochondria; these last few years she's spent most of her time at St James's Hospital, badgering the doctors to tell us she has something life-threatening.'

'That's where she was meant to have been the morning I met Fi at Stephen's Green,' Paul put in.

Rory winced. 'What, when I was doing my Sherlock Holmes impression?'

Paul smiled. 'That's right. She'd been on at me the night before, when we went to see you DJ – "You don't love me, I could die tomorrow under the doctor's knife, I need to see you, blah, blah, blah...."'

'Honest to God,' Fiona said, setting her cutlery down. 'That's how she goes on.'

Rory flushed with embarrassment. 'Aoife, I'm really

sorry. Paul, I was in the loo at the time and I heard that conversation; and I thought – well, with the "Of course I love you"s and the pleading not to hang up, I thought you were talking to another woman.'

'Why didn't you just ask me in the club?' Paul said.

'I was just about to get behind the decks, and it was too much for me to deal with right then. Anyway, I wanted to be sure – and look where that got me: I add two and two and get four hundred.'

Paul smiled. 'Look, I'm no more married than I am the man in the moon. What exactly did my mother say that made you think I was?'

Rory thought hard. 'I'm not sure I remember word for word.'

'I know it's not your fault; my mother could convince you black was white if she wanted to. I'd just love to know what she said, that's all.'

'She never said outright that you were husband and wife,' Rory admitted apologetically. 'She just said that Fiona was "more than a girlfriend", and I took that to mean that you were married. I said as much, and she never corrected me.'

'That sounds about right. And she was on form that day, believe me,' Fiona went on. 'She demanded that Paul go with her to the hospital, but he told her that he'd meet her at the Green. She never even got out of bed that morning – told me she was dying – and I had to go meet him and bring him back. But when we got back to the house, she was up and about, acting like nothing had ever happened and asking if Paul had had a nice night with his floozy. No girl's ever good enough for Paul, according to her; I think she just can't stand to see him happy.'

Aoife was counting her blessings; at least her own mother was only half-mad.

'And here's the best bit about the old witch,' Fiona said, polishing off her salad. 'The only reason we were both living at home was because she told us she had terminal cancer. So we moved back in; she might be a pain in the backside, but she's still our ma. But after a couple of months she didn't seem to be getting any worse. We didn't know what to do. In the meantime, Paul had arranged to move in with a mate of his who has a little terraced house in Killiney; he was just waiting for the right time.'

'And then last week,' Paul said. 'I went to her doctor to see if there was a chance that the cancer had gone into remission, and I was informed that the woman is as fit as a butcher's dog.'

'Can you believe it?' Fiona asked. 'She'd lied to us all along. But she wouldn't admit it; she said that she'd been saying her rosaries and it had just cleared up.'

'Yeah, it was a fecking miracle,' Paul said. 'I told her she was a lunatic, and I moved my stuff down to Killiney.'

'I moved out the same day,' Fiona told them. 'I'm starting a nursing course in Leitrim after the summer, and I'm staying with a friend on the south side until then. I had all my clothes in a bin-liner, ready to be loaded into the car, and she threw the lot of them out the window onto the street. They were soaked when I picked them up – it had been lashing rain that morning – and the entire street was out having a good gawk while Ma screamed at me through the window. I was mortified!'

Paul began laughing, and Aoife and Rory joined in. 'You can just picture the street, can't you, Rory?' Fiona said mischievously. Aoife looked at the other three. She knew that what she was hearing was the truth, and that Rory knew it as well, and it was a great relief.

'Paul,' Rory said, as the starter plates were being cleared. 'I just want to apologise for throwing a spanner in the works.'

'It's fine. I know you were only looking out for Aoife – and if I'd been honest in the first place, none of this would have happened.'

Once Rory had recovered from his embarrassment at being faced with two people he had stalked across the city, he was back to his old self. Aoife noticed that he might have met his match in Fiona.

'Do you get told you look like your one out of Riverdance?' he asked Fiona, looking at her long ringlets.

'Do you get told you look like your *man* out of Riverdance?' she inquired, not missing a beat.

'Flatley!' Rory exclaimed in disgust. 'I might have just met you, but I'll put you over my knee and give you a good hiding for that sort of comment.'

By the end of the meal, Rory and Fiona were locked

in a good-natured war of words; as they left the restaurant, Rory linked her arm and announced that the two of them were going to continue their battle over a pint or three.

As they headed off, still arguing loudly, Paul ran his fingers through his curly hair and held his hand out to Aoife. 'Come here,' he said. 'I hope that everything we told you makes sense. And I hope you know that I didn't tell you all this in the first place because I thought you might run a mile if you knew I was a twenty-seven-year-old man living with his mad mother. I just want you to know it's not like that. I moved out of home when I was nineteen, and I only went back because – well, you know the rest.'

'I think you've pretty much explained everything.' Aoife smiled as they wandered towards the Ha'penny Bridge. It meant a lot to her that Paul had gone to such lengths to set the record straight. 'And if I think of anything else, I can always call Fiona.'

Aoife and Paul stood at the middle of the bridge, looking out past O'Connell Bridge. The sky over the DART line was a deep red, and the Liffey was high enough to look like a river again, rather than the set of intermittent puddles it had been the last time Aoife had paid any attention to it.

Paul put his arm around his girlfriend and pulled her close. 'How good does Dublin look?'

Aoife shrugged. 'I suppose it looks pretty good.'

'Pretty good? It looks fecking beautiful.' Paul kissed her. 'And it could all be yours, my pretty.'

'Oh, yeah – Dublin's lying at my feet for the taking, isn't it?'

'Dress designer to the stars, friend of Bono ... what more do you want?' Paul smiled and pushed Aoife's hair back from her face. *He is such a ride*, she thought, her stomach doing flip-flops. She couldn't believe she could feel like this; she was mad about him.

She smiled. 'I've got *one* famous person wearing *one* dress for *one* night; that hardly makes me Stella McCartney. And I'm not Bono's friend; I'm just his ineffectual stalker.' *Shame about the five grand,* she thought; it would have been more than useful – but she couldn't have everything. She was more than happy with all the things she did have. The bank manager could wait another couple of weeks for his full payment.

Paul laughed and leaned against the railings of the bridge. 'Well now,' he said mysteriously, raising an eyebrow at Aoife. 'When you turn up at Dublin Castle on Tuesday night, bring a change of clothes – clothes befitting a guest at such an occasion – and you might get to meet your man after all.'

'What do you mean?' Aoife almost shrieked with excitement.

'I'm not saying anything more.' Paul turned back to look at the river.

'Ah, you can't do that to me! What do you mean?' Aoife pleaded.

'I mean that I'm going to do my best to get you an introduction, but I can't promise anything. I'm not saying any more, because if I don't manage it, then you'll only be disappointed.'

'Aw!' Aoife protested, but she was smiling.

'Come on.' Paul grabbed her hand again.

'Where are we going?' Aoife asked, as they headed along the quays.

'To get a taxi. I'm taking you home, to my new humble abode.' Paul smiled at Aoife, but she didn't need to smile back; she was already grinning from ear to ear.

Chapter Forty-Four

Aoife had been in Dublin Castle for two hours, passing champagne flutes as instructed by Róisín, the woman who, alongside Paul, was running this mammoth operation. There were over a hundred waiters and waitresses there; most of them had been assigned tables, but as Aoife had admitted that she couldn't do silver service (she didn't want to run the risk of launching carrots onto the head of some visiting dignitary) she hadn't been given a specific task. Róisín had told her to circulate, topping up wine and clearing empty glasses.

Aoife – who, in her regulation bow tie and pinafore, looked like a stuffed penguin – had just relieved herself of champagne-carrying duty; she had been holding the tray for so long that her left arm was nearly the length of Mr Tickle's. She had been looking out for Bono and for Dervla Cannon in the hall where the drinks were being served, but there was no sign of either of them.

She was now checking the tables in the main hall. There were huge crystal vases of flowers dotted around the room, and the smell of lilies hung in the air. The grandeur of the hall, and the sense of occasion, momentarily overwhelmed Aoife.

Paul had been nowhere to be seen for the past hour or so; but as she neared the end of the hall, one of the doors from the kitchen opened and he hurried in.

'Aoife, there you are,' he whispered. 'You need to go and get ready.'

'What?' Aoife looked confused. 'I'm meant to be –'

Paul obviously didn't have time for her protestations. 'Look, Aoife. If anyone finds out what I've done, I'll be shot. Now go and get changed, go back into the outer hall, tell Carmel to cover for you – not that it should matter; there's practically one waiter to every guest – and then come back in here when the guests are called in. Just think that you're allowed to be here; you're a designer.'

'I'm not a fecking designer, I'm a waitress!'

'Aoife, shut up or you're going to lose me my job. It's done now; just do what I say and it should be fine,' Paul implored. 'There's a seating plan in the corner; your name's on it. Now go on, before I get killed!'

'What if any of the other waiters recognise me?'

'Aoife …' Paul was becoming exasperated, and Aoife could hear people milling around near the door, ready to come in to dinner. 'Just do it.'

'OK! OK!'

Aoife ran into the toilet with her bag, reached into it and pulled out a very simple blue satin slip-dress, trimmed at the neckline with black lace, that fell just below her knees. She pulled her hair out of its ponytail and brushed it straight. She rapidly applied dusky eye make-up and some lip gloss, and pinched her cheeks to make them look as if she had skilfully applied blusher. She hopped from one foot to the other, pulling on her satin stiletto sling-backs – she had bought them ages ago, but she had always felt they were too good to ruin by actually *wearing* them. Quickly checking her reflection and smoothing the front of her dress, Aoife decided that she looked pretty good, even if she did say so herself.

After the meal, she decided, she'd have to make a beeline across the room for Bono and have a quick chat – and she'd probably have to fend off another fifty people vying for his attention. Never mind, she thought; it would be easier as a guest – especially with the help of a few glasses of wine – than it would have been had she been serving his spuds.

Out of force of habit, she checked her mobile phone; it had been in her bag, on 'silent', since she had arrived at the Castle. She had a text message from Rory: 'Cheque ready & w8ing – lick Bono's face & I'll throw in an xtra grand.'

Aoife grinned. She had been over the moon to find out that Rory still had an income and that they both still had a home – and that Rory's father was hitting several roofs over what Niamh had done – but she still had no intention of taking his money. It was time for her to stand on her own two feet. She texted him back, 'Don't want ur money, but will lick his face anyway! x'.

She stuffed her waitress uniform into her bag and considered leaving the bag in the toilets, but then she had a vision of the Bomb Squad turning up to blow up the loos, which wouldn't have been the done thing at all. She ran into the changing room, threw her bag in the corner and, ignoring a quizzical stare of recognition from one of the waiters, ran into the outer hall.

Looking around the room as the crowd milled towards the door, Aoife spotted Carmel heading towards her with a tray of champagne.

'You look beautiful,' she told her.

'Thanks a million,' Aoife said, taking a glass of champagne.

'And guess who's over there.'

Aoife followed Carmel's gaze. 'Oh, my God!' she said slowly, feeling her skin pucker into goosebumps and a smile spread across her face. 'It's Dervla Cannon!'

Dervla Cannon was about five foot ten, with shoulder-length blonde hair. Her golden skin was accentuated by the bold red of the dress – *Aoife's* dress! She was talking with a gaggle of women, who seemed to be complimenting her on it; she turned so that they could admire the embroidery on the back. *She looks beautiful*, Aoife thought, feeling herself swell with pride.

'You have to talk to her, Aoife,' Carmel said. 'It's too good an opportunity to miss.'

'I will.' Aoife nodded. 'Just let me get this down my neck.'

Before she had a chance to approach her first customer, Dervla Cannon and her group had gone into the main hall, and Aoife was left holding an empty champagne glass. Carmel gave her another. 'You'd better go in. Here, neck this; one for the road.'

Aoife walked into the main hall. The champagne had eased her slight feeling of foolishness at being alone – and seeing her dress on Ireland's favourite clothes-horse had helped. She went up to the maître d'. 'Aoife Collins,' she said timidly, and then instructed herself silently and firmly to get a grip.

'Over there, Ms Collins; Sandra will show you to your table.' Aoife smiled at Sandra – who, thankfully, she didn't recognise.

As Sandra pulled out her seat, Aoife was suddenly overwhelmed with guilt. She was gate-crashing, not just a dinner, but a charity dinner where the tickets were a thousand euro each. She vowed that, when she got home, she would empty her money-box and send it all to the Drop the Debt campaign – or she might persuade Rory to give the ticket price to the charity, seeing that she wasn't going to take the money.

The middle-aged couple opposite Aoife introduced

themselves as Conor and Moira; she smiled nervously and wondered who would be at the three empty places at their table. She craned her neck, looking around the room. She couldn't see Bono anywhere. *Why am I surprised?* she wondered. But she did recognise half the people in the room, from the TV and magazines. She saw Bertie Ahern being escorted to the table next to her and thought, *Typical – that man'd turn up to the opening of an envelope*, before deciding that, as he was the Taoiseach, it was fair enough. She saw Bob Geldof taking a seat at the far end of the room. She watched as Gerry Ryan's wife chatted to Dervla Cannon. Even without being able to hear them, Aoife knew they were discussing her dress. She thought her head was going to pop.

The doors were closing, and most people had shuffled into their seats, but the three seats at Aoife's table were still vacant. Aoife's eyes fell on the little place-card in front of her. 'Aoife Collins,' it read. A warm glow filled her as she thought about the trouble Paul had gone to. She glanced across at the name to her right. 'Radine Burke'; *Never heard of her*, Aoife thought. At that moment a very glamorous middle-aged woman, accompanied by a man who appeared to be Pierce Brosnan's doppelgänger, took the seat.

Aoife glanced at the space to her left. She could hear footsteps over her left shoulder, but she didn't want to embarrass herself by turning around and staring. She'd be better off finding out the person's name, she thought.

She peeked at the place-card to her left. There was just one name on it – no first name or second name; just plain 'Bono'. Aoife nearly fell off her chair.

Someone was pouring wine into one of the many Waterford Crystal glasses in front of her; she felt a hand on her back and glanced around. It was Paul. He gave her a smile and a wink, and moved on to fill the glass of Aoife's dinner companion.

'Good evening,' he said, picking up the place-card to check that he had the right seat.

'Hello,' Aoife squeaked.

'Bono,' he said, offering his hand.

No shit, Shergar, Aoife thought. She shook his hand firmly. 'Aoife,' she said. And then she added, wanting to fulfil every condition of the bet, 'Aoife Collins. *Very* pleased to meet you.'

Chapter Forty-Five

It had been a week since Aoife had met Bono. She hadn't been alone – the world and his granny had been at Dublin Castle that evening – but she, *she* had sat next to him.

Every single person that Aoife had talked to that week knew every detail of her meeting with Bono. Rory had heard it all.

The night of the meeting, he had been out celebrating his new-found fortune with Gavin and Dave; he had been lying on his bed, enveloped in something between a merry glow and a drunken stupor, when Aoife arrived home. He hadn't been particularly responsive to her shaking; only when she'd nearly rocked him out of the bed had Rory finally woken up.

He had sat up in bed, rubbing his eyes, to be greeted by a barrage of words. 'I did it! I finally did it! I didn't just talk to him for three minutes – in between interruptions, I reckon we talked for a good fifteen minutes! He was very interesting– Jesus, the stuff he knows – and everyone wanted to talk to him; you could see them all looking over and wondering who I was! And, to put the fecking tin lid on it, didn't I go over to Dervla Cannon and introduce myself – and she was telling me how she loved the dress, and how she's going to ask Mari about my other stuff – and all the time, I'm there thinking, "I should be serving the food!" And I said to Bono, told him straight out, "Everyone thinks they know you, don't they, or at least they reckon they've met you?" I didn't mention our bet, but –'

'Aoife!' Rory had shouted at the top of his lungs. 'Put a fecking sock in it, will you?' Aoife had stopped in mid-sentence. 'Now,' he had begun more slowly, realising that he was actually awake. 'One thing at a time. How did you get to meet Bono?'

Today she, Rory and Paul sat together in the Clarence Hotel – Rory had decided that it was befitting to the occasion. Aoife was wondering out loud which fixtures and fittings Bono had had a hand in choosing.

'He's not your friend, you know,' Rory told her. 'You just spoke to him and sat next to him.'

'I know.' Aoife shook her head at him in mock disgust. 'I'm not stupid.'

Rory turned to Paul. 'This is the woman who declared that – what was it? let me get this right – "I don't know if he's fantastic or just all right or a

complete bollix, because I haven't got a Bono story!"
That's what she said, and she was proud of it. Now
look at you,' he smirked, turning to Aoife. 'You're a
fame groupie, that's what you are! You'll be throwing
your smelly knickers at Westlife next.'

'I will not!' Aoife laughed, outraged. She was
delighted with herself all round. Rory and Paul had
been getting on well; Aoife wasn't being unrealistic,
thinking that they'd go off on male-bonding weekends
and be best buddies for all eternity, but she was happy
that there weren't any hard feelings.

'So,' Rory asked. 'When's your appointment with
the bank manager?'

'Tomorrow morning. I can't wait,' Aoife said with
glee. 'I've never gone into a bank feeling like that. I'm
usually skulking at the counter, begging them to
increase my overdraft. But not this time.'

Aoife's dress had made it onto the pages of *VIP*,
Irish Tatler and *Image* magazine. She wasn't named, of
course, but it was fantastic all the same. There had
already been a lot of interest in the pieces she had
made for Mari, and it looked as if she might have a
very good foot in the design door.

'So, what then?'

'Well, once I've smoothed things over with them,
I'm going to take the bank loan that I hope to Jaysus
they're going to give me, buy loads of material and
make loads of clothes.'

'Aoife, take the five grand.'

'No, Rory. End of story,' Aoife said. 'Paul, tell him.'

'I'm not getting involved in this,' Paul said, holding his hands up.

'So you're just going to get into more debt to pay off your debt? That's logical,' Rory told her.

'Look, just give a grand to the charity for the ticket and that's your bit done. Anyway, once I've got a bit of a collection together, I'll go round all the other independent boutiques in Dublin – Blackrock, Dalkey, Howth … the place is swimming with them.'

Aoife was happily resigned to the fact that she was going to be working at Blues for the foreseeable future. She would be making clothes – and, for the most part, getting paid for it. And she wasn't just going to sit back and let things happen at their own pace. She had enthusiasm and drive – and, if that wasn't enough, she had the memory of terminally boring work conversations at Join the Dots, to remind her of where she didn't want to be.

A waiter came over to the table with a champagne bucket and three glasses. As he placed them on the table, Aoife noticed an envelope with her name on it, beside the bucket.

'What's this?' she asked.

'It's an envelope; what's it look like? Open it,' Rory instructed.

Aoife did as she was told.

'What are we celebrating?' she asked, tugging at the paper and nodding at the glasses.

'Everything, I think; don't you? Just open that thing, will you?'

Aoife pulled out three pieces of paper. The first was the crumpled bet that she and Rory had made. She smiled, remembering that evening and thinking of everything that had happened since. Her brow furrowed as she unfolded the second piece of paper. 'What's this?'

'It's a letter from my solicitor to you.' Aoife absentmindedly glanced at the third piece of paper; it was a bank receipt for five thousand euro that had been paid into her account. She snapped her head up.

'No, Rory – you haven't, have you?' She looked from Rory to Paul for confirmation that she wasn't seeing things.

'Right,' Rory said, taking a deep breath and looking like he meant business. 'I want you to listen to me for once in your life, Aoife Collins. Firstly, you can live with me for as long or as short a time as you wish. I will accept rent from you every month. From now on, I will not try to support you financially; you will support yourself.'

'Yes, that's already agreed, but –'

Rory gave her a stern look. '*But* we have a legally binding agreement that, should you manage to get yourself a Bono story, I will pay you five thousand euro. And that, my sweet, is exactly what I've done. It's all in there.' Rory pointed at the solicitor's letter and handed Aoife and Paul glasses of champagne.

'I'll drink a toast, but I'm not taking the money. I'm going to put it back in your account.' Aoife clinked her glass against Paul's and Rory's.

'Do that and I'll sue you.' Rory said, straight-faced. 'It's all there, in writing; you haven't got a leg to stand on.'

Aoife took a sip of her champagne. Half of her was secretly delighted that Rory was honouring the bet; the other half was telling her she had to give back the money. She gave him a sidelong glance.

'You'd never sue me; you wouldn't dare,' she said, calling his bluff.

'I wouldn't, would I?' Rory took a sip of his champagne and raised an eyebrow at Aoife.

'How much do you want to bet?'

Everyone's got a Bono Story...

What's yours?

Tell us your Bono story
to be in with a chance to

Win a weekend in Dublin!

INSTRUCTIONS

1. To enter the competition go to www.bonostories.com
   and submit your Bono story.
2. The entry does not give rise to any contract between
   Gill & Macmillan Ltd. ('Gill & Macmillan') and the entrant.
3. The competition will be run and determined in
   accordance with the Rules oveleaf.

RULES

1. The instructions overleaf form part of the Rules.

2. Only entries submitted to www.bonostories.com will be considered. No entries received by any means other than the website such as by hand, ordinary post, courier, facsimile, etc., will be accepted or considered.

3. All entries must be submitted to www.bonostories.com prior to or not later than 31 August 2004 ('the Closing Date').

4. Gill & Macmillan reserves the right to extend the Closing Date if necessary.

5. Multiple entries will be accepted, but each such entry must be submitted to www.bonostories.com.

6. No cash will be offered in lieu of the prizes available in the competition.

7. Gill & Macmillan will in its absolute discretion decide any matter or question concerning the running of the competition, these Rules, their interpretation or any ancillary matter and any such decision or necessary opinion of Gill & Macmillan will be final and no correspondence will be entered into concerning such a decision.

8. Gill & Macmillan will have no responsibility for, and is not obliged to take into account, any entry that fails to be properly submitted to www.bonostories.com.

9. Gill & Macmillan will notify the winner within 30 days of the Closing Date that he/she has been successful.

10. The competition is open to residents of the Republic of Ireland (and the United Kingdom), except the author, employees of Gill & Macmillan and their families, and employees and/or administration of www.bonostories.com and this competition.

11. The winner's name may, at Gill & Macmillan's discretion, be used for publicity purposes.

12. The details of this prize can be found at www.bonostories.com. Gill & Macmillan and www.bonostories.com are free from any liability involved in travel to/from and participation in the prize.